STRONGHOLD

The Maiyochi Chronicles
Book Two

PHILLIP L. JOHNSON

Black Rose Writing | Texas

This is a work of fiction. Names, characters, businesses, places, events, and incidents are
either the products of the author's imagination or used in a fictitious manner. Any
resemblance to actual persons, living or dead, or actual events is purely coincidental.

ISBN: 978-1-68513-158-6
PUBLISHED BY BLACK ROSE WRITING
www.blackrosewriting.com

Printed in the United States of America
Suggested Retail Price (SRP) $21.95

The Maiyochi Chronicles: Stronghold is printed in Book Antiqua

*As a planet-friendly publisher, Black Rose Writing does its best to eliminate unnecessary waste to
reduce paper usage and energy costs, while never compromising the reading experience. As a result,
the final word count vs. page count may not meet common expectations.

To Easton Lennox Johnson,
a true blessing from The One Spirit.

STRONGHOLD

The Maiyochi Chronicles

Book Two

PROLOGUE

Cafran was already in a foul mood.

He was a neophyte, yes, but a neophyte in the priesthood! That alone should be deserving of a goodly portion of respect, and at most times it was. He served Jusaan - one of the Holy Counsel of Nine. That Jusaan was one of its most junior members should mean little in terms of respect. Just to be counted among the Nine was considered by many to be the pinnacle of a life's work.

Cafran had worked hard - both openly and from the shadows - to attach himself to one whom all knew as an ambitious young priest, maybe a future High Priest if attrition be left to run its natural course. And if it did, Cafran could count on a lifelong position of influence inside the Citadel. The very least he could expect would be an appointment to one of the outlying villages where, if the village leaders were sufficiently subservient to the Temple, he would rule his own serfdom, answering only to The Nine and having the ear of the High Priest.

At most – should he even dare to dream it – an appointment to the Holy Council itself!

What Cafran never envisioned was having to accompany his mentor on a journey such as this; many leagues from the Citadel and the civilized confines of Stronghold, traveling with an expeditionary force into the wilderness of the Ursal Mountains. How had he come to such a fate?

Cafran was finding that being close to the seat of holy power was no guarantee of influence, or even understanding. Why his mentor had committed himself to this torturous existence, even temporarily, he had not a clue.

It had been difficult enough seeing to his own needs while also ensuring the comfort of his master in this bug-infested wilderness, surrounded by the coarseness and filth of well over one-hundred soldiers and their animals. As usual, Petri was no help. He was as lazy as they come and, were it not for Cafran's constant berating, would be content to lie about and soak up the stench of both man and beast that was forcing its way into the tent they shared.

Sharing a tent. Another of the many indignities he was forced to suffer.

And not only was he forced to share a tent with one who was beneath him, but circumstance had forced him to commandeer Petri's smelly cot. It seemed no amount of perfume or incense could remove the stench of the junior acolyte, and every night since Jusaan had offered Cafran's tent to their "guests" was a night of misery. How fortunate was Petri to have a rug and clean blanket on the floor of the tent for his comfort.

All these thoughts did nothing to lift Cafran's spirits as he took his leave of Jusaan's tent, trudging through the slowly lifting darkness toward the flimsy dwelling he now shared, and the wagon standing beside it. Once at the wagon, he removed the cover from a crate and, under the dim light of a single candle, carefully eyed its contents. Opening a small door, he reached inside and carefully removed the appropriately marked bird from the lot within. Having already placed a strip of parchment into a tiny bamboo cylinder, he attached this to the messenger's leg with a ribbon of garnet and gold; colors identifying this message as for the eyes of the Royal House alone.

In case this smelly creature does not make it to the chamber of the King's scribe, he thought, frowning with distaste at the bird he held cupped in his hands.

Having closed and re-covered the crate, Cafran blew out the candle and carried the pigeon to a clearing beyond the confines of the camp. Confident he had not been followed, he tossed the bird skyward and watched as it rose into the air. It circled once, twice, then found its bearings and was lost to sight in the dim light beyond the northern tree line.

And now there is water to be fetched, food to be prepared, and the wagon must be packed for today's journey, Cafran thought unhappily.

As he moved off toward his tent to begin the day's labors, he considered Petri.

The loaf is still sleeping while I've been attending to these important tasks. No matter. I'll have him awake and hopping soon enough!
The thought of disturbing the slumber of his junior servant brought the first smile of the morning to Cafran's face.

Chapter 1

His nose told of the presence of wood, smoke, oils, and incense.

The wood he had gathered just before dark on last evening. It had been used to feed the fire, the smoldering remains of which were no longer sufficient to hold back the cold of the night, even as it continued to send subtle wisps of smoke rising into the early morning air. The oils were a mixture concocted by the priests and had been liberally used on the leather divan, the stools, and the tables. It gave off a rich cinnamon scent. It was much different from the flowery sweetness of the incense. Its pungent odor clung to the blankets, the pillows, the rugs, and the very walls of the tent which he and Hanshee now shared.

Having identified these scents, Raymond felt a moment of satisfaction. He was attempting to hone his skills as a warrior. This morning's lesson: how to awaken.

Focusing on maintaining his breathing at an even pace to simulate continued sleep, he listened for what sounds could be heard in the still morning air. The closed confines of the tent served to muffle all but the loudest and sharpest of noises but, as he listened carefully, there could be heard the still-sleepy footsteps of one – no, two – of the camp's earliest risers. A rhythmic slap accompanied every other stride as they trudged by in the direction of the swift- flowing stream beside which camp had been made two evenings ago.

Those two are cooks, thought Ray. *The sound of the oversized leather water bags they carry, striking against their legs as they walk, is the tell.*

Further away there was the sharp thunk that spoke of the splitting of firewood. This was soon followed by the ringing clack of one piece thrown atop another, probably upon the remaining embers from last night's fire. Raymond could visualize the sparks and ashes rising as the dry wood impacted the still hot coals; could almost hear the crackle and pop as the smaller pieces quickly caught and held a flame.

Concentrating still more, he was able to pick up the indistinct background noise of the encampment as it came alive. He heard someone clear their throat, and someone else grunt in acknowledgment of a morning greeting, but nothing else jumped out from the myriad of small noises that made up the slowly growing hum of morning activity.

He knew the morning was cool and crisp. Inside the tent, the temperature had been steadily dropping since the demise of the fire that had burned brightly at its center. Now his shoulders, neck, and face, uncovered by the woolen blanket which held the morning cold at bay, felt the chill. It told him what awaited him when he came completely out from under its folds. With his eyes still closed, he was sure his every breath was revealed as a fleeting mist in the cold morning air.

Raymond recalled Hanshee's earlier teaching:

"The ears should awaken first, so as to listen to the surroundings, while the body remains motionless. Then the nose should awaken and smell the different fragrances which ride the winds. Of course, the skin should have already told its tale. Is it hot or cold? Dry or damp? Only after these senses had performed their task were the eyes allowed to open, fully alert and already having a sense of what would lie before them. Yet the body still has not moved, save for the easy breath which has not changed, and therefore has not told anyone or anything watching that the warrior is awake, ready to glide silently to a place of

hiding or spring suddenly into action, depending on the demands of the moment."

Raymond had taken account of his surroundings with his other senses and, already having a good idea of what awaited him inside the confines of the tent, had only to open his eyes.

"Aaaugh!"

Raymond's whole body jumped in reaction to the face not six inches from his own!

The ever-observant Hanshee had read some telltale sign his companion was awakening and, crouching silently, had positioned himself directly in front of Ray's face. When at last his eyes opened, Ray was staring into the wide eyes and flared nostrils of Hanshee, the 'joker', who now rolled back on his haunches and burst into laughter at Ray's startled reaction.

Trying to gather his composure after his initial shock, Raymond first attempted a look of annoyance. This made Hanshee whoop even more loudly and Ray, realizing there was no escape from being the butt of this joke, finally smiled and shook his head.

His whooping laughter having trailed off, Hanshee rolled over on his side, propped himself up on one elbow, and regarded Raymond with a smile of amusement.

"I was trying to..." Ray began.

"...awaken as a warrior should," finished Hanshee, still grinning as he regarded him.

Raymond fixed him with questioning eyes. "How did you know?" he asked.

Hanshee raised his eyebrows in mock questioning.

"How did you know I was awake?" Ray repeated.

Hanshee's grin faded and his eyes looked to nothing as he focused on this question, appearing to quiz himself. Finally nodding with certainty, he replied, "I felt you awaken."

Now it was Raymond's turn to raise his eyebrows.

"Huh?"

"It is the only way I can explain it," Hanshee began, his eyes drifting away from Raymond, seeming to focus on nothing, as if checking his calculations in his mind. Satisfied, he again met Raymond's gaze. "I felt you awaken, and observed your attempt to hide your awakening until you knew your surroundings, as a warrior should." In a single fluid movement, he rose from the floor of the tent and started toward the flap. "It was a noble effort," he said as he stepped through the tent flap and into the morning cold.

Raymond was left wondering if Hanshee had been serious.

He felt me wake up? he thought, as he flung the blanket back and swung his legs over the side of the cot.

It was a fine cot, light and sturdy, made of leather pulled taut over a bamboo frame held together with wooden pegs and tightly wound strips of leather. It was easy to break down, carry to the next camp, and set up again. Even so, Ray was sure there were only three or four in the entire camp of over one-hundred fifty men, not counting the surveyors and map makers. All the rest would be content to make their bed on the ground, using their bedroll, and whatever cushioning could be scrounged from nature. Only a priest would insist on sleeping in such comfort within a military encampment.

There were two cots in this tent, and Ray looked over to the one provided for Hanshee's comfort. He smiled to himself as he thought of the look they would be receiving from the acolyte, who had to endure yet another night on the floor of a shared tent. He would follow Hanshee's lead and simply smile and nod in their direction. Hanshee appreciated the joke, all the more amusing since he never slept on the cot set up for his use. Noting again that Hanshee's cot was pristine, Ray stood, stretched, donned a heavy robe, and made his way toward the tent flap.

At least he complemented my effort…didn't he? Ray wondered.

Stepping through the flap, he was greeted by the cold and the mingled odors of the encampment. The smell of men, animals, and their waste produced a stench all its own, one he and Hanshee were shielded from at night by the strong scent of the incense permeating their borrowed tent. It was always somewhat of a shock first thing in the morning but, in truth, Ray had become used to the smell. After the initial distaste, he was able to ignore it for the rest of the day.

He paused at the exit, confirming his breath was revealed as vapor in the dim coldness just before full sunrise, and then made his way to the east. He walked just past the camp's perimeter, over to a large evergreen, where he took immense pleasure in relieving his full bladder. He watched as the steam rose from the stream and from the puddle forming between the exposed roots of the tree. Finished, he made his way back to the tent to wash and dress.

He passed others on the way but, after three weeks of travel, the fact of the two strangers in the camp was no longer a point of curiosity. Most of the soldiers ignored Ray's presence, speaking among themselves as if he were not there. They were content in their knowledge this stranger did not understand their tongue.

They were wrong.

Raymond understood everything that was said by those now around him. Given time, he knew he would understand any new languages he was exposed to. He had no explanation for this, as so much of his life over the past three months could not be explained. In fact, he felt it was essential to his sanity that he not attempt an understanding at this time. He knew it would prove to be fruitless, as had his earlier attempts, and the rigors and hostilities of this new environment required him to focus his energies where they would pay the most dividends.

Hopefully, there would come a time when he could afford to relax his body and mind, and more fully turn his attention to the puzzle of why he was here, how he got here, and where "here" was.

Reaching the tent, Raymond scanned his surroundings for his companion. He spied Hanshee moving toward him with what appeared to be water bags newly filled from the swift part of the stream laying just beyond the tree line beside which the company had camped. As he watched, he noted the way the soldiers were quick to make room for the stranger, quick to speak a morning greeting if their eyes should meet, and quick to be about their business, though with many a backward glance at the 'warrior-priest' who moved so freely among them.

They all remembered - would probably remember until their dying day - the scene at the dried lake bed where Hanshee revealed to the assembled soldiers what he was capable of. Though these men were all hardened warriors, none now harbored any desire to challenge "the Panther," the name they had taken to calling Hanshee amongst themselves. All of them had witnessed how he toyed with the sadistic giant Botha, punishing and humiliating him before finally laying him low. And Botha had been the most feared warrior among them. The respect which Hanshee had earned from those who witnessed that day could be ignored by none, not even Lord Galin.

Hanshee moved with nimble, measured steps among the throng of fighting men, showing an easy smile of contentment to those who dared to glance his way. He nodded placidly to obvious greetings as he approached the tent and, as he drew closer, Ray was quick to pull aside the tent flap for his teacher to enter. This was a move befitting the acolyte of the warrior-priest. Raymond quickly followed Hanshee inside the tent and, moving to one of the small leathern tables, grasped and presented a wooden bowl which Hanshee filled with the cold, clear water.

"Thanks," Raymond said, raising the bowl to his lips and relishing the cool wetness as it made its way down his throat. He had no idea he was this thirsty.

"Dajee," replied Hanshee, as he had the first time Raymond had offered him thanks for a cool drink.

Ray dimly recalled that day. He had been injured and drugged at the time. Apparently, Hanshee had pulled his body from the river. Over the course of several days of Hanshee's constant attention, and with the contents of what Raymond came to call his "magic pouch," Hanshee had brought him back from the brink of death. He had spoken in a language Raymond could not then understand, the first word being "dajee."

Raymond was now fluent in Hanshee's tongue. He knew "dajee," roughly translated to "honor" or "duty." In the case where it was first used, in reply to an obvious word of thanks, it was meant to convey the thought that, in serving him, Hanshee had performed what was considered a duty among his people; to lend aid to any sick or injured one may come upon in one's travels. Of course, this only applied when the sick or injured was not an enemy, and when lending aid would not expose one to danger.

Finishing his drink, Raymond retrieved the water bag from where it hung and poured some into a second wooden bowl, larger than the first, which had been provided for washing. Following his benefactor's lead, Raymond washed in the morning and again in the evening, usually as soon as camp had been made. Hanshee was a stickler for cleanliness. He seemed to take advantage of almost every pause during their day to attend to some matter of hygiene. This must be why, though having made their way through the wilderness, and having a good portion of the wilderness attempt to take up residence on their persons, he never appeared to be dirty.

Using the cloth provided for this purpose, Ray washed his face and head and neck. In the warmer months, Hanshee had advised him about carefully searching those places most likely to harbor ticks, but this was less of a concern in the late fall and winter months. Ray then washed each upper extremity, beginning at his shoulders and working down. He followed this with a thorough washing of his torso and each leg. He saved the crevices of this body for last, before using the remaining water to wash out the cloth.

Satisfied with his hygiene, he turned toward Hanshee who, having finished his own morning cleansing, was patiently awaiting Ray's attention. Raymond took a seat on the edge of his cot, this being much more comfortable for him than the cross-legged seat Hanshee had assumed on the rug spread over the dirt floor. Hanshee added more kindling to the embers of last night's fire, which had been made in a shallow brass bowl provided for that purpose. He stoked the pile until it glowed brightly. After a while, a tiny flame could be seen growing from its center.

"What have you heard?" Hanshee began, after he had settled in.

"I only left the tent to relieve myself," said Ray. "I didn't really have a chance to overhear anything."

Raymond wondered why Hanshee had asked. He must be aware that, since he chose to get the water this morning, Ray had no opportunity to mingle among the soldiers and pick up the gossip of the camp, as had been their usual routine. Hanshee addressed this right away.

"I went for the morning water so to see with my eyes what our future holds. This is our second morning encamped here, and none are moving to break camp. This is strange if we are as close to their garrison as your listening has revealed."

"I can only tell you what I hear," replied Ray. "Two nights ago, when we first made camp here, the soldiers spoke of a halt. Some of them were upset because, according to them, we are only three hard days' march from what they called 'the gates'. I'm guessing they were referring to their castle, or their fortress, or whatever you want to call their main camp. Some of them are eager to make it back. They questioned the purpose of this expedition from its beginning."

"Then why we linger here is a mystery," said Hanshee. "But it is not a concern. Our situation has not changed. Rash judgments are still to be avoided. Patience remains our best course."

****

It was about an hour after the morning meal when a soldier appeared at their tent. Hanshee, ever alert, heard footsteps stop before the flap and waited while the soldier mulled over whether he should stick his head in or call out to whoever was inside. His respect for the prowess of "the Panther" carried the day. Hanshee listened as the soldier tried loudly clearing his throat. Receiving no response, he tried calling out to whoever was within.

"M'lords?" was the first tentative call.

The soldier was reaching to pull back the flap for a look inside when Raymond turned the corner and approached the tent. Startled, the soldier released the flap and jumped back with a curse.

"Damn, man!" he exclaimed in his native tongue, before composing himself. In a halting voice, he half-spoke, half-mumbled the unfamiliar words that had been given to him.

"Your presence is requested," he said in the language of the priesthood.

He peered at Raymond to see if these words, given to him by Jusaan, had any meaning to him. Ray understood, even if the speaker obviously did not, but he maintained the illusion of ignorance. He smiled at the soldier and ducked inside the tent to get his master. Hanshee had heard everything, including the summons spoken in what was close to his native tongue, and knew it was Jusaan who called for their presence. Gathering his robe about him, he shrugged a response to the question in Raymond's eyes before leading him out of the tent. There, the soldier repeated his message in the same clumsy manner. Hanshee smiled benevolently and motioned for him to lead the way.

Jusaan's tent was on the opposite side of the acolytes' tent from the one shared by Hanshee and Raymond, so they felt mild surprise when the soldier walked past it and continued into the depth of the encampment. As they passed by the cooking fires, Raymond saw they were headed toward the large tent, which bore a banner of forest green trimmed in bright gold, the banner of the First Expeditionary Legion. As they approached the tent, Raymond could see a trio of men standing before it. Two of them he knew: Lord Galin, commander of the military force, and the priest Jusaan, who apparently had summoned them at Galin's request. The third man was unknown to Raymond. By his bearing, he was a soldier. He stood with his hands clasped behind his back, his legs straight, with his weight resting on the balls of his feet, in a position Ray thought he recognized as "at ease."

The stranger's attire, while practical, seemed designed to catch the eye. He wore a blood-red tunic that hung to just above his knees. Over the tunic was a breastplate of polished metal, gold in color if not in fact. Armor matching the breastplate protected his forearms and shins. Under his left arm was cradled a red-crested helmet. His harness, from which the hilt of a short sword protruded, was made of rich leather, polished to a gleaming shine with oils and waxes made just for this purpose. It was matched by leather sandals, the binding of which snaked up his sturdy calf muscles, ending just below the knee.

The uniform was topped off with a cloak, the same blood-red as the tunic. It was held in place by circular pieces of metal attached to the shoulders of the breastplate. These metal discs bore an emblem, a smaller version of the one centered on the breastplate. It was of a fist with its thumb upward, closed around the hilt of a knife, which pointed downward.

The messenger who had summoned Hanshee and Ray escorted them to a position about ten feet behind Jusaan. There he stopped, awaiting recognition from his three superiors. The colorfully clad warrior was speaking in low tones, not quite a whisper, but quietly enough to ensure a level of privacy among the three. When he stopped, Galin turned toward the messenger and curtly nodded. This was a signal giving permission to send Hanshee and Ray forward. The messenger did so with a sweep of his arm, a grand gesture that seemed out of place coming from a foot soldier in this setting. Hanshee nodded in acceptance and stepped forward, with Raymond close upon his heels.

Having accomplished his mission, the soldier searched Galin's face for a sign of dismissal. Galin's attention was on Hanshee as he, at Jusaan's direction, took the position to the left of the priest. This made the circle of three into a circle of four, with Raymond taking up position directly behind Hanshee.

Galin did not like this priest, who had so handily shown him up by the relative ease with which he had bested his chosen man, Botha. He did not like the respect his men now bestowed upon the ragged traveler, nor the way Jusaan treated him as almost an equal. Knowing Jusaan as he did, this meant some game was afoot, and the fact that he could not put his finger on the priest's motives annoyed him. But Galin knew the benefit of patience and hid his annoyance behind a calm demeanor. Seeing the expectant face of the foot soldier, he waved him away before turning to the scarlet-crested newcomer.

"These are the two you have been sent to retrieve." Galin glanced sideways at Jusaan after making this statement. He had no illusions as to how the Royal House knew of the arrival of their guests out of the southern wilderness. "My men will see to a change of your horses. While you wait, you may avail yourself of our chow line, though I am sure it will be lacking in comparison to the fare of the royal kitchen."

The brightly garbed soldier, an officer in the Citadel Guard, heard the insult and the challenge in the words of Galin. He leveled as stiff a gaze as he dared to give at one who was technically his superior.

"Lord Galin, your stew pots are as mother's milk to one who has served, fought, bled, and shed blood, for the empire. Tell your cooks I will have a double portion, as well as a portion for the journey back."

This brought laughter from deep within Galin's chest, and he slapped the guard's shoulder in appreciation of his courage and wit.

The exchange was lost on Jusaan, who now eyed the royal guard with a mixture of concern and pity. Many are the times he had eaten in the royal kitchens. The fare there was passable, at best. The bags of spices and herbs he had his acolytes secure prior to the journey ensured his every sumptuous meal was fit for a high priest. To survive in this wilderness, even on the royal fare, would be a challenge to his palate and his will. It truly had never occurred to him to sup from the same stew pots as these... heathens.

All the better, thought Jusaan. *I'll now not be obliged to share the remains of my morning meal with this man, though he be here on my summons.*

With this thought, Jusaan turned his attention to Hanshee, regarding him with a long-practiced gaze of kindness and sincerity.

"My brother," he began in a language close to Hanshee's native tongue, the traditional language of the priesthood. "I have wonderful news! This man has just arrived to escort us to the Citadel. There we will be met by His Holiness Lord Mayhew, High Priest of the Order, chief above The Counsel of Nine, a most humble servant of The One!"

As Hanshee nodded in understanding, he continued.

"If you will have your acolyte secure for you what belongings you will need, the two of us can be off as soon as the horses are prepared. The King's chariots are swift. We should be at our destination before the sun sets. Our servants will secure the remainder of our belongings."

Though now well-schooled in keeping a passive and uninterested demeanor, Raymond could barely hide his surprise upon hearing Jusaan's plans. He almost spoke up, but for Hanshee, who somehow sensed his companion's fears and reached back to grasp Ray's upper arm. The message inherent in the iron grip was one of composure, and Raymond swallowed his words even as Hanshee pulled him forward until they stood side by side. As Hanshee turned to Jusaan, his expression changed. No longer was he smiling placidly. Now his gaze was focused, his jaw hardened. He spoke to Jusaan in a tone not exactly threatening, yet forceful nonetheless.

"He will come," said Hanshee, maintaining his grip on Ray, making it clear who "he" was.

This caused Jusaan to pause and arch an eyebrow in curiosity, wondering what type of relationship these two had shared… alone…in the wilderness.

Ray continued to bite his tongue, the iron grip on his arm reminding him that his role in this drama was of a faithful servant with little understanding of what was transpiring.

Seeing the determined look in Hanshee's eyes, Jusaan began to backtrack.

"Of course, my brother, your acolyte may come along. It is just that the chariot…well…I believe it is built for no more than three. The added weight will surely slow us down."

"He is needed," Hanshee said. "He will come." As he spoke, he nodded his head in agreement with his words, keeping Jusaan captive with his piercing gaze, waiting for him to relent.

Jusaan could see the writing on the wall. He needed this Hanshee fellow to like him, to trust him, ideally to depend on him. Separating him from his companion might have accelerated this process, but now it was clear he had no intention of leaving his acolyte behind. Jusaan needed his cooperation for his plans to come to fruition.

Best not to stir the waters too fast, or too soon, he thought. *It is a small matter to allow the acolyte to accompany his master. His calming influence may make for a more receptive Hanshee in the long run.*

"Yes, my brother, I see. Of course, he will accompany us."

Hanshee continued to nod his head in response to Jusaan's capitulation. His eyes softened, and a smile of placid contentment returned to his face.

"Now, my brother," Jusaan said. "Have your acolyte prepare your belongings. We leave within the hour!"

Chapter 2

After two days at the encampment, the horses were strong and well-rested. With the able guardsman at the reins, they made good progress across the hilly terrain. There were four passengers in the chariot: the King's guard, the priest Jusaan, Hanshee, and Raymond.

At Jusaan's insistence, Hanshee and Raymond left behind their borrowed robes and now wore the clothes they had been found in, with the sole addition of a cloak to protect them from the wind stirred up by the ever-moving chariot. This was needed since neither had been dressed for the cold weather. Prior to their capture, they had been accumulating skins with which to fashion some type of protection against the elements until they made their way beyond the southern mountains.

It was part of Jusaan's plan that Hanshee be presented to those of the Royal House as he had first appeared to Jusaan: the very image of a warrior-priest of old. The proper impression, made from the beginning, was crucial to achieving what had been so serendipitously placed within his grasp.

Jusaan still could hardly believe his good fortune.

When High Priest Mayhew had learned of the planned expedition to the southern mountains, he had petitioned the King for permission to allow one of his priests to go, *"to attend to the spiritual wellbeing of our men at arms"*. In actuality, it served two purposes: providing eyes and ears to another of Galin's machinations, and removing from the royal court one whose naked ambition was becoming a nuisance.

Jusaan remembered his reaction when the rumors of this expedition first reached his ears. He chuckled at the thought of some poor lesser priest having to abandon all that was comfortable - not that a priest of such shallow standing understood real comfort - to go trekking through the wilderness, possibly for months, just so he could report back to the High Priest that the trees were still tall, the soldiers still uncouth, and despite all precautions, the dirt and insects still managed to find their way next to your skin.

The thoughts of others suffering such indignations had bought smile after smile to Jusaan's lips. This was before word reached him through a messenger, straight from the mouth of Lord High Priest Mayhew himself, that it was he who was slated to accompany the expeditionary force. Instantly, all joy was sucked from his life.

Upon hearing of Jusaan's dismayed reaction, the lord high priest decided the time was ripe to drop yet another thunderbolt upon him. Near the end of a meeting in the chamber of The Nine, Mayhew made an unexpected appearance. Waving away formality, he allowed the meeting to continue to its end. Then, as the others prepared to leave, he signaled for Jusaan to stay.

"How may I be of service, Your Grace?" Jusaan asked warily, bending and kissing Mayhew's proffered hand. An impromptu meeting with the lord high priest was highly unusual, and Jusaan was caught off guard.

"Please be at ease, my son," Mayhew said, while the others were still within earshot. They were all curious to know what would cause the high priest to break with his usual formality and appeared to take a little longer than usual to clear the room.

"I have been considering the value of appointing a military liaison from among our number," Mayhew said, once he and Jusaan were alone. "Such a one would need to have intimate knowledge of the machinations within the Council of Seven, with special attention paid to Lord Galin who, despite his relative youth, holds inordinate sway within the council and with the king. What think you, Jusaan?"

The Council of Seven consisted of the commanders of the seven military forces of the nation of Pith.

Jusaan was taken aback by this query, but his response was both fluid and diplomatic.

"It is easy to see the wisdom of such an arrangement," he replied. "A fledgling priest would be wise to embrace such an opportunity to display his fealty to The One Spirit by operating as the eyes and ears of his most humble servant, the lord high priest. I know just the candidate."

"Then you shall train him to take your place... after a time," said the high priest, slamming the door to the trap shut.

"But... but, Your Grace..." Jusaan stammered, his mind reeling. "Would not a member of the council be of greater service to Your Grace, and thus to The One Spirit, here in the temple, closer to the intrigues of the court, where the seeds of any real threat to Your Grace and the council will surely be planted?"

"Did you not just speak to the wisdom of my proposal, to the opportunity availed by this service, and of fealty to The One?" the high priest asked, using Jusaan's own words against him. "You would leave to a junior priest the task of ferreting out the schemes and intrigues of Lord Galin and the rest of the Council of Seven? No! This assignment calls for qualities not yet developed in our junior ranks, along with the deft touch of experience. You are already scheduled to accompany the First Expeditionary Force into the southern mountains, are you not? We will use that adventure as your trial by fire, shall we say?"

Mayhew fixed Jusaan with a pointed stare.

"Do not underperform."

Jusaan was no fool. From the high priest's first appearance at the meeting, he had sensed a trap. He had tried to avoid it. He had failed. No purpose would be served now by allowing his disappointment to show.

"Your Eminence is kind to bless one such as I with this opportunity," Jusaan lied. "My service to The One shall be exemplary."

"As is expected," the lord high priest curtly replied, as he spun away in dismissal of his underling.

Mayhew had been very pleased with himself. With little effort, he had placed what he hoped was a permanent spy within the ranks of the military. This was a position the Council of Seven had resisted for some time. Simultaneously, he had also removed a potential nuisance from the Temple of The One Spirit. The lord high priest was a keen observer of men and their natures. One did not ascend to the position of ultimate spiritual authority without this attribute. His observation of Jusaan had shown the council priest to be highly motivated, highly intelligent, extremely ambitious, and very manipulative; traits that should serve him well as the Temple's military liaison. They were also traits that would necessitate he be closely watched should he spend his days in the Temple.

That one is much too much like me," Mayhew had thought smugly as he left the chamber.

Jusaan remembered the smile playing across Mayhew's lips as he departed the chamber that day. He was sure the lord high priest was aware of their similarities. No doubt, this was why he viewed Jusaan as a potential threat.

If the lord high priest were here now, I would thank him, Jusaan thought.

Though clever in arranging his banishment, Mayhew had unwittingly opened the door to his blessing... and an opportunity undreamed of.

Wham!

Striking a fallen limb, the chariot pitched to one side, then to the other, shaking Jusaan from his thoughts. He shot a glance to his right, to the unconcerned profile of the guard as he steered the chariot down the center of the rutted path that eventually would give way to a proper road. Leaning backward and shifting his glance farther to the right, Jusaan noticed his priestly guest was not so at ease as he was when his feet touched the earth. Using a heavy leather strap for balance, Hanshee kept a death grip with both hands on the chariot's rails. As Jusaan's presence was often required at short notice at one place or another, he had experience riding in the Temple's chariots, though not over such rough terrain as this. He found humor in the predicament of his guest.

Hulking warriors give him no pause, but a horse and chariot... Jusaan's chuckle was cut short by another bump in the trail, causing the vehicle to continue to rock from side to side.

Hanshee tightened his grip but remained stoic.

Jusaan cast a glance over his shoulder to where the acolyte squatted in the rear of the chariot. A wide leather band was suspended across the rear of the vehicle. By leaning his hips against it, Ray-mond - *was that his name?* - achieved some semblance of balance. He still found it necessary to squat while holding tight to the rails at either side, his arms almost at full extension. His expression told a story of fear, mingled with resignation and determination.

Together, the four of them made a curious sight, with only their driver standing tall and easy, the reins in hand, appearing to enjoy the ride.

****

They had been traveling this path for more than half the day, stopping only at the sun's zenith to rest and eat. The horses had been pushed hard and desperately needed tending. While the guard saw to their care, Jusaan enjoyed the light lunch his subordinates had packed for him.

Hanshee and Ray didn't feel the least bit hungry after their first chariot ride. They staggered from the vehicle on wobbly legs, thankful to stand upon the good earth once more, even as they looked ahead with dread at climbing back into the contraption. But climb back aboard they did, continuing to endure the lurching chariot as the sun dipped lower in the western sky.

The chariot rolled past forested hills on which stood the occasional homes of citizens of Pith who preferred a life of more freedom on the edges of civilization. These structures spanned the gamut from humble single-family cabins to great estates that were home both to lords and servants and whose fields could stretch to the horizon.

Soon the trail became a proper road and the chariot raced past farms and orchards, through crossroads and a few larger settlements that could rightly be called towns. All of these served to break up the monotonous leagues of hills and forest, which up to then had represented the bulk of their view from the swiftly moving chariot.

It was very late in the day when the chariot pulled off to the right and down a narrow road leading into a small valley. Here stood a wood frame house, a modest dwelling, with a stone chimney from which curled thin white smoke. A stone's throw away stood a barn, a much larger structure, whose rear doors opened up into a corral holding horses that raised their heads from their hay to inspect the visitors. A pasture located across from the two buildings held even more horses, a few cattle, and some sheep and goats, all enclosed by a weathered fence running its entire perimeter.

As soon as the chariot came to a halt, Raymond untied his support strap and gingerly stepped down to the ground. Still holding firmly to the chariot's side rail for support, he let his eyes wander around the grounds. Hanshee soon joined him at the rear of the vehicle. Ray took note of the fact that Hanshee stood straight and tall and no longer showed the effects of the bumpy ride.

"Oh, you like chariots now?" Raymond asked, nodding toward the chariot.

Hanshee turned and eyed the conveyance.

"It was first difficult," he said, "but I am adapting."

Springing deftly to the ground, the guard turned a critical eye toward the pair.

"Riding a proper road is much nicer, is it not?" He grinned, as if they understood him. He seemed satisfied they had successfully completed the second leg of their journey.

Turning to Jusaan, he said, "Lord priest, please instruct our guests to take this time to stretch their legs and rest. I will see to the changing of the horses before the last leg of our journey to the Citadel."

With that, he strode off toward the house, bellowing for the stable master.

Looking past the guard, Raymond eyed the barn. There, he noticed a small head peering at them from beyond the open door. As quickly as it appeared, it was gone, leaving Ray to wonder if he had really seen it in the first place. About this time, the door to the house swung open to reveal the figure of a squat elderly man struggling into his coat while cheerfully calling out to the guard.

"Commander! I see you've made it back! Please know I was praying for your safe and speedy return!

He stumbled on the stairs while shrugging the garment over his shoulders, righted himself, and approached the waiting guard with a smile of pure joy on his face.

"We have your mounts ready to go, we have – Boy! – the boy will get you taken care of quick as you please. BOY! Just let me go find his lazy arse."

The stable master started for the barn, his joyful expression changing in mid stride to an evil scowl. When he has halfway there the boy – he whose head Raymond had seen – came tentatively forward, his eyes cast down toward the dust of the yard. As he passed the stable master, the old man swatted him on the side of the head with a calloused hand, knocking him stumbling in the direction of the chariot.

"Get those damn horses untied and taken care of!" he shouted before turning back to the guard, his scowl now replaced by his joyful face.

"The boy needs a bit of prodding now and again," he smiled.

Ignoring this harsh treatment, the guard asked, "Is there more watered wine?" He recalled its cool sweetness from his stop here the day before.

"Why yes, commander! It's right inside on the table. If you don't mind helping yourself, I'll get your horses tied on and ready to go. You just take your time and enjoy the wine!"

As the guard strode toward the open door, the stable master let his eyes cut to where the boy was removing the harnesses from the two horses. Satisfied another blow was not needed - and the boy being out of reach in any case - he spared a glance at the passengers. His experienced gaze quickly passed over the two whose plain cloaks did little to hide their strange garb, and came to rest on Jusaan.

"Your Grace!" the stable master cried out as he hustled over to the priest seated on the rear edge of the chariot. "My pardon, Your Grace," he said, taking the priest's extended hand and pressing it to his bowed forehead. "I did not notice you there. That lazy boy is a powerful distraction." He cut his eyes at the child. "I hope your journey has not been too trying?"

"The Ursal Mountains are always trying," replied Jusaan, soaking up the stable master's fawning as his due. "Fortunately, some of us are heartier than others." He cast a derogatory glance toward Hanshee and Raymond. "You mentioned wine…?"

"Yes, Your Grace." the stable master said. "It's right inside. Just let me wash and I will serve you, though it may delay my tending to the horses."

"Do not trouble yourself, man," said Jusaan, maintaining his pretense as a hearty traveler. "I am quite capable of serving myself. Is it this way?" he asked, gesturing toward the house as he started off in its direction.

"Yes, Your Grace," said the old man. "Careful on the steps!" he called as he turned toward the stable.

Jusaan drew himself up in indignation as he continued toward the house.

Does this fool think me a delicate child who cannot climb steps? Still, he took extra care as he lifted the hem of his robe and made his way up the ancient wooden steps which led into the house.

Raymond followed Hanshee's lead and had a drink of cool water from the well on the far end of the trough from which the horses drank. As he drank, he watched the boy expertly working with the horses.

He appeared to be on the young side, maybe nine or ten years old, having not yet reached puberty. Despite his youth, he went about his duties with skill and confidence, as if he'd spent the entirety of his young life living with and tending to horses. Having removed the harnesses and placing them in an orderly fashion on the front of the chariot, he took both horses by their soaking wet bridles and, encouraging them with a gentle voice and a firm hand, led them toward the stable where he would rub them down and brush them out while they ate from bags of oats.

Just outside the stable door, the boy passed the stable master, who was coming the other way with two replacements. He veered to the side as the old man threw a kick his way and yelled at him to be patient as he led his horses out. The boy deftly evaded the stable masters boot.

Raymond was watching and muttered, half to himself, "The boy knew that kick was coming."

Hanshee, having witnessed the same, remained silent but continued to watch as the boy stared quizzically after the two new horses before turning and leading his charges into the dark interior of the stable.

The stable master got to work harnessing the two horses to the chariot as Jusaan and the guard, carrying a good-sized wine bag, emerged from the house. While the guard looked on at the harnessing, Jusaan approached Hanshee.

"Were you not thirsty, my brother?" the priest asked. "There is enough wine for all."

"We slaked our thirst from the well," Hanshee replied. "The cool water was refreshment enough."

Seeking to mask his thoughtlessness, Jusaan turned toward the stable master.

"We require another wine bag for our continued travel. See that one is prepared," he barked before turning to Hanshee with a smile.

"Of course, Your Eminence," the stable master replied as he struggled with the harness, "but I be but one man, and that lazy boy…"

As if on cue, the boy suddenly appeared beside the guard. "Those two are not your horses," he said.

The stable master, while reaching under one of the horses for the cinch, froze. Slowly, he turned his head until he could fix the child with his stare.

"What did you say, boy?" the old man asked menacingly.

"I said those are not the horses he left with us yesterday." the boy said, this time more boldly.

Before the stable master could respond, the guard spoke up.

"I believe you are right, boy," he said as he eyed the two horses. "They be similar, the same color and such, and both be geldings, but mine were at least a hand taller with longer legs."

There was a moment of silence before the old man piped up.

"I believe you are right, commander! I would have mistaken these horses myself!"

"Boy!" the stable master yelled, as if the mistake were not his. "Get your arse in the barn and bring me the commander's horses! Right this instant!"

Turning back to the group, he spoke with authority. "We'll get this cleared up, right quick!"

Raymond had seen and heard enough.

From his treatment of the child, to his obvious dishonesty, he felt this old liar needed to be confronted, but due to his continued charade, he dared not speak up. He looked to the guard, who he thought would be angry this old thief had tried to trick him, but the guard simply chuckled at the stable master's transparent attempts to appear innocent.

As the only other authority figure present, it was clear Jusaan could not care less which horses were attached to the chariot, so long as they could continue on to the Citadel.

Taking his lead from Hanshee, who was content to stay out of matters that didn't concern them, Raymond took a deep breath and let it out slowly, resigning himself to the fact that the attempted thievery would go unpunished.

Presently, the child returned from the stable with the correct animals and took up the task of harnessing them. The wily old man returned the imposters to the stable before proceeding to the house to retrieve another bag of watered wine. Upon his return, all was completed and, as the four travelers again secured themselves inside the chariot, the guard reached under his tunic and produced a purse from which he took two coins of gold.

"For your trouble, and for the wine," he grinned as he flipped a coin to the old man.

"And for you, boy, for your sharp eye and steady hand," he said, flipping the other coin toward the boy.

With the speed and coordination of a man in his prime, the old stable master plucked the spinning coin from the air before the child could make ready to catch it.

"The boy is young," the old thief said with a sheepish grin. "He could lose it. I'll keep it safe for him."

Roaring with laughter, the guard took the reins and deftly guided the horses into a turn toward the narrow road leading out of the small valley.

"God speed, commander! God speed, Your Grace! Pleasant journey!" the stable master called after the departing chariot.

Raymond did not dare look back. He knew the child would pay hell for exposing the old man's scheme.

And he probably won't even wait until we're out of sight, he thought, forcing himself to look straight ahead.

Chapter 3

Back on the main road, the chariot continued heading north. The fresh horses and relatively smooth surface made for a swift passage and, after cresting a low hill, the four looked upon the Stone Walls of Pith in the distance. These were not walls in the sense that the Pithians had built them. Rather, it was a natural rock formation, sheer on its face, extending upward to heights of two hundred feet or more, dwarfing the trees at their base. The tops of the walls were jagged, a natural dissuasion for any man to attempt to cross, even if he could find the nonexistent holds for hands and feet.

As the chariot proceeded, Raymond could see that the road ran directly toward the wall before forking short of its base. The wider and presumably more heavily traveled fork continued forward until reaching the wall, before veering to the west and running along its base. The narrower fork, which appeared to have seen less use, led off to the southeast, disappearing into a stand of elm trees. It was this lesser fork which the chariot took, and soon the four were surrounded by the tall, thick trunks and leafless branches of the wintering trees. A short ride through this miniature forest brought them again in sight of the wall.

From this distance, maybe six-hundred feet, an arched passage leading into the wall was visible. It was about twelve feet at its crest and about twice that in width. On either side of the passage stood two men; regulars of the military by their appearance. They wore clothing and armor similar in design to that of the chariots' driver, but of a grayish color and not nearly as highly polished. At their waist they wore swords. A lance and buckler could be seen leaning against the base of the rock wall behind both men.

To the right of the archway, about forty feet from the end of the road, there stood a sturdy wooden structure made of thick logs. Its dimensions were about thirty feet square, with a sloped wooden roof and stone chimney from which a plume of gray smoke rose.

As soon as the chariot came into sight, the men standing on either side of the archway sprang into action. Taking up their buckler and lance, they hurried inside the dim archway. They were soon joined by eight more men who emerged similarly equipped from the log structure. The shadowy confines of the archway made it difficult to know what went on beyond its entrance but, as they drew closer, Raymond found he could see about the first ten feet into its interior.

As he watched, the men used ropes and pulleys to quickly move a large log into position. When they finished, the log spanned the entire width of the passage at about two feet from the floor. Attached to its outward-facing side were several wide bucklers, spaced about a foot apart. The purpose of log and bucklers, though apparent, was driven home to the travelers when five feet of iron-pointed lance was extended from between each suspended buckler, toward the opening.

A lone soldier, obviously the leader of this group, strode out from the log building to stand before the formation. He was differentiated from the others only by the red crest on his dull gray helmet.

He took a moment to inspect his defenses, giving a scowl of dissatisfaction before turning to confront the oncoming chariot. The chariot driver pulled up about fifty-feet shy of the arched entrance, and steadied his horses as the lone soldier, a captain, approached. When the captain reached the horses' heads, the driver snapped out a salute, right fist closed – palm up – striking the center of his chest. This salute was mirrored by the captain, who spoke first.

"Hail, Hendric. You've made good time. We did not expect you 'til the morrow."

"I pushed the horses," the driver, Hendric, responded. "Maybe too hard, but it was my wish to be within the Citadel gates before nightfall." He reached to a hook in front of him and then straightened, tossing the larger of the wine bags to the captain.

"For you and your men, Ailean. They were quick and ready."

Ailean hefted the bag and glanced in the direction of his men before responding.

"I'll thank you not to share your opinion with them, as I want them to *remain* quick and ready." He then took stock of the other passengers.

"Your Grace," he said to Jusaan with a formal nod of his head. He eyed Hanshee and Raymond without comment before again addressing Hendric.

"You won't make the capital before nightfall," he said, "but you'll be resting not long thereafter."

Hendric snapped the reins and spurred the horses toward the arch, now unobstructed as its guard had quickly broken down their defenses and formed a line to either side of the entrance. Some saluted as the chariot rolled past, but all closely examined those riding within, wondering at the occupants who were allowed to use a portal designated for only the most important of the citizenry of Pith.

As the chariot entered the cool darkness, Raymond noticed the sound of the horses' hooves and chariot wheels changed. They had left the hard-packed earth and were now rumbling across wooden planks, not unlike a bridge. Up ahead could be seen a dull light, apparently the exit. Without torches the interior of the passage remained all but unfathomable.

Just before the exit, the horses' hooves, then the wheels, left the planks and traversed hard-packed ground once more. The chariot emerged into a large open space where there were more soldiers.

Theirs was a larger force than their brethren on the other side of the passage. They had a larger barracks, capable of housing upwards of thirty men, along with their equipment. There were also stables for their horses, a few wagons, and a storehouse for food and other supplies.

Raymond and Hanshee made these things out in the quickly dimming light of the shadows cast by the western sun against the rock wall towering above them. Hanshee seemed to take extra time in his assessment, as if mapping the area and its layout. He continued to look back the way they had come. Curious, Ray turned to see what Hanshee was looking at.

The first thing he noticed was a large disc-shaped stone beside the entrance to the passage. Standing on its side, this stone was positioned to be rolled into place before the tunnel, thus blocking any movement in or out. Attached to the stone, through precisely cut holes, were heavy ropes. Some of these ran from its top to a series of pulleys similarly attached to the stone wall and down to a large spindle to which a four-horse team could be harnessed. At a signal, a taut rope would be cut, allowing the weight of the stone to cause it to roll across and block the exit. Once in place, it could only be moved by the horse team.

To the other side of the entrance stood what looked like a large barrel. Standing upright on sturdy wooden stilts, its bottom was about five feet taller than the height of the arch, with the barrel itself being about twelve feet in diameter and in height. It reminded Raymond of a smaller version of the water towers back home. From its bottom extended what appeared to be piping. A closer inspection would have revealed large sections of bamboo attached end to end, the joints tightly sealed with wax, then bound with leather. This piping reached the top of the arched passageway, then curved to follow the contour of the ceiling inside. Puzzled, Raymond turned to Hanshee to get his reaction. Hanshee offered no explanation, simply making a mental note of the contraption before moving his gaze elsewhere.

By this time, the chariot had reached the edge of the clearing and turned right toward a road that was slightly broader than the one on the other side of the passage. This road wound its way downhill. Since the initial slope was fairly steep, the road progressed by going from side to side, the hairpin turns on either end allowing for a change of direction. The thickness of the surrounding forest ensured that wherever the road led remained a mystery.

Just as the last rays of evening light were about to fade, the chariot emerged onto a gentler slope. It was still impossible to get a complete bearing, with all the trees and undergrowth on either side, but it could be seen that the road now extended straight before them for several leagues. From this vantage point, Raymond could just make out where the slope appeared to end on the floor of an immense valley which continued on for a great distance. At some point, the road blended into the surrounding landscape, becoming invisible well before reaching the foot of a mountain range barely discernible due to distance and the growing darkness.

The sun had now completely set and, in this world without incandescent light, the blackness could sometimes seem complete. Raymond had been a dweller in this land for several months now and was no longer intimidated by the darkness. He knew his eyes would adjust and the stars, and especially the moon, would provide adequate light to move about if one was careful. Even now he could still make out the tops of the trees against the darkening sky, so he was aware when they emerged from the wooded slope and into a land of row upon row of smaller trees. They were now traveling through an orchard, and these squat trees with their empty limbs allowed more light to filter through to them.

Off to his right, between the barren boughs, Raymond was aware of a faint glow against the darkening sky. As the chariot made its way closer to the valley floor, the orchards gave way to terraced fields, and Ray now had an unobstructed view in the direction of the glow. It was still there, along with several points of light that appeared to be contained in shadow beneath it. This glow, and these lights, appeared to float above a strip of unfathomable darkness.

That could be a high wall, thought Raymond, *with what brilliance there was within reflected on the night sky. And those points of flickering light could be single lamps, visible to us from towers higher than the city walls.*

Though not certain that what he surmised was true, Raymond felt a sense of dread begin to grow within him. Since his arrival in this land, his one and only experience with what these people called a city had been a nightmare of confusion turning to anger, surprise turning to fear, and fear turning to stark terror after Ray had witnessed a level of violence and savagery he never dreamed existed. He looked over to Hanshee who appeared placid, mesmerized by the scene which had held Ray's attention.

Of course, the violence had been necessary.

They would both be dead now if Hanshee had not acted swiftly, decisively, and with deadly force. Raymond thought he had come to terms with what was sometimes required to survive in this place, but he now had to make a conscious effort to control his anxiety.

This is different, he thought. *We are being escorted as guests, not sneaking in as strangers. Control yourself; control your nerves. This will work out.*

Raymond looked up and saw that, while he had been lost in thought, the chariot had eased onto a side road and was now headed directly for the high wall. As they came closer, Ray could see his first guess had been correct; this appeared to be a huge city.

It was not huge by the standards he had grown up with; the area it encompassed would not compare with the downtown district of even a medium-size city back home, but it was impressive. Imagine ten square miles containing towers and cathedrals their pinnacles and spires reaching toward the heavens. Then add buildings to house the city garrison and all that is needed to maintain the city's infrastructure. Add the numerous other dwellings needed for forty thousand inhabitants, including stables for horses, theaters and arenas for entertainment, shops, taverns, and slums - because every city has its poor. Imagine all this and more, enclosed by an imposing stone wall sixty feet high and fifteen feet thick at its base.

Now approach the wall from a distance and watch as it become larger and larger, seeming to grow with each passing moment, until you find yourself standing at its base, looking up in awe of its sheer mass as it draws your eyes up and up, high above to its lowest battlements, and higher still to its tallest towers.

Imagine all of that and you would understand, as Raymond did, the meaning of insignificance.

Presently, a series of lights up ahead captured his attention. Torches placed along the wall at twenty-foot intervals gave evidence of their approach to the two sentries stationed outside the wall, standing before an iron gate blocking the way into the city. As the chariot drew closer, the sentries assumed defensive postures.

As Hendric pulled the horses up, his crimson and gold uniform became visible in the semicircle of light before the portal, causing both sentries to relax their stance and snap a wordless salute. One reached out and pulled on a cord hanging from the wall to the left of the portal. With a series of tugs, he produced a code audible only on the other side of the wall. This task complete, the sentries resumed their positions on either side of the portal. As the four travelers watched, the heavy iron gate was smoothly raised into position, with only its deadly spiked bottom still visible at the very top of the entry.

Hendric returned the sentries' salute and guided the horses into the darkness of the interior of the wall. Again, Raymond noticed the almost immediate transition from stone floor to wooden planks inside the short tunnel. Before he could give this much thought, the iron bars of the gate clanged down behind them and a second set, about thirty feet ahead, opened before them, allowing them to proceed into the stable yard of the Royal House of the Citadel.

No sooner did the chariot come to a stop in the torch lit yard than two grooms came sprinting across the loose gravel surface. One took up a position at the horses' heads, a hand on each bridle, while the other stood at the rear of the chariot, awaiting directions from Hendric. As neither groom was of the military, a half bow took the place of a salute. With a nod of his head to the grooms, Hendric addressed Jusaan.

"These boys will see you to the temple entrance," he said as he unhitched his leather chariot belt. "I go to report your arrival, thus ending my service to you this night."

This was spoken with a touch of formality and with discernible satisfaction. Hendric then moved away from the chariot, allowing the groom who stood behind it to assume his place at the reins. As Raymond watched Hendric walk through a portal in the side of the large building across from the stables, the chariot started forward.

The temple was at the far end of the citadel grounds, past the Royal House, the building which Hendric had entered.

The Royal House, home to King Ammon IV and the formal government of Pith, loomed huge, even in the darkness. The groom kept the horses at a respectful walk as they passed from one pool of light to the next, temporarily lost in the shadows between. When they passed before the main entrance, ablaze with lamps and torches, Raymond could see a half-dozen guards outfitted as was Hendric and standing at their assigned posts. There was one each positioned in front of the four massive columns supporting the portico, with two more before the heavy main doors. As one, their eyes followed the chariot as it passed before them, and their eyes remained on it until it passed out of sight into the shadows between the torches.

The horses plodded forward until the chariot reached the end of the Royal House. There the chariot pulled up before a side entrance to the building just beyond it, the Temple of The One Spirit. Here three young acolytes rushed out. They ignored all the chariot's occupants, save for the priest, Jusaan, who was a member of the Council of Nine. The first acolyte to arrive took his place at the heads of the horses, while his companions waited at the rear of the chariot to be available when needed. After Raymond and Hanshee had stepped down onto the loose gravel, an acolyte came forward to take the wine bag which had accompanied Jusaan since leaving the stables where they'd changed horses. The remaining acolyte extended his hand so Council Priest Jusaan would be steadied and regal as he descended from the chariot.

His feet once again on solid ground, Jusaan dismissed the chariot. After a sigh of relief at being back in familiar surroundings, he began barking commands.

"These men are guests of the Temple," Jusaan said with a stern face. "Specifically, they are my guests. Any discourtesy done them will be as a discourtesy done me. For now, they will be housed in the empty servants' rooms across from my quarters. You will arrange for hot baths, followed by hot meals from the royal kitchens."

He cast a glance at Ray before again addressing the acolyte. "Mend and clean their apparel, see that their bedding is comfortable, and post a servant outside their quarters to meet their every need this night."

This latter was as much to prevent Hanshee and Raymond from wandering about, and others from snooping, as to address the guests' needs, but this was tacitly understood, and need not be spoken aloud.

Jusaan turned to Hanshee and, in the ancient tongue, explained all that was to be provided them this night. Hanshee, with a slight smile, bowed his thanks.

Having given all needed orders and explanations, Jusaan made his way quickly to the side entrance, trailed closely by the second acolyte. The acolyte to whom Jusaan had given his instructions watched his master depart before turning toward Hanshee, who he assumed was the leader. Having glimpsed part of his heathen attire underneath the borrowed cloak, the servant's face nevertheless remained courteously expressionless as he addressed him.

"If it would please m'lord, I will escort you to your quarters." He turned and started for the door only to realize, after several steps, he walked alone.

Turning back, he saw Hanshee and Raymond still standing where he had addressed them and staring after him. In his haste to follow his orders, the servant had turned away quickly and so was completely unaware Raymond had begun to follow, only to be instantly checked by Hanshee's iron grip on his arm. At first puzzled, it suddenly dawned on the servant there must be a language barrier at work here. He made an exaggerated gestured for the two to follow and, watching until they complied, again turned and led the way into the Temple.

Entering the doorway, they found themselves in a narrow but well-lit passageway which, after a few steps, led to a much wider hallway. This hallway was almost twenty feet across and appeared to run the length of the building. The walls on either side provided room for appropriately spaced chairs and couches, along with pedestals which supported ornate vases and beautiful sculptures in wood and stone. The walls on both sides were adorned with intricate paintings and colorful tapestries, most depicting scenes of battle and conquest incongruous in a temple of faith.

The trio followed this hall for quite a way, passing closed doors and narrow stairs leading both up and down, until they reached a wide staircase, its steps and bannisters fashioned out of polished hardwood. They ascended for several flights, enough to make Raymond wonder how someone as pampered as Jusaan could endure making this trek several times a day.

Finally, on what Raymond thought to be the ninth level, they left the stairwell and proceeded down a hall of similar size as the first, but less ornate. On the left were door after door. The right side also had doors, but they were spaced much further apart. After passing three doors on the right, and maybe nine or ten on the left, they came to a door on the left situated directly across from the fourth door on the right. Here the servant produced a key and, unlocking the door, ushered Raymond and Hanshee inside. Believing he would not be understood, the servant nevertheless paused to give polite instructions.

"Please consider this dwelling as your home for the night, and do not hesitate to make yourselves fully comfortable," he said, motioning toward a small wooden table with two chairs next to it. "Your needs will be provided for momentarily."

With that, he spun on his heel and exited the quarters, closing and locking the door behind him. Raymond and Hanshee stared at each other, each listening for the servant's footsteps to recede before speaking in their own 'private' language; Hanshee's tongue.

"Much thanks for stopping me from following him outside," Ray began. "I could have…"

"Dajee, Way-mon," Hanshee said. "You have endured much and your mind has not yet been trained. We will endure this also, and whatever else comes."

Having sensed the apprehension Ray had been feeling ever since he had recognized a city wall in the darkness, Hanshee continued. "We are safe, for now. Biding our time and keeping our secrets, we will endure and learn. When the time comes, we will again make our way west, to the Blue Mountains, to my home."

Before Ray could respond, there was a knock on the door. The pair stood silent as the key was turned and the door swung inward to reveal the first acolyte, the one who had followed Jusaan. Having satisfied himself that this was the correct room, he stood aside and waved in two women with bundles in their arms. They hurried past Hanshee and Ray and were quickly followed by four young men, each carrying one end of a large metal tub half-filled with steaming water. Their muscles strained as they shuffled awkwardly through the doorway with their heavy burdens. Finding room beyond the table and chairs, the four eased the tubs to the floor so they sat side by side. They then bowed to no one in particular and took their leave.

The two women had gone about making up the two heavy cots in the second room of the two room apartment with clean sheets and blankets. When they returned to the main room, they positioned themselves, one behind each tub, and waited.

After the young men carrying the tubs made their exit, there was room enough for two other women who were waiting outside to come in. They entered, each carrying a large vessel in either hand. In addition, each woman had a canvas bag slung around her neck and hanging off one shoulder. After placing the vessels on the table, they reached into their bags and pulled forth carved wooden cups and heavy glass goblets, spoons and knives, and hand-size towels, all of which they arranged on the table before bowing and taking their leave.

Hanshee and Raymond watched this whirlwind of activity with wordless fascination. Once the table had been set and the women had closed the door behind them, the two found themselves still staring at it, anticipating another knock which would set off yet another parade of eager-to-please servants. When after a few moments no knock came, the friends turned their eyes to each other, with Raymond breaking into an amused grin.

Still smiling he turned to the table and the drinks awaiting his parched lips, but gave a startled jump when he noticed the two women, smiling patiently, still standing behind the tubs.

Hanshee, being ever-aware, knew the women were still there. He burst into laughter at Raymond's startled expression. The two women also laughed demurely. Then the elder of the two spoke while motioning toward the water.

"If it pleases m'lords," she said, "come and test the water for your baths."

Raymond stared at her quizzically, pretending he didn't understand. To further sell the ruse, he turned a confused look to Hanshee, as if asking for a translation. Hanshee shrugged and returned his look of confusion before both turned back toward the tubs and the women stationed behind them.

The two women exchanged nervous glances. Then the one who first spoke stepped forward and gently took Ray by the hand. Her smiling face exuding reassurance, she led him to the tub and dipped his hand in the water.

"Whoa!" Ray exclaimed, snatching his hand from the scalding water and the servant's grip. The two women, their eyes wide with surprise, were frozen in their tracks as Raymond examined his tender hand. They remained motionless for one beat...two beats... and then...

"Bwaaahahahaha!"

Hanshee's riotous laughter exploded in the room, echoing down the wide hallway outside. By this time, Raymond was used to Hanshee's sense of humor, and his contagious laughter. He instantly saw what his companion found funny in this situation, and began to chuckle in response to Hanshee's roars. As Hanshee continued on, Ray found himself involuntarily chuckling even more. He was trying not to lose himself in the mirth, but he knew he wouldn't be able to hold out for long. Moments later he had joined Hanshee in full-throated laughter as the tension and apprehension of the past few weeks fell away.

The startled women stared wide-eyed at the pair before turning to each other. Were these madmen? Why were they roaring with laughter over a simple bath? The surprise and worry on the face of each fed the concerns of the other. Puzzled, they turned toward their laughing guests, desperately trying to understand what they found so funny.

Seeing this, Hanshee, still laughing, pointed his finger at the two while looking at Ray. His eyes flitting between Hanshee and the women, the stinging in his hand forgotten, Raymond slumped onto one knee as tears began streaming down his cheeks.

The women continued to watch the strangers, their eyes narrowing in suspicion until, first one, then the other, began to giggle. That made Hanshee and Raymond laugh even harder. Soon all decorum was lost as the two servant women, one holding onto the rim of the tub, the other holding onto her back, laughed uncontrollably while stealing glances at the two strange travelers.

Hanshee, his back now against a wall, continued to point at the women and laugh as he slowly slid to the floor. Raymond, down on one knee and clutching the back of a chair for support, had almost gotten hold of himself when he looked up and saw the younger of the two women laughing so hard that a bubble of snot exploded from her nostril. This sent Hanshee into convulsions of laughter. He completed his slide to the floor and fell over into the fetal position, screaming with mirth. Raymond, seeing the snot bubble and Hanshee's reaction to it, pointed at his partner as he himself descended into great bouts of laughter which left him gasping for breath.

Amid all of this hilarity, no one noticed the door opening, or the acolyte, the one who had escorted them to the room, peering in with wide-eyed astonishment. Not knowing what to make of the situation, he first assured himself no one was being killed. Then, shaking his head in silent sympathy for the afflicted, he gently closed the door.

Eventually, the four regained their composure. The eldest of the two women found the strength to add one of the large pitchers of cold water to her tub. Testing it with her hand, she coaxed Raymond to disrobe and get in. Hanshee had no problem with the steaming-hot temperature of his bath, and was soon immersed in the tub beside Ray's. The two of them relaxed in the water while the woman set about the task of scrubbing them from head to foot with large, stiff-bristled brushes. This was made all the more difficult since they were still experiencing mini-fits of laughter each time any two of them made eye contact.

Raymond felt more relaxed with every passing minute the woman worked the brush on him. He'd always heard laughter was cathartic. Now he wholeheartedly agreed. All the tension and stress, the fear and anxiety he had built up over the course of the last few months, seemed to drain from his body as the result of his fit of laughter.

Maybe I'll call it a mirth attack, he absently thought, his mind seeming to drift ever farther away, as his body became more and more relaxed.

Whatever it was…damn, I needed it.

Chapter 4

After giving detailed instructions to the acolyte, Jusaan waved a hand in dismissal and walked down the great hall on the first level of the temple. Reaching its end, he withdrew a key from inside his robe and unlocked a gold-painted door hanging on ornate hinges. Passing quickly through and closing the door behind him, he proceeded to a similar door set into the wall to his right. The same key unlocked this door and revealed one of the perks of the senior members of the priesthood. Stepping through the threshold, Jusaan was instantly hailed with a respectful, "Your Grace." Nodding in acknowledgment, he proceeded to a sturdy wooden cage fitted snugly between four thick beams extending upward toward the upper floors of the temple.

The area inside the cage was sufficient to accommodate several individuals and was lit by four lamps, positioned one to each corner. The flickering light revealed walls of polished wood, decorated with ornate carvings and inlays of gold and colorful stones, as well as iron reinforcement, all done in such a way as to transform a basic cage into a safe and luxurious transport fit for the holy servants of The One Spirit.

Atop the cage was a brace of solid iron supporting a flywheel about a foot in diameter. A thick rope had been looped around the wheel and from there rose into the darkness above. To the side of the cage, the man who had greeted the priest was positioned beside a similar rope running down from above and passing through two flywheels before rising back up into the darkness.

Jusaan gingerly made his way into the cage and braced himself with the aid of the many short lengths of rope hanging from its ceiling. He nodded to the man who had positioned himself beside the closest of the flywheels. After acknowledging the priest's consent, the heavyset man grasped a handle extending horizontally from the wheel. Putting all of his muscled bulk into his work, the man began to crank the wheel which, aided by a system of weights, was intended to raise and lower the cage. There was a slight lurch before it lifted from the floor and began its journey toward the upper levels of the Temple of The One Spirit.

Jusaan smiled in contentment as he felt himself rising toward his destination. He loved this contraption, this lift, and he loved even more the fact that only the lord high priest and members of the Council of Seven carried keys granting access. There were similar lifts at strategic locations throughout the temple, though most were much smaller and without ornamentation. They were for the rapid transport of food, wine, and other essentials. The servants, along with the various junior priests and acolytes had to traverse the seemingly endless stairs connecting the building's many levels.

As the lift neared the tenth level, Jusaan pulled a cord which rang a chime, signaling that the lift should be brought to a halt. Stepping onto a ledge, he again produced his key, which he used to open the door before him. Passing through, he entered a richly decorated foyer. Stepping quickly, he crossed this space to face a huge double door in a wall paneled in oak.

After taking a lantern from the table beside the door and coaxing a light, Jusaan reached into his robe and produced a different key. This he used on the three locks that secured the portal. Upon hearing the last lock disengage, he pushed the heavy doors inward, took up his light, and entered the temple's library.

Here the most valuable religious and historical artifacts of Pith were stored, most in boxes so finely crafted as to be airtight. Valuable objects of lesser metals and wood were wrapped in oiled cloths, with only objects of gold, ivory, or of special significance open to view on permanent or semi-permanent display.

Jusaan made his way between tables, pedestals, and cases, to a door in the back of the room. There he used the same key which had opened the outer door to pass through and into a vast storage area. It was easy to find the relic he desired, for it was of special origin and highly significant. It was sealed in an airtight container, dusty with age and from lack of use, though it was one of the most important artifacts stored there.

Jusaan was very careful in removing the container from the shelf on which it rested. Just as carefully, he carried it to a wide table in the center of the room. Hanging his lantern from a hook above the table, Jusaan took the time to admire the box on the table before him. Placing his hands on either side of it, he caressed the intricately carved wood from which the lid was made. Lifting gently but firmly, he felt the lid begin to separate from the lower portion of the box. Alternately applying pressure first to one side, then to the other, he carefully worked the lid upward. Only when he sensed it was about to release did he pause, the weight of his actions finally catching up to him.

Jusaan realized, with as much trepidation as anticipation, that the decisions he would make this night - the wheels he would set into motion in this room - could ultimately lead to his elevation as lord high priest.

They could just as easily lead to his destruction.

These ruminations made him hesitate and gave him second thoughts. He allowed this doubt to rise to the surface of his consciousness.

Was this the way? If so, why was he afraid? When The One had finally recognized him, sent fortune to favor him, presented to him a pathway to follow in order to realize his greatest ambitions, had he not the stomach and the heart to seize it?

Wait, a voice spoke to him from his own mind. This *is not just about you…not simply a matter of satisfying your ambitions.*

The forces he was about to unleash, properly controlled, had the potential to set the empire on a path to unrivaled greatness. If uncontrolled, the empire could be consumed by flames of its own making. He was afraid that if he started down this path, there could be no turning back. He was afraid because he knew he was already too far down the path and, for him and therefore for Pith, there *was* no turning back.

With this last thought echoing through his mind, Jusaan lifted the lid that concealed the four leather scrolls within.

****

When Jusaan finally reached his chambers, a messenger from the Royal House awaited him. He had expected this. With the dust of the road still upon him, he pushed away thoughts of a hot bath and a change of garments and allowed the servant to escort him to the first of the many trials along the path which he had chosen this night.

From the door of his quarters overlooking the great sanctuary, they turned left and proceeded down a long hall. Reaching its end, they turned right, moved past the servants' hall, and proceeded down the wide staircase to the eighth level. This entire level was devoted to the quarters of the lord high priest, with a few apartments for his personal servants. The only other feature was a foyer leading to a covered archway. It was the only known passage by which the Temple and the Royal House were connected.

The royal messenger led Jusaan across the archway, which formed a bridge one hundred feet above the cobblestones of an alley between the two buildings. At its other end was an identical foyer in the Royal House, adorned with couches, chairs, tables, sculptures and tapestries. Upon an oversized high-backed chair sat Lord Cecil, chief advisor to the King and arguably the second-most powerful personage in the kingdom. Any argument would center on whether he was *the* most powerful.

Cecil did not stand when Jusaan arrived. He would not have stood for the lord high priest himself, except where protocol demanded. He made a point of eyeing the council member as he was led before him by the royal messenger.

Coming to a halt, the messenger bowed deeply before addressing the chief advisor.

"Lord Priest Jusaan of the Council of the Nine," he said, gesturing toward the priest who had come to a halt beside him. He then turned to Jusaan and with a sweeping gesture toward the older man said, "Lord Cecil, Chief Adviser to the Marble Throne of Pith." Having completed the introductions his duty required, he again bowed low before disappearing into the Royal House.

The pair remained silent as the advisor continued to eye the priest. When satisfied his stare had achieved the desired result, Cecil spoke.

"How much have I wagered in indulgence of your foolishness, Jusaan?"

"Should you not offer me a seat before we discuss important matters?" the priest asked, attempting to put the advisor on his heels.

"Sit or stand, priest," Cecil said. "Your posture changes your situation not in the least!"

Recognizing these words for their true meaning, Jusaan chose a seat close to Cecil and slowly, carefully sat down. Taking time to gather his thoughts, Jusaan lifted his eyes to meet the adviser's stare before speaking.

"You require an explanation."

It was a statement, not a question.

"Indeed," shot back the older man. "I require a very good explanation, considering your request."

Reaching into the folds of his robe, Cecil produced the small wooden tube made from young bamboo, further hollowed to reduce its weight. Jusaan recognized it as the tube in which he had placed his message to the Royal House while he was encamped with Galin and his forces in the Ursal Mountains. Jusaan watched as Cecil's thick fingers removed a wooden plug, the original having been of wax, and shook loose the roll of thin paper concealed inside. Carefully unfurling it to its full length, Cecil let his eyes scan the miniature document before once again raising them to Jusaan.

"Of highest importance to the Royal House. Prophesy! Send transport for two," Cecil recited, his eyes boring into Jusaan's.

"One of your station would be a fool to send such a message directly to the Royal House," Cecil stated flatly.

"A fool?" Jusaan questioned. "In what way?"

Cecil's stare turned cold. Brandishing the message before him, he asked, "You would secretly approach the Throne on a matter of prophesy? You would circumvent the council and assume for yourself the mantle of lord high priest?"

Leaning into the priest's face he continued, "You would demand expulsion from the Temple? You would invite execution? You think yourself *not* a fool? You think this wisdom? Think again."

Having driven home the consequences of his actions, Cecil was surprised to see no fear in Jusaan's eyes. Slowly he leaned back in his chair, intensely curious as to what secret knowledge lay at the foundation of such audacity.

Having calmly withstood the chief advisor's admonitions, Jusaan gazed beyond him as if in deep thought. Presently he spoke, weighing every word.

"Whether I be wise or foolish has yet to be judged," he began, "but judged I most assuredly will be. Yet only in the context of loyalty and self-sacrifice can my actions be truly judged, so let me not be judged by those for whom self-preservation comes before duty, and let me not be judged by those who see their own aggrandizement in the downfall of their fellows."

"What I am poised to bring forward," Jusaan continued, "can only be judged by one who dwells above the petty entanglements of station, privilege and ego. One whose wisdom has been long established, and whose devotion to Pith is unquestioned."

There were insults and compliments aplenty in this statement. Cecil knew that answering to them would be likened to self-incrimination. No fool himself, he saw the path the priest had chosen, and understood what he was requesting. He knew that such a path was a plea for the headman's axe, unless the unknown information being bartered here was of such value as to bring instant validity, instant relevance, and therefore instant authority to he who had discovered it.

Jusaan was intelligent and ambitious. Cecil found it difficult to believe he was also suicidal.

Cecil carefully rolled the message back up and, placing it again inside the small bamboo tube, tucked it into an inner pocket of his robe. Only then did he respond to the council member.

"I brought you here in order to hear an explanation, and as yet you offer none. Instead, you cast aspersions on those of your caste and, laying the foundation of your own destruction, request a judgment by the King. Am I not correct?" Not waiting for a response, Cecil continued. "But I grant you this; by your boldness and audacity you have made your point and, should your explanation impress, you will have your royal audience. However, it is only through me that this audience is possible."

The chief advisor's eyes bore into the priests. "You now have my pledge," he said. "Impress me."

****

Cecil was impressed.

So much so that he granted the additional requests Jusaan had made. It was now his place to arrange the audience, prepare His Majesty, and let the King's judgment decide the future of the empire.

A smile came unbidden to his lips. The next few days could be both momentous and entertaining!

Chapter 5

Raymond didn't know what time it was.

The darkness inside their sleeping quarters would have been absolute, save for the trickle of moonlight that came through the sliver in the outer wall passing for a window. Trying to count the hours from their arrival until they were left to sleep, and knowing their usual sleeping habits, he figured it to be about an hour, maybe a little less, before sunrise.

His mind drifted back to the previous night, and he wondered at the changes in himself. When he considered it, last night was his first real contact with a female since he woke up in this place. He had seen many women and girls in Aggipoor, the first city they encountered. He had even briefly interacted with a tavern maid there, but at the time he wasn't disposed to admire feminine beauty, or to allow himself to experience physical attraction. He had been concerned with finding out where he was and getting back to where he should be.

Last night it had felt good to be touched by a woman and, even though it was only a bath, his body had responded. He wasn't ashamed or embarrassed, like he knew the old Ray would have been, and he and the servant woman had laughed at what her fingers found under the bath water.

This must happen to her all the time, Ray had thought, since she must also be required to bathe the priests. But, for all he knew, the priests may have experienced no reaction at all. *Hadn't priests moved beyond such needs?* Raymond shuddered at the thought, silently vowing to never pursue the priesthood.

His mind continued to wander, back to when he had awakened on the river bank. He remembered the confusion and creeping dread that had blossomed into outright fear and panic, emotions that, for a time, were never far from the surface of his thoughts. Over time, he had come to terms with the fact that he was in a different world, possibly a different time. This place bore no resemblance to the world he knew, the world of motor vehicles and fast food and television. Not knowing how he arrived here, he had no idea how to get back.

You can't get there from here, was the old punchline that kept repeating itself in his mind but, unlike the times back home when he had heard it, this time it wasn't a joke.

He had spent the last three months, not sure even if it was three months, in a state of high stress and anxiety. Looking back, it was a wonder he had been able function at all. It was Hanshee who had saved him. He pictured his benefactor, who slept on the other side of the room, bedding down on the floor and leaving the cot untouched, as was his custom. Hanshee had picked him up and dusted him off, literally and figuratively. He had provided for all of Ray's needs: food, water, shelter, medicine, guidance, protection, as well as acceptance, sympathy, structure, training, focus, companionship, confidence, and even friendship.

Raymond was glad he could include friendship in the list. There were times when he wasn't so sure about Hanshee's intentions, or about their relationship. When he had witnessed, up close, the violence Hanshee was capable of, he had experienced terror as he had never known it before. He had feared for his life. For an instant, his only thought had been to get as far away from this man as possible, but Hanshee would have none of that. Only by staying close to him was Ray's life saved.

Again.

Lying there in the darkness, Raymond thought about how his life had changed, how he himself had changed. The last three months of travel by foot and living off the land had transformed him physically. His body was now lean and hard. He guessed he was about twenty pounds lighter than he had been before, yet he felt just as strong as he'd been before he woke up on the river bank, maybe even stronger.

Nature is its own gym, he mused.

He was fit, was relatively sound of mind, considering his circumstances, and had his friend by his side. Now they had found a place, not of their choosing but still a place, where they might find respite. Here they would bide their time, gather their thoughts, and plan their future course.

It would be easier if they knew why the priest Jusaan had taken such an interest in them. That Jusaan and Hanshee came from the same ancient people didn't explain anything at all, as far as Raymond could tell. Jusaan appeared to have some secret scheme, one of which even Lord Galin seemed unaware. This had the potential to lead to costly complications, but it remained the only explanation as to why they were extended the hospitality they now enjoyed.

After their bath, the servants had dried them with linen towels. They were given clean clothes, as their other garments had been taken for cleaning and repair, even their shoes. Though he wore little, Hanshee was loath to part with his undergarment, skirt, and harness, all of good leather. The servant who had tended to him did her best to persuade him, and eventually he relented, though he held tight to his weapons and to the "magic pouch," as Raymond thought of the bag Hanshee carried over his shoulder. Ray knew it contained herbs and the ingredients for potions. Hanshee had even produced gold coins from the pouch when needed!

After parting with their clothes, they were provided with traditional undergarments. Raymond thought they fit like snug diapers. Robes of heavy wool embroidered with silk provided a hedge against the cool night air.

Not long after they were dressed, two new servants arrived with trays of hot food and a pitcher of wine. The meal consisted of dried fruit, a thick stew, warm bread, and pastries. Ray found it delicious. Having gone almost an entire day without food, he and Hanshee ate near to bursting, while discussing the events of the day and evening, and making plans for the coming days.

During the meal, it was decided that Raymond, while still pretending not to understand the Pithian tongue, should look for a way to communicate directly with the servants, but never with the guards. This was another lesson passed to him from Hanshee.

"Those who serve are often looked down upon and ignored," Hanshee had said. "It would be they who would be privy to many secrets of the Pith, secrets their masters would be unaware they knew. They would be more likely to share these secrets, inflating their own importance in our eyes, and in their own.

"But never attempt to speak with the guards," Hanshee had continued, "nor lead them in any way to believe you understand their tongue. Well-trained guards are like pups, wanting nothing more than to please their masters. It is their nature to be suspicious of all outsiders. Though I doubt they know our secret tongue, still we will guard our words when we speak around them."

Not being a man of the city, Raymond wondered where Hanshee had garnered wisdom such as this, and he asked as much.

"My words are not so much lessons of guards and servants as lessons on the nature of men," Hanshee had said. Peering at Raymond, Hanshee seemed to sense his processing, and accepting, this new lesson. He smiled affirmation at his pupil.

"The servants who bathed us," Raymond had volunteered. "They spoke quietly to each other. Not much. Not enough for my understanding. Only enough to know it was not the Pithian tongue. If I can hear enough of their tongue, I could learn it. Then we would have more eyes and ears to aid us."

Hanshee broke into a big smile. "You spoke those words as would I, as if you were one with the People of the Earth."

Puzzled, Raymond had thought back to what he had just said and how he said it.

"You're right," he said. "You must be influencing me."

"As a teacher should." Hanshee exclaimed. He rose lithely from his cross-legged seat on the floor. "Now it is time to rest. We know not what the morrow brings, but whatever it be, rest will make it easier."

With that, Hanshee had prepared for sleep, using the sheets and blanket from one of the cots to prepare a makeshift bed on the floor. Months of living in the forest had acclimated Raymond to sleeping on the ground, but the cot still looked wonderful.

He was asleep before his head hit the pillow.

Now, lying in the still darkness just before dawn, Ray thought he heard movement outside the door. Opening his eyes, he watched as a shadow noiselessly glided across the darkness of the bedchamber and out into the larger room. He heard a key inserted into the lock. Light from the outer hall flooded into the sitting room as the door opened and someone stealthily entered. They paused after a few steps, then silently retraced their steps back into the main hallway. The door quietly closed, again leaving the chamber in darkness.

The brief light had shown Raymond that Hanshee was not on his bedding on the floor, meaning the shadow which had flitted silently across the bedchamber was he. As Raymond waited, he heard the striking of a flint. A lamp was lit, brightening the outer chamber and casting faint light into the bedchamber. Ray rose from his cot and entered the sitting room, where he found Hanshee standing over a bundle on the table.

"Our garments have been returned," he stated, and held up Ray's underwear as proof.

Raymond took the proffered garment and examined it. "At least it's clean," he said as he reached for his cargo shorts, his boots, and what was left of his socks and shirt.

"Hanshee, my clothes are in pretty rough shape," Raymond began, "and while your leather holds up well, it is unlike anything I have seen others around us wear."

Hanshee seemed to peer into Ray's mind. Then he asked, "You wish to continue wearing the robes we have been given?"

"If we did, we wouldn't stand out so much," replied Ray. "They would probably be more comfortable around us if we tried to adopt some of their ways."

"Yes, Way-mon," Hanshee nodded in agreement. "If those who host us are comfortable with us in their midst, it will help our stay with them, however long it may last, to be…uneventful."

This brought a smile to Raymond's face. He was happy to be in a position to contribute what knowledge and ideas he could in this foreign place. He felt that, out of necessity, Hanshee had been carrying him for far too long.

They were about to put their old clothes in the sleeping chamber when there was a knock on the door. After a short pause it opened, revealing the same two servants who had helped them bathe last night. Now they carried bowls of water for the morning wash. As they entered the room, the elder one spoke to Hanshee, who responded with a quizzical look. This brought a smile to her face. She turned to her companion and said something, causing them both to burst into giggles.

Hanshee turned to Raymond, who responded in their language, "Not yet." He had no idea what the woman had said to Hanshee; he hadn't been exposed long enough to the language the women spoke to be able to understand it. He did, however, feel it was appropriate to try to initiate some level of communication.

After the women had placed the bowls of water on the table, Raymond stepped forward, gestured to his chest and said, "Raymond." He then gestured toward his companion and said, "Hanshee."

The women looked on curiously as he repeated this basic introduction. Then he pointed to the older of the two and waited, his eyebrows raised. She caught on immediately. Pointing a finger toward herself, she said "Laretha." This led to delighted giggles from her and her companion.

Turning to the other woman, Ray pointed to her, his eyebrows raised.

Laretha pointed to her companion and said, "Meesha."

Smiling brightly, Meesha nodded in agreement. She touched her chest and repeated, "Meesha."

There was much smiling and nodding among the four of them as they acknowledged this beginning of communication. Then the servants went about their duties, filling the large bowl from the container of warm water they had brought with them, and leaving the container of drinking water on the table. They cleaned up the residue of the evening's meal, chattering as they worked, while casting occasional glances at Raymond and Hanshee. Ray listened intently to every word passing from their lips.

When she finished clearing the table, Laretha turned to them and rapidly spoke a few words. She and Meesha giggled, knowing the two men hadn't understood. They departed, still giggling.

Raymond did not understand this special gift he had with regard to languages. It had appeared out of nowhere. He didn't know if it was triggered by the number of words he heard or the length of exposure he had to a strange tongue. At times it had seemed like both. Whatever was the case, he was feeling frustrated it had not kicked in yet.

He caught a quizzical look from Hanshee and shook his head.

"Not a word yet," Ray said.

"Keep listening, Way-mon," Hanshee replied. "It will come."

The two servants had brought clay vessels with lids, which they placed on the floor. Ray figured they were to be used as chamber pots, and he and Hanshee gladly put one to use. Replacing he lid, they placed the used pot outside the door.

They used the warm water in the bowls to wash themselves. As they finished, .Laretha and Meesha returned with the morning meal of dried fruit, cheese, bread and pastries. This was to be washed down with watered wine. The servants departed and the pair dug into a meal worth killing for after months spent in the wild.

It was not long after they finished that Jusaan paid them a visit.

He was preceded by a personal servant, who inspected the quarters for the requisite level of cleanliness that would allow for his master's presence. Satisfied with what he found, he departed, only to reappear moments later, opening the door for Jusaan. The priest entered the apartment with a serene smile on his lips and a deep nod of his head to Hanshee. The servant entered behind him and made his way to the nearest chair. Pulling it out, he made a great show of using his handkerchief to wipe it down before offering it to his master with a bow.

Raymond, having fallen into character as Hanshee's acolyte as soon as Jusaan made his entrance, had to stifle a chuckle as he waited to see if Hanshee would require him to pull out a chair for him and dust its seat. Hanshee saw the expression on Raymond's face and gave him a stern look. Ray bowed as if accepting admonishment and went into the sleeping room. There he stuffed a pillow in his mouth so his laughter would be contained. Hanshee cast a look of annoyance at his departing back, then took the seat opposite Jusaan.

Jusaan smiled and spoke courteously. "Honored guest, I hope your quarters have been to your liking and all of your needs have been adequately met. These servants' quarters are small, servants having so few needs. But rest assured if all goes well, I will shortly be moving you into apartments more fitting for one of your station."

This was spoken in what Jusaan referred to as "the old tongue," which was closely related to Hanshee's native language. Raymond, with his newfound gift for languages, understood what he heard Jusaan say from his position in the next room. Though he recognized a familiar word or two, the servant of Jusaan did not understand what was said.

After Hanshee nodded his head in acceptance of the hospitality, Jusaan continued.

"I have made arrangements for an audience for you and your acolyte before the marble throne, with his Royal Monarch, Leader of the Forces of Stronghold and Defender of the Faith of The One Spirit, King Ammon IV of the Pithian Empire!" Jusaan finished with a flourish and, leaning back in his seat, prepared to watch as awe and amazement flooded the features of this savage priest.

Hanshee's expression did not change and Jusaan looked to his servant in puzzlement, finally muttering, "Perhaps my translation is at fault..." Nevertheless, he plunged on; "Your audience with the King has been arranged for the second hour after the noon meal. He requests you be attired as you were when first brought to the encampment in the Ursal Mountains."

Finally, Hanshee spoke.

"To meet with your king is a great honor, is it not? I will gladly meet with him, and be attired as he wishes."

"Both of you," Jusaan interjected, making sure the priest was aware his companion was included. "Your acolyte should attend and also wear his traditional garb."

"This will be done." Hanshee nodded in agreement.

Signaling for his attendant, Jusaan stood. Looking down at the still-seated Hanshee, he said, "I will send a man to escort you at the designated hour, probably accompanied by Citadel Guards. Please, do not be alarmed. Any armed men are only for your safety, as well as for ceremony."

Seeing Hanshee understood and would comply, Jusaan bowed his leave as his servant opened the door and stood aside to allow him to depart.

Upon hearing the door close, Raymond came back into the room. The awe and amazement Jusaan had expected from Hanshee was clearly reflected on Ray's face as he wordlessly locked eyes with his companion.

"At the second hour after the noon meal," Hanshee said, "it begins."

Chapter 6

Galin was a different kind of warrior, it was said.

Though thoroughly cold-blooded when applying his craft - the arts of death, destruction, torture, rape, pillage and carnage - he was widely recognized as the most jovial of men. He was always quick with a smile or a hearty laugh. He appreciated a good joke, and was known to love good music, good drink, a good meal, and good company. He was fond of a good story and was known to spin a few himself. His poetry, some claimed, was as smooth and as sharp as his swordsmanship. It was as though his profession as a taker of life had left him with an oversized joy for living.

When it came to his business, though, he did not like surprises. Surprises like the special courier from the royal court, who had awakened him before dawn with orders bearing the seal of the chief advisor to the King. These orders requested his presence within the Citadel by noon. He was to bring Lucius, his trusted sergeant and his right hand in many ways.

Galin had turned this over in his mind for a while, wondering why the two of them should be summoned at this time, and concluded this had something to do with the priest Jusaan and the captives from the Southeastern Ursals. He had no actual basis for this belief, only that a courier had arrived to transport the scheming priest and his 'guests' in the same way the morning before.

"And that," Galin had said to Lucius, "is too much of a coincidence to be ignored."

His men, an elite offshoot of his command, the First Expeditionary Legion, had at least a two-day march before again seeing Stronghold's gates. Galin prided himself on enduring as his men endured, and they loved him for it. He would always see his command through to the end, accepting the salute of the last man as he passed through the gates. Alas, this was not to be for the so-called "mapping expedition" now near its end. The thought of breaking his tradition only added more fuel to Galin's foul mood.

He had given the needed orders and, taking only essentials, he and Lucius had been driven by chariot toward the southern gate. They made good time and arrived at the Citadel as the noon meal was ending.

As he strode through the wide halls of the Royal House, Galin hardly spared a glance for those he passed. He headed first for the offices of the Citadel Guard, for some explanation as to why he had been summoned. He harbored no illusions and was not surprised when the officers told him they knew nothing of his orders. Judging by their surprise at his sudden appearance, they had not expected his presence in the Citadel that day. He had expected as much. This detour had been as much a way to deal with the time before the audience with the King as a mission to find answers.

Of course, he could have used the time to bathe and change into clean attire before standing before his King, but he wished to present himself fresh from the field, with the dust of the road still clinching to his clothes and skin.

The dedicated commander, summoned from the midst of his duty.

Lucius had left his side when they dismounted the chariot. One of his most endearing qualities was his ability to ferret out secrets, information, and answers, when none other seemed able. Even now he was making his rounds throughout the grounds of the Royal House, to the places where he could move quietly and fairly unnoticed; the guard stations, the stables, the kitchens, and some of the servant quarters. He had a way with people, especially the workers, which almost guaranteed that if secrets were to be had, he would have them before long. Galin had only to be patient and a goodly portion of whatever was afoot would eventually be revealed to him.

Whether this would occur before the commander was forced to confront the reason for his summons was still in question.

As Galin rounded a corner inside the Royal House, he saw up ahead the corpulence of Cecil. The chief advisor stood before the southern entrance to the throne room, surrounded by lower ministers and servants to whom he was giving instructions before waving them away to perform his bidding. Not yet ready to approach him, Galin ducked through an archway to his right, and out onto a terraced garden, where carefully pruned shrubs and miniature evergreens still spoke to the illusion of warmer weather. He needed to hear from Lucius, and maybe gain some idea of what lay ahead.

Lucius did not take long to appear, leading Galin to wonder just how the sergeant always seemed to find him. Smiling at his right-hand man, Galin wasted no time.

"What have you learned?"

"Only that Jusaan arrived last night with two mysterious guests," Lucius began. "He housed them in the temple, in quarters close to his own. Few have seen them, as they have yet to leave their quarters. There is a royal audience set for the second hour after the noon meal. None can say the nature of the audience, as word has not yet filtered down that far. Apparently, it was hastily arranged, which points to the arrival of Jusaan and the two prisoners… uh… guests."

"As I surmised," said Galin.

He looked at Lucius, who returned his look expectantly, but Galin had no further orders for him. Lucius was aware the true nature of the "mapping expedition" was to remain a secret. Not knowing the particulars of the audience left Galin with but one piece of advice for the soldier.

"Let us go then, and attend to our duty before the Throne," he said.

Leading the way back into the Royal House and toward the throne room, Galin saw that Cecil still stood before the heavy oaken doors, as if awaiting his arrival. Putting a smile on his lips, he approached the advisor with a proud and steady stride.

"Lord High Minister and Chief Advisor!" Galin spoke in greeting as he came to a stop before Cecil. "We set forth as soon as we received the summons of the Throne." He included Lucius with a gesture.

The sergeant bowed respectfully, "Lord High Minister."

Cecil ignored the sergeant, locking gazes with Galin. They were almost of the same height, but while one was lean, well-muscled, and bronzed by the sun, the other was portly and pale, his times spent in direct sunlight few and far between. Yet Cecil's bearing was as a titan, and Galin knew that to challenge the chief advisor here, where his word was second only to that of the King, was to court embarrassment and defeat.

"Lord Galin," Cecil said. "I was made aware of your arrival more than an hour ago. Enough time to clean oneself," he made a show of looking the officer up and down, "or to slake one's curiosity." This last was said with a knowing smile.

"Always abreast of the comings and goings in your realm," Galin said with a respectful nod, the smile still playing across his lips.

"Woe be unto me should you ever catch me in your realm, eh, commander?" Cecil said with a chuckle. Galin chuckled too. Cecil almost never left the confines of the Royal House.

"If you would follow me," Cecil said, and seemed to draw himself up to stand taller. Then he led them through the ornate double doors and into the throne room.

****

The servants, Laretha and Meesha, had arrived just before the noon meal. Hanshee and Raymond were resting, something they were unaccustomed to doing, quietly speculating on what lay ahead at the audience with the King. The arrival of the women was a welcome surprise, but the greater surprise was the entourage accompanying them.

It was as the night before, with strong young men bearing tubs half-filled with bath water, although not so hot as before. The women brought fresh undergarments, oils and fragrances. It was a welcome sight for Hanshee and Raymond, as it broke the monotony of the last several hours and also presented another opportunity for interaction with the two woman, something they had been discussing off and on throughout the morning.

Raymond did not have to be coaxed this time. After checking the temperature of the water, he disrobed and immersed himself in the soothing bath. He saw that Hanshee had done the same and, as the other servants took their leave, Laretha and Meesha took their places, scrub brushes in hand, behind the two tubs.

As the two servants began their work, Raymond noticed the bristles on the brushes they used were not as stiff as those used to scrub the dust and grime of the road from their bodies the night before. He was appreciating the sensation when the women stopped scrubbing. Meesha spoke to her companion in quick, clipped bursts. There was a pause, and then Laretha responded in almost conspiratorial tones. More words were exchanged between them and then, amidst a chorus of giggles, they switched positions, with Laretha behind Raymond and Meesha behind Hanshee.

Raymond glanced at his friend, and saw Hanshee return his look with a huge smile on his face. Ray met the smile with one of his own. He appreciated the playfulness, and the company, of the young women. Hanshee arched an eyebrow his way, wordlessly asking a question. At Ray's startled expression, Hanshee burst into hearty laughter, splashing water as he shook.

"Do not be afraid Way-mon," Hanshee said between chuckles, in his own tongue. "I was simply curious. Did you understand their words?"

Raymond laughed. "Not yet," he said.

Not understanding what was said, but rightly interpreting the innuendo, the two women again erupted into a fit of giggles as they began scrubbing the men clean. Raymond closed his eyes and surrendered to the feel of the brush and the softness of Laretha's hands as they scrubbed and kneaded his muscles. He was first pushed forward until his chest rested on his knees while she scrubbed his head, neck and back. Then he was allowed to recline as the women switched positions from the head of the tub to its foot, and began scrubbing their guests' feet and legs.

Raymond watched as Laretha caressed his feet and lower legs. The water had splashed upon the thin robes the women wore, causing the material to cling to the curves and crevasses that would normally remain concealed. Ray felt his body involuntarily responding to his bather's touch and he smiled dreamily up at her face. Catching her eye, he was rewarded with a smile, as she worked her way down his left leg. His anticipation grew as she passed the knee and began to scrub down the length of his outer thigh... then underneath... then the top... and then...

With a mischievous giggle, Laretha released his left leg and began scrubbing his right foot. Raymond could not believe what she had done, but then he began to giggle too and their giggles turned to laughter at the teasing she was inflicting upon him.

Still laughing softly Raymond closed his eyes and absently said, "You'll pay for that."

Suddenly all motion stopped!

Ray opened his eyes and looked around, finding both women with eyes wide and mouths agape, staring directly at him. Hanshee stared too, but his eyes were guarded slits in his wary face as he processed what he thought he had heard.

Then it dawned on Ray.

Damn' he thought, desperately searching for an explanation for what he had just done, and what the two women had just heard.

Laretha turned to Meesha and spoke quickly. Then turning toward Raymond, she again spoke quickly, looking at him as if expecting a reply.

Now Raymond was puzzled. He didn't recognize what she had said. He felt like he should, but he didn't. Involuntarily he opened his mouth to give the reply he knew was expected, but he found he had nothing to say.

Again Laretha spoke, this time more slowly, and Raymond understood not just her words, but also the reason for his confusion.

He responded slowly.

"Yes," he said, "I do speak the language of the cities to the south."

"Aaaiiii!" Laretha screamed in happy astonishment. She turned to Meesha and spoke quickly in their usual tongue, not the language of Pith. Then she turned back to Raymond and began what sounded like a rapid babble.

"Slow down!" Ray exclaimed over the torrent of words.

Laretha paused, took a deep breath to collect herself, and began again at a more measured pace.

"You speak the language of my people!" she exclaimed, both a statement and a question. "How is that so?"

"Tell me of your people," was Raymond's cautious reply.

"We...my family, left the southlands years ago," Laretha said. "It was before I was born. They settled here in Pith. I have not heard my native language, outside of the home of my father. for so long."

As she spoke, she looked at Raymond in wonder, as if waiting for him to speak again and delight her. Then a look of mild confusion crossed her face. "You are not from the southlands. Where are you from? How did you come to learn my native tongue?"

Raymond beamed up at Laretha as she rattled off question after question, feeling relieved he now had an explanation for his earlier slip of the tongue. He turned to Hanshee, who was still wearing a look of guarded confusion, and to Meesha who, having completely forgotten Hanshee, looked from Laretha to Ray and back to Laretha.

Realizing everyone was staring expectantly at him, Raymond gathered his wits and began.

"M'lord Hanshee," Raymond said, gesturing toward his companion, "is a wandering priest banished long ago from his homelands far to the west," he waved his hand, making a guess as to which direction was west. "He was sent forth to wander, and to atone, and to learn of the eastern peoples; peoples like the Pith. In his travels, he came upon me," he touched a hand to his chest. "I was drowning in a deep and swift river and m'lord pulled me from the current."

Raymond had always heard that sticking close to the truth was the easiest and best way to lie, and the story he was telling could be repeated without drawing any suspicion. But now he was feeling more confident, and the embellishment just seemed to flow.

"I myself was a warrior," he continued, "and a great hunter among my tribe. There was a famine in my land and the greatest of us ranged far and wide in search of game to feed our people. Alone, I tracked a heard of elk. They were huge, with great antlers," he held his hands to his head, palms out, fingers spread, in what was meant to mimic the antlers of a gigantic bull elk. "I tracked an enormous elk for many, many...," Raymond was stuck on a word for 'miles'... "over a great distance. I tracked him for many days, through distant lands, until I reached the great river, the River of Dreams," he said, using Hanshee's description of the river where he was found and rescued.

"It was there, in my struggle with the great elk, that we both fell into the river and Hanshee," he said, again pointing to his friend, "a great warrior-priest of the people of the Western Mountains, pulled me from the swift waters and saved my life." He smiled a big smile in Hanshee's direction.

"Among my people it is a custom to pledge your life to one who has given it back to you," Raymond continued, using the tried-and-true theme from many a book and film, "and so I have pledged myself to m'lord Hanshee, as his friend and acolyte, to serve him and learn his ways."

Raymond finished with a flourish and sat back in the tub, looking from one face to another with a smile of satisfaction, before he remembered only Laretha could understand any of the story he had just told.

Once she was sure Raymond had finished, Laretha turned to Meesha and began relaying the story in the language they shared, shooting a glance at Ray before placing her spread hands to her head, palms out, in imitation of the "great bull elk" Raymond had sought.

Raymond looked on in fascination, barley stifling a laugh when she mimicked his great elk. Then his eye was caught by Hanshee who cast an intensely quizzical look his way.

Understanding Hanshee was left out, Raymond began explaining the story to him, using language not quite so bold.

Once he finished, he turned back to Laretha, who had more questions.

"But how did you come to speak the language of my father?" she asked.

Raymond had been so caught up in his telling of the story, he had forgotten the reason he had told it was to answer this very question.

"I have a gift for tongues," he said truthfully. "M'lord and I spent some time in a city several days' travel from the eastern foothills of the Ursal Mountains. Aggipoor, it was called. It was there I learned to speak your father's tongue."

This was true, and Raymond decided no embellishment was needed.

"I did not understand you at first," he continued. "You speak so quickly and somehow differently from how they speak in Aggipoor."

"My father says I speak our tongue like a Pithian," Laretha said shyly. "He teases that I can barely speak our native tongue."

That explained why I had trouble understanding, Raymond thought, *until she spoke more slowly and deliberately.*

Now it was Ray's turn to ask questions.

"Tell me, what language do you and Meesha speak with each other?"

He was curious about this and felt it could be asked without revealing he understood the Pithian tongue.

"Part of Meesha's family is from the Plains Nations," Laretha offered in explanation. "They are enemies of the Pith. Many here refuse to learn their language and customs because they are enemies. She was taught their language by her grandmother, and she taught me."

She dropped her head as she spoke the next words.

"Meesha and I consider it our secret language. We speak it only to ourselves and not at all when the priests are near."

Raymond smiled knowingly. It seemed everyone had secrets in this place.

He reached out and took one of Laretha's hands in his.

"Let us two do the same," he said. "Let no one outside this room know you and I can speak with each other." He spoke these words with great sincerity as he looked into her eyes, and was met with a smile and eyes holding a promise; *It will be our secret. Our secret will be safe.*

"Aaaiii!" Meesha spoke hurriedly to Laretha, then rose from the floor in front of Hanshee's bath.

Laretha explained to Raymond, "We have little time. We must bring you the noon meal and prepare you for the Lord Priest Jusaan!" Then the two women rushed from the room.

Hanshee and Raymond sat in the now-tepid water, in a startled daze as the door closed behind the two servants. Then Hanshee turned to Ray, placed his open hands to his head, palms out, with his spread fingers wiggling, and roared with laughter!

Chapter 7

The richly appointed carriage lurched again as it struck another upturned stone, and Lord High Priest Mayhew fought back the urge to curse the driver.

Two of the three retainers who rode with him had caught wind of his ill mood and studiously avoided eye contact. The third, blissfully unaware of the mood in the carriage, raised his head from his reading with a joke.

"I believe the coachman is testing his aim on every hole and stone!"

He smiled from one to the other, expecting all to delight in his sense of humor. What he found in their faces caused him to drop his eyes back to his reading as if nothing had been said.

Lord Mayhew was irritated, and not simply from the bumpy ride.

He had given the driver instructions to return with all speed to the Citadel, so was in no position to complain about a bump or two. What really irked him was the need to cut his holiday short in the first place. And this, due to a problem he had all but solved prior to leaving the temple!

Just this morning, feeling particularly refreshed after a late night of festivities, followed by a sound sleep, a courier interrupted his late-morning meal in the most barbaric fashion, slamming his fist against the closed door as if hell itself were erupting outside!

"Enter!" he had shouted, the remainder of his words muttered, and so drowned out by the creaking of the door's hinges.

The breathless courier rushed in, took a knee and bowed his head before the lord high priest, who was seated on the edge of his bed, enjoying salted meats and pastries.

"My pardon, m'lord," the courier began. "A bird has just arrived from the Temple, with a purple ribbon attached." As he spoke, head still bowed, he extended an arm toward Mayhew. In his outstretched hand was a small canister with a purple ribbon.

Though the courier was just following orders – Mayhew's own orders - Mayhew was annoyed with the abrupt change in the morning's mood. He snatched the ribbon from the courier's hand, fumbled open the canister, and unrolled the small parchment inside.

The purple ribbon meant none were to open the message, which should be delivered directly to his grace with the best possible speed. Usually this meant the sender, in this case one of his spies within the Temple, thought its contents important enough to require immediate attention. As Mayhew read the message a second time, he found his annoyance deepening.

Mentally donning his position as high priest of The One Spirit, he addressed the still-kneeling courier.

"You have done well." Mayhew said in a soft and even tone. "You may go."

"Thank you, m'lord."

As the courier exited the bedchamber, Mayhew crushed the message, canister and all, and hurled it across the room toward the fireplace.

In the darkness of night, Jusaan has arrived at the temple, he thought, seething with indignation. *Curious... maybe highly suspect... that the troublesome priest had found some excuse to circumvent his express orders, but worthy of a purple ribbon?*

This was hardly an emergency, Mayhew thought, and he would happily deal with the disobedient underling immediately upon his return to the temple. This thought brought back some of his lost serenity. Mayhew again settled into his meal, taking a small bite of the sweet pastry and a sip of the watered wine.

Bam! Bam! Bam!

The pounding on the door rang out, just as Mayhew was about to finish his meal. Without thought, he reacted.

"Damn, damn, DAMN!" he snarled. "Who disturbs me now?!"

The shaky voice of the servant was heard through the heavy door.

"A thousand pardons, m'lord," he said weakly. "Another bird has just this moment arrived."

"Damn you, man! Bring me the parchment and be gone!" Mayhew roared.

The hinges creaked as the courier opened the door and sprinted into the room. Assuming the supplicant position, he allowed his master to snatch the small tube with a purple ribbon tied around it from his trembling hand before swiftly rising and dashing through the open door, careful to close it behind him.

This time, in his haste and anger, Mayhew almost ripped the delicate parchment in two. Taking a deep breath, he managed to settle himself enough to carefully unroll and examine the message.

It was not from the Temple.

It was from his spies in the royal household, and though the paper was too small to provide much detail, the message gave rise to instant alarm.

Leaping to his feet as quickly as his pudgy body allowed, Mayhew tugged on the cord dangling beside his bed. Simultaneously he tuned to face the wall opposite the door the courier had used. There stood another, smaller door that opened on well-greased hinges to reveal his chief attendant.

"Prepare my bath, and clothes fit for travel" the high priest barked. "Send word to the stable to prepare my coach. We leave for the Citadel within the hour!"

The long ride, though lacking in comfort, provided Mayhew time to consider.

The second message, the one from the Royal House, informed him of an audience before His Royal Highness King Ammon IV. Most matters concerning the Throne were handled behind closed doors, with the King's chief advisor taking the lead, the better to control the parley, the outcome, and the message.

It was highly unusual to grant an audience on short notice. These were semi-public events, and the eyes of the court would be riveted upon the proceedings. For this reason, they were granted judiciously, planned fastidiously, and handled with care. In the case of visiting royalty, or a summit of some kind, these affairs were mostly pomp. Occasionally serious matters merited a public audience. The repercussions of such an event could be profound and far-reaching.

Mayhew could not shake the feeling he had ever since first reading the note, that somehow Jusaan was involved in this. It wasn't that he did not believe in coincidence, but for the priest to arrive in the dark of the night and the very next day a surprise audience with the King was scheduled?

Something must be afoot, he thought. *It must be something dangerous, if the unruly priest sought to bypass decorum and himself meet with the King.*

Tradition held that all matters of the Temple concerning the Royal House be run through the high priest. Of course, small matters had always been delegated to underlings by both parties, along with the preparations for ceremonies and grand events. But with momentous decisions, with grand proclamations, whenever the Royal House and the Temple were bonded in public, the high priest bore the standard for The One Spirit.

Only my absence made this possible, Mayhew fumed.

But no. In his absence, delays could be requested, messages could be sent. The machinations of the court put on hold until his hasty return. That was what made this most troubling.

What has occurred that could not be held until my royal summons and arrival? he thought.

A part of him said this scenario, as he had laid it out in his mind, was mostly speculation. Those two messages were not necessarily connected. He could be rushing to the Citadel for no reason whatsoever. But Mayhew knew he was right to fear chicanery. He felt it deep within his bones and he truly feared not reaching the Citadel in time.

Startling his companions, the lord high priest leaned his head out of the coach window and addressed the driver.

"Can you coax no more speed from those beasts?" Mayhew yelled.

The other passengers could not make out the drivers reply, garbled as it was by the wind, the sound of the wheels on the road, and the motion of the coach, but they heard clearly as the lord high priest screamed his response.

"Kill them if you must, so long as they perish in the courtyard before the Royal House!"

With a crack of the whip, the carriage hurtled toward the Citadel and the royal audience.

Chapter 8

The throne room was huge.

It was a room befitting the monarchy of Pith and the seat of Pithian power, the Marble Throne.

Jusaan had led Hanshee and Raymond to the main entrance, which faced west, and before oaken doors ten feet wide and twice as high. These opened inward, into a room designed to both awe and humble those who entered. Raymond likened its dimensions to that of a football field turned sideways, so that the distance from the main doors to the back wall, from west to east, was roughly half the distance from the southern to the northern wall.

As they proceeded into the room, seven huge stone pillars, roughly six feet in diameter, rose on either side of them. They marked a wide path, cushioned with rich carpets, leading from the main entrance to the stone and marble steps by which one ascended to the dais supporting the fabled Marble Throne of Pith.

As he looked closer, Ray could see that the pillars divided the room into roughly three equal parts. Only the wide center isle was lit, with torches set into holders attached to the pillars. Mingling with their flickering light was the steady glow of ornate lamps hanging from silken ropes strung from pillar to pillar. The pillars rose upward as far as the eye could see. There was no telling how high they rose, for they, along with the room's ceiling, were lost in the darkness above.

Standing midway between each pillar, bathed in a pool of light emanating from the lamp above each head, was a soldier of the Citadel Guard. Each was resplendent in crimson tunics, with their highly polished helmets, breastplates, and bucklers, the color of gold. With a short sword on their hip, and a gold tipped lance in hand and tilted toward the center aisle, they presented an image of both splendor and resolve.

As the party proceeded toward the dais, Raymond could see the flickering light from the torches had brought to life intricate paintings decorating the pillars with scenes of hardship, battle and conquest. The first images they passed were of a vast grassy plain, and a large group of dark skinned warriors who were driving a similarly hued people, men, women and children, adorned in crimson and gold, away from a group of thatched huts and into the wilderness. Additional paintings on this pillar showed images representing the hardships of the nomadic existence apparently forced upon the people in crimson and gold.

On the next pillar was a different scene.

The nomads were now in a wide mountain pass, high peaks to either side. They were locked in battle with a force of fair-skinned warriors. The surrounding scenes depicted the life-and-death struggles of individuals in this battle, the final scene depicting an apparent victory for the people wearing crimson and gold.

This pattern continued on the ensuing pillars, with scenes of hardship, battle, and celebration. The pillar second from last documented a pitched battle occurring before a natural wall of sheer stone. A representation, Raymond guessed, of the high stone walls which had greeted them as they approached Stronghold the day before. The surrounding paintings depicted another battle, this one appearing to last through the night and into the next day. The forces in crimson and gold were backed up against the stone wall, besieged on three sides by a great host composed of forces under at least three different flags.

Some of these paintings held meanings Ray could not fathom, but one of the last showed a gap opening in the great stone wall allowing the cornered forces in crimson an avenue of escape for their women and children. The last depiction on this pillar showed the warriors of crimson and gold defending the gap, with the forces aligned against them breaking on the stone walls to either side, and many tumbling into a crevasse that had opened at their feet.

The last pillar bore a single image of a mighty fortress of such grandeur that it had to have been constructed by those touched by The One Spirit, for man on his own could not hope to achieve the splendor and strength of the nearly divine image depicted therein. The fortress seemed to rise from a mountainside and in doing so, somehow became the mountain, its towers and spires and minarets rising into the heavens. It was surrounded on all sides by the high stone walls of the earlier pictures. They seemed to cradle it, embracing it as would a mother protecting her child or, in their majesty, a deity protecting his chosen.

The Citadel of Pith, the words sprang unbidden into Raymond's mind.

Roughly twenty paces past the last of the seven pillars, wide steps of gray granite rose from the floor. At the center of these steps, the granite had been replaced with marble naturally streaked with thick veins of crimson and gold. The marble had been laid so precisely that to run a hand across its surface would fail to reveal the place where the granite ended and the marble began. These steps led upward to a dais made of the same material, on which sat the Marble Throne of Pith.

Carved from a single block of red marble, richly inlaid with polished oak and pure gold, the throne was both a work of art and a testament to the perseverance and strength of those who held it dear. No banners or ostentatious displays surrounded it. None were required. The throne stood alone atop the dais, towering above the room, giving all within an unobstructed view of an icon symbolizing the power and the pride of Pith.

Sitting proudly upon the throne was His Majesty King Ammon IV of the empire of Pith, Ruler of the Chosen, Commander of all Forces of Stronghold, and Defender of the Faith of The One Spirit.

As Raymond continued to keep pace behind Hanshee and Jusaan, two Citadel Guards who had been positioned on the throne side of the last of the seven columns, stepped forward and crossed their lances in Jusaan's path. Jusaan advanced until he stood directly before the crossed lances, then came to a halt. Hanshee and Raymond stood one pace back and on either side of him. Sensing movement to his right, Raymond shifted his glance and observed a man, large in both height and girth, emerge from the darkness.

Cecil entered the pool of light illuminating the space before the marble steps. He was resplendent in white robes trimmed in crimson and gold, and carrying two objects reverently before him.

In his left hand he held a wooden staff.

It was at least six feet long and, near its top, was as big around as the wrist of a large man. It tapered down to a golden tip a fraction of that size. The tip was inlaid with gold trailing up the length of the almost black wood in beautifully thin lines, some ending in swirls, some continuing in spirals up the length of the staff, finally ending near the very top where the wood had been carved to a flared head. It was here, in the broad flat head, that a brilliant blood red stone was imbedded. With waves of gold appearing to emanate from its edges, it was likened in appearance to golden rays of light from a crimson sun. This image was maintained on both sides of the broadened head.

In his right hand, Cecil carried a short sword.

The sword was of polished iron and had been sharpened to a razor's edge. Its hilt was gold, with gold inlay decorating the black oak comprising the grip. At the base of the hilt was the same symbol of golden rays surrounding a crimson sun as on the staff.

With solemn, measured steps, Lord Cecil proceeded to a point at the center of the first marble step before turning to his right so that he stood facing the throne. He then cast his eyes upward and, in a baritone voice that resonated within the huge chamber, he petitioned his King.

"Hail, Ammon the Fourth, Monarch of the Empire of Pith!" he began. "There is one who begs your audience this day. He is Jusaan, a priest of The One Spirit, seated among The Council of The Nine. Absent the lord high priest, he requests a break with tradition to directly petition Your Highness on a matter he deems of great importance to both the Temple and the empire."

Cecil paused to let his words sink in. From the corner of his eye, Raymond was sure he saw Jusaan cringe. Then Cecil extended both his arms toward the throne, offering up the two totems of sword and staff to His Majesty. He held them there, not an easy task considering their weight, and completed his oration.

"Be it your patience," Cecil motioned with the staff, "or your judgment," he motioned with the sword, "we await your will."

The last echoes of Cecil's words had died before the King stirred. Slowly rising from his cushioned perch upon the Marble Throne, King Ammon IV descended the steps toward his chief advisor. When the monarch reached the bottom step, Cecil bowed his head and, trembling with the effort, further extended both totems toward his liege. Ammon IV nodded graciously and accepted the staff. Lord High Minister Cecil, his relief at being relieved of his burden almost palpable, took a step backward. Turning again to his right, and with the same measured steps, he moved into position at the side of the marble steps.

Now the two guards who had held their crossed lances before Jusaan and his small company, withdrew them and stepped backward to their original positions beside the seventh pillar. Jusaan stood silently, awaiting the King's pleasure.

"Come forward, lord priest," said the King. Jusaan complied, motioning Hanshee and Raymond to follow.

Moving forward, but still behind and to the left of Jusaan, Raymond could not help but consider the voice of the King. It had not sounded...'Kingly', or regal, or maybe there was some other, better word for what he was hearing. But, to his thinking, the King sounded like a man. Simply a man.

Raymond fixed him with his eyes, noting that he was a tall, gaunt man, his face lean with high cheekbones that emphasized the hollows underneath. But his eyes were different. If anything on this man were to be proclaimed regal, it was his eyes. They sought out what they would, then bore into what they found with a stare more akin to a bird of prey than a human being. This was a gaze so intense, it held Ray's eyes while not looking at him. So intense, Ray did not notice the three guards emerging from the darkness on each side to converge on them as they reached a position about fifteen feet in front of the King.

Ammon IV nodded his head, halting Jusaan and his party in its tracks. The guards came to a halt also, on either side and slightly ahead of Jusaan, weapons at the ready.

"Lord priest," Ammon said to Jusaan, "I have been apprised of your request and find it to be extraordinary."

He fixed Jusaan with that avian stare and continued.

"There has not been a time, in my reign or that of my father - be he blessed by The One - that it has been seen fit to dispense with custom and allow a mere priest to approach the Throne on affairs of the Temple. Knowing of your travels and arrival only last night, along with the absence of the lord high priest, I can only surmise your reason for this breach of decorum is quite compelling in your eyes. So compelling, you would eschew the council and the blessing of High Priest Mayhew and approach the Throne directly.

"I place great trust in my chief advisor," King Ammon said, nodding toward Cecil. "He has deemed your plea worth hearing, though he has tempted my ire by refusing me details as to why this is so."

This last was said as somewhat of a private joke between His Majesty and his advisor, as both smiled when it was spoken.

"The effect of your decision," the King continued, "and his council, is that the weight of this entire proceeding has been placed upon your shoulders. I hope, for your sake, your shoulders are up to the task."

Ammon IV's gaze took on a new level of intensity as it seemed to bore into Jusaan's very soul.

"Impress me, priest," Ammon said, "and mayhap your King can spare you the wrath of High Priest Mayhew."

The King spoke these last words with a flatness that left no doubt he would not intercede should the council priest fail in this test. By his tone, it was apparent King Ammon IV did not expect to be impressed.

The great hall was silent as a visibly shaken Jusaan paused to gather himself before beginning.

"Thanking Your Highness for granting this boon to the Temple," he began hesitantly. "If it please Your Highness, allow me to present Lord Priest Hanshee, along with his acolyte, Way-Mon."

Jusaan made these introductions in a slightly more confident manner, pausing before finishing in a voice both strong and clear. "Lord Priest Hanshee is a Warrior-Priest of Old... from the motherland."

Raymond heard gasps from the darkness on either side, as those concealed therein were struck by this revelation. The gasps quickly turned into a low buzzing of murmured conversation, an indication the darkness concealed more than just a few onlookers.

The effect Jusaan's words had on the King were even more surprising.

Ammon reacted as if facing a strong wind, visibly catching himself from taking a step backward and losing his balance. After righting himself, the King leaned forward, eyes wide and mouth agape, focusing intently on Hanshee. His eyes flitted briefly to the strangely garbed Raymond before settling again on this "warrior-priest of old."

Taking advantage of the astonishment of all present, Jusaan moved quickly to cement his claim.

"With your indulgence, Your Highness," Jusaan said, "and with the permission of his commander, Lord Galin, of the First Expeditionary Legion, I would present to you Citizen Lucius. It was he who commanded the advance scouting team that first encountered our guests."

As he spoke, Jusaan waved his hand toward the darkness on the right. Presently there appeared the squat soldier who had commanded the archers who first came upon Hanshee and Raymond in the forest of the Southeastern Ursal Mountains.

Jusaan had planned this moment to perfection. He had petitioned Cecil to call in both Galin and Lucius as witnesses to the capture of Hanshee and his acolyte. The claim he was making had ramifications beyond what the King's ministers and advisors - those now watching from the shadows - were prepared to consider. Had Jusaan made these proclamations alone, he would have been jeered by these men, his sanity questioned, his position in the Temple forfeit. But with witnesses such as Lucius and Lord Commander Galin, there could be no easy dismissal. Behind their testimony, his claims must be given serious consideration.

The key was to have them both present, and to get statements favorable to Jusaan's position. For this reason, he had called for Lucius first.

If Jusaan had called for Galin first, he would be placing his fate squarely in the commander's hands. No stranger to the court, Galin would have sensed the politics of the situation and, following his embarrassment in having pitted Botha against the warrior-priest, could have doomed them both with a lie. A lie Lucius would most likely support as it came from his commanding officer. Otherwise Lucius, a wide-eyed neophyte in the court of the King, would not fathom speaking dishonestly before His Highness.

Jusaan had watched Galin carefully while embedded with his force. That was the reasoning behind his assignment to the expedition. What he had learned in their brief time together was that Galin was indeed a commander of men and, as such, placed a high value on the virtues his position demanded. Loyalty was foremost. Once the die had been cast, Galin would forgo politics and support his man, laying at Jusaan's feet the victory he so desired.

Unaccustomed to matters of the court, and having never been in the throne room before, Lucius was understandably hesitant when coming forth. The guards parted, allowing him to stand beside Jusaan, who greeted him with a warm smile. Facing the King, Lucius began a formal military salute before catching himself and instead executing a low bow from the waist. Upon straightening, he brought his right hand crisply to his chest, fist clinched, palm up, and shouted, "My life I give for Pith!"

King Ammon IV smiled down at him. One or two of the guards let their composure slip with a quick grin at the soldier's zeal.

Jusaan spoke quickly, confidently assuming charge of the proceeding.

"Citizen Lucius," he began, "are these two men those your patrol found in the forest of the Southeast Ursal Mountains, clothed then exactly as they stand before you now?"

Lucius looked Hanshee and Raymond up and down for a long time, not replying until giggles were heard from the darkness. Then he turned and faced Jusaan.

"Save for a bundle of furs carried by this one," he pointed at Raymond, "and a bow and some quivered arrows carried by this one," he indicated Hanshee, "they stand exactly as they were found that day, Lord Priest."

Raymond had wondered why it had been so important to Jusaan that they wore their own clothes when appearing before the King. The priest had even requested Hanshee wear his sword and his pouch. The question and answer confirmed it must be important in some way, though Raymond still could not grasp why. Perhaps if he were not so focused on projecting an air of ignorance, pretending to be someone to whom the language being spoken around him was incomprehensible, he would be able to better process what was going on. He noted Hanshee did not have that problem, as he truly was ignorant of what was being said. So much the better, Raymond figured, that Hanshee was the focus of their curiosity. This made it more likely any slips in Ray's demeanor would go unnoticed.

Jusaan now felt he had the occasion well in hand and addressed his King once more.

"If it pleases Your Highness, I would like to call forth Lord Galin, Commander of the First Expeditionary Legion and a member of the Council of Seven."

Galin strode gracefully from the shadows with a smile of greeting for his King, in whose presence he had spent many an hour. The guards quickly parted for the commander, allowing him to walk directly up to King Ammon. Upon hitting his mark, he placed his right fist on his chest and bowed deeply, holding it just a moment longer than he had to before rising. "My liege," he said, his tone reverent.

The King smiled benevolently upon Galin, causing Jusaan once again to feel uneasy. He hoped he had not made the classic mistake of attempting to "drown a fish in water," as the saying went. Knowing there was no other way than to trust his instincts, he made ready to continue with his plan.

"It is good to behold you once more, Lord Galin," the King said, placing his hands on the commander's broad shoulders. "How went your latest excursion?"

"A mapping expedition, my liege," Galin replied. "A simple housekeeping matter, really."

"And does my house now extend south beyond the Bruin Peak and into the southeastern foothills?" the King asked coyly, a knowing look on his face.

Galin greeted this inquiry with a winning smile.

"Not yet, my liege," he said, "but on the day when you proclaim it does, we will be as comfortable there as in any new extension to a home."

Ammon chuckled at this reply. He was well aware of Galin's restlessness, and his ambition. Long ago, Galin had put forth his dream of conquering the southern plains, bringing new vassals and new resources into the empire, and positioning Pith strategically above the main trading routs from the Great Inland Sea. The fact that such a move would have the consequence of forcing the three great nations to their west to once again join together against them seemed never to dissuade his favorite commander of those dreams.

Jusaan, sensing his opportunity to once again steer the audience in the direction of his choosing, prepared to speak up and refocus the King's attention to the matters at hand. As he took a breath before plunging in, Ammon IV turned in his direction and spoke.

"Lord Commander," the King said to Galin, motioning to Jusaan and his guests, "what say you to the claims of Lord Priest Jusaan and the testimony of Citizen Lucius? Are they to be believed?" He asked this question with a furrowed brow, searching for words of truth from one he trusted.

Galin turned his gaze on the trio and then, shaking his head in astonishment, squarely met the eyes of his King.

"I was not present at the capture, my liege, but my man Lucius speaks truly. He came upon them in the Southeastern Ursal Mountains, and they wore this same attire when presented to me in camp. From the very first Jusaan viewed them as special, that I can say, but as to his claim of this one," he motioned toward Hanshee, "being a warrior-priest of old? My liege, I am but a soldier. Who am I to say?"

Ammon gave a heavy sigh, his continence again becoming firm.

"Thank you, Lord Galin," he said, as if reaching a harsh but necessary decision.

Galin bowed.

"I am ever at your service, My Liege," he said before turning toward Jusaan and favoring him with a triumphant grin. Then he and Lucius excused themselves from the group standing before the King.

Ammon IV silently looked from one to the other in the small group before him and Jusaan felt his plans, and maybe even his life, slipping away. Grasping at what he saw as his last play, he spoke unbidden to the King.

"My King," Jusaan quickly said, "I have proof."

Having opened his mouth to give the order to have the priest and his dupes removed, Ammon was taken by surprise, as much by Jusaan's gall as by his words.

"Proof?" the King asked, not bothering to hide his skepticism. "Proof, did you say? Where is this 'proof'?"

"If it would please His Majesty, I have asked the Temple's liaison to the royal court to be present with an object of utmost importance to our history. It is the Chest of the Four Scrolls of Prophesy."

With these words, the shadows again erupted in gasps, followed by the sound of many voices murmuring in tones of astonishment.

Knowing this statement had taken everyone aback, Jusaan signaled almost desperately to the shadows on his left, from which appeared a small man wearing priestly robes. He was a lesser priest, one whose nondescript appearance made him easy to overlook and thus valuable as a spy for Mayhew in the royal court. Jusaan waved him forward aggressively, knowing that in the airtight box the junior priest carried close to his chest lay his last hope for survival this day.

The liaison's progress was checked by the three guards, who did not immediately allow him to pass. Only after the King nodded his head in assent, did the guards part ranks and allow the priest to proceed.

Junior Priest Emrey first turned to Ammon and bowed low. Straightening, he turned to Jusaan and presented him with the ancient box, before once again bowing to the King. This done, he left the group, squeezing between the guards.

With his eyes focused on Jusaan in a mixture of anger and curiosity, Ammon IV spoke brusquely.

"Bring a table!"

Two servants appeared from the darkness, carrying an intricately carved table. Another followed with a lamp. This time the guards moved aside without being told. The table was placed before King Ammon. Once it was positioned, the lamp was placed at its center and quickly lit. Impatiently, King Ammon motioned for Jusaan to bring the box forward. Slowly, and with exquisite care, he placed it on the table before the King. There the two of them stood, separated by the table, staring down at the ancient airtight chest with its intricate carving; a box holding so important a part of their nation's history.

Jusaan looked up and found King Ammon IV staring at him, the anger now gone from his eyes, replaced by anxiety, curiosity, and wonder.

The King looked again at the box and back at Jusaan before nervously licking his lips.

"Open it," he said.

Jusaan looked down on the box for the second time in less than a day. For some reason, opening it in the library had been a much easier task. He had no explanation for the sudden sweat beading his brow, and the trembling of his hands as he reached for the lid. He carefully pried first one section, then another, slowly forcing the top up and allowing air to seep into the interior. This continued for what seemed a very long time until, with an audible pop, the lid came completely free. Jusaan delicately placed it to the side, beside the now-open box. He paused, allowing his King to drink in the sight of Pithian history he himself had beheld the night before.

The four scrolls lay neatly side by side in the tight confines of the ancient box. Each was wound evenly around a hardwood spool. The scrolls had been made from animal skins that had been worked until they were thin and supple. They had survived the rigors of time much better than scrolls of papyrus would. The ink used upon them would hold fast to its shape and color, preserving the words and images on them for an extraordinarily long time. This had been the purpose of transferring the original scrolls, made of papyrus, onto leather many centuries ago.

Raymond studied Ammon IV's expression as he looked upon the scrolls for the first time.

As a child of royalty, the King had been exposed to the same education as aspiring priests and therefore had knowledge of what would be found within the box. But this was different. The scrolls of his youth were mere copies of those now lying before him. They were probably copies of copies, well-worn and passed down from one child of the Royal House to another. There was no weight of years by which they developed a mystique about them, no weight of history which demanded reverence. Ammon IV looked upon these sacred texts with a combination of awe and wonder. He wanted to reach out and take one up, but for the first time in his life of royal privilege, he felt unworthy.

Finally tearing his eyes away from the contents of the box, King Ammon IV spoke to Jusaan. The disdain previously noticeable in his voice had dissipated, replaced by respect for the history of his people and for one more qualified than he to address it.

"Which parchment do you seek?" the monarch asked, already knowing the answer. "Which parchment contains the Fourth Prophesy?"

Jusaan heard the change in the King's tone and saw the change in his demeanor. Being a priest, he was familiar with the effect often wrought in people when exposed to the antiquities of the Faith. Being a priest, he was well schooled in how to use such a moment and how to manipulate such feelings of reverence.

Now, Jusaan thought delightedly, his face a solemn mask. *Now is the moment to grasp for what has been decreed from on high to be mine!*

With hands steadied by a newfound sense of confidence, Jusaan reached into the box and extracted the scroll he had identified the evening before. He placed it carefully on the table, beside the lamp. With his hands poised to spread open the aged skin, he paused to look at the King. He found him transfixed, his eyes glued to the scroll in excitement and anticipation. Satisfied, Jusaan waited a moment longer, savoring this moment, and heightening the suspense. Then he gently unrolled the Scroll of the Fourth Prophesy, whispering a single drawn-out word:

"Behooold!"

King Ammon IV leaned forward, eager to behold the Scroll of the Fourth Prophesy in all its glory!

But this scroll was much different from those copies he remembered from his youth. It was so different that the scrolls he had learned from could hardly be called copies.

The scroll before him lacked the bold proclamations and clear messages he had expected. This writing was small and crowded, a mixture of dialects born of the same mother tongue but confusing, nonetheless. There were other differences, in the form of many illustrations in the margins, some so small and delicate as to be unfathomable after so much time. Others, though at one time probably of great practical use, now having no meaning in the current world of the Pith.

Confused, King Ammon scanned the document again and again, searching for something familiar, something to allay his growing feeling of disappointment and dread. His eyes became frantic, seeing the document unfurled before him but recognizing nothing. Desperately he again sought the face of the priest Jusaan.

"What is this?" he spat. "What are you showing me? This...this is meaningless! It's gibberish!"

Jusaan met the King's wrath with a confident smile as he unrolled the last part of the scroll, a part that, up to now, he had held in place with one hand.

"Look here, Your Majesty," he said, pointing to the newly uncovered portion of writing.

There, at Jusaan's fingertip, were the words with which Ammon had been familiar since childhood:

"And lo, the time shall come when our labors will have reached fruition, and the People will be called home. We will be called to turn our faces toward the far lands of the high mountains of our birth, and called to reclaim our birthright, and return to the Motherland triumphant! And we will know this time is upon us when I return to my People, to lead them home."

Jusaan read this passage – the final passage of the scroll - aloud, giving the King time to compose himself and once again assume a regal demeanor. Then he moved his hand once more, unrolling the final bit of the scroll and uncovering the last illustration.

It was larger than any of the scroll's other illustrations, and it depicted a man. Not any man, but a legendary hero of the ancient tribe of the Pith. Here was the warrior-priest, Usaid, resplendent in his minimal leather garments, his medicine pouch slung over his shoulder, his weapons at the ready, his dark features chiseled and plain, his body lean and hard, and his posture proud and regal.

It was the Warrior-Priest Usaid, his likeness preserved on this scroll so that all who read it might know his countenance.

The King's eyes were glued to the illustration, intently studying every detail. When he was satisfied... when he was sure this image was burned into his mind... he raised his eyes and beheld Usaid in the flesh! Standing before him in the throne room of the Royal House was the living, breathing image of the great warrior-priest of old in the form of Hanshee!

Eyes wide with wonder, Ammon studied the figure standing before him as intently as he had examined the illustration. The King's mouth opened and closed as he struggled to give words to his astonishment. Tearing his gaze away from Hanshee, he cast his eyes toward Jusaan.

With a furrowed brow and a plea in his voice, he asked his question

"How can this be?" he begged. "Where is he from? How came he here?

Jusaan had watched as the familiar passage settled his King, waited as the twin images, one on an ancient scroll and the other of flesh and blood, again sent Ammon's mind reeling with shock and astonishment. Now, knowing the foundation laid, he leveled a steady gaze at his sovereign and sealed his victory.

"You may ask your questions of him yourself, Your Highness," Jusaan said. "He speaks the ancient tongue."

The ancient tongue! Ammon thought as his eyes snapped back to Hanshee.

The current language of Pith was a bastardized version of the speech of the many different tribes and peoples who had been assimilated during the centuries-long pilgrimage beginning in the motherland and ending at Stronghold. Through it all, their original language, what was referred to as "the ancient tongue," had been kept alive by the priesthood, and by members of the royal household, whose children were exposed to a portion of the extensive education given to priests. Through the years since his boyhood, Ammon had no cause to speak his people's native language. Never a very apt student, what little skill he possessed had eroded with time. Still, his curiosity demanded he attempt to speak with this man, as a final test.

Searching his memory for the right words, his voice tentative and sounding anything but regal, he slowly and carefully addressed Hanshee.

"What is your name?" Ammon asked, looking deeply into the dark eyes of the stranger. "Where…are you …from? Who are your…people?"

Raymond, having understood all that was said around him, knew what to expect, but Hanshee was taken aback as the monarch attempted to converse with him in his own language. He returned the King's quizzical gaze with his own iron stare and replied, "I am Hanshee, a warrior-priest of Clan Dula, of the People of the Earth. I am Maiyochi. I come from a place far to the West, beyond the great desert, beyond the Blue Mountains."

Ammon could only understand some of what Hanshee said. He turned to Jusaan for a full translation. Having barely avoided being forcibly removed from his presence, the priest was more than happy to indulge his sovereign's dependence, while reinforcing his importance as the man who had recognized Hanshee and presented him to the King, and the only one who was trusted by both.

Ammon listened to Hanshee's words, faithfully presented through Jusaan, and smiled in satisfaction. The entire chamber, those visible and those shrouded in the surrounding darkness, held their tongues and even their breaths as the King pondered that which this royal audience had brought to light. All eyes in the group before him studied his face for some sign of his thoughts and for how it would bode for them.

Finally, the King turned to Jusaan and fixed him with his raptor stare.

"Priest," he began, "I *am* impressed. Though you took an awful chance, I have decided you were indeed wise to bring these strangers to the Citadel, and to request my audience. Through your actions, the empire may have been greatly served."

"I am but a vessel for the will of The One Spirit," Jusaan replied modestly, while inwardly exalting. "In truth, I am humbled to be chosen by Him to bring His blessing to my people."

"His will be known, His will be done," said the King. "I have much to consider and will be meeting with my advisors, the Temple, and the Council of Seven in the coming days. I will trust to you to provide the safety and comfort our new guests so richly deserve until such time as they are summoned again."

Jusaan's face was a picture of iron control, concealing a mighty struggle not to beam with joy at his victory.

"I am honored, Your Highness," he replied.

Turning to the captain of the Citadel Guard, Ammon gave additional orders.

"Assign six of your best to provide the needed security at all times for our honored guests. These guardsmen will answer first to Council Priest Jusaan," the King said, using a more respectful title for the priest. Turning to Cecil, he again spoke.

"I would meet with my advisors after the evening meal," he said. "Summon all available from the Council of Seven to meet with me in the morning."

"Couriers will be dispatched within the hour, my liege," Cecil replied.

The King waved a hand in dismissal. He turned to leave, then paused.

"One more thing, Cecil," King Ammon said, having noticed a questioning look on Jusaan's face. "Upon his return, advise Lord High Priest Mayhew he is to forgive Council Priest Jusaan this breach of etiquette, as he has performed an invaluable service to the Temple, the Throne, and the empire."

Smiling as he saw relief sweep over Jusaan's features, King Ammon IV, the Royal Monarch, Ruler of the Chosen, Commander of All Forces of Stronghold, and Defender of the Faith of The One Spirit, turned and strode toward the door which led, through hidden staircases and secret passageways, to his private chambers, picking up guards and servants as he went.

Holding a position of salute until the King's departure, Cecil turned and eyed Jusaan.

"Well done, priest," Cecil said with a small nod of his head, before turning in the opposite direction from where the King had gone, and walking into the shadows.

Still feeling eyes upon him from the shadows beyond the lights, Jusaan continued to hold his composure, allowing himself only a sigh of relief before addressing Hanshee.

"Our sovereign, King Ammon IV, has extended his welcome and his hospitality to you," Jusaan said. "Last night, it was necessary to guard your presence in the Citadel, thus the servant's quarters to which you were temporarily assigned. Now, as an honored guest of the Temple, I will see that your accommodations are more in line with your station. Please follow me."

With these words, Jusaan led his small party, now joined by two of the Citadel Guards, back through the throne room. Waiting immediately outside was Errol, a member of Jusaan's staff, who had been seeing to his needs until Cafran's return. He rushed forward to receive his orders as soon as the priest emerged.

"These guards will accompany you as you escort our honored guests to the visiting priest's suite of rooms," Jusaan told him. "You will see that they are made comfortable, that all of their belongings are transferred there, and that all of their needs are addressed."

Errol bowed. "Of course, Your Grace."

It was then that Hanshee spoke up. Jusaan had already turned to go, but the priest halted and turned back to Hanshee, a gracious smile on his face.

"Yes, my brother," Jusaan said. "How may I be of further service?"

"We have grown accustomed to the two servants who provided for us last evening and this morning," Hanshee said. "Could it be arranged that they continue to see to our needs?"

Jusaan was momentarily taken aback, as this was the most Hanshee had spoken to him since his discovery. He tried to recall which servants had waited on the warrior-priest and his acolyte. Then he remembered. Aha! Two young women. Very attractive young women, too. Jusaan bowed.

"Of course, their continued services will be provided," he said knowingly. He turned to Errol and said, "See that the same two servants of the Temple as before are assigned to them."

Bowing once more to Hanshee, Jusaan took his leave.

Errol watched his master disappear down the corridor before turning a nervous smile toward his quests and giving an overly cheerful, "Follow me, please." He took several steps before realizing he was not being followed. With another nervous smile he motioned with his hand, and remained in place until Hanshee and Ray followed. Then the small procession made its way toward the temple.

****

The horses were thick with lather and gasping for breath when the coach finally came to a stop in the courtyard before the main doors of the Royal House.

Mayhew did not wait for his servants to depart the carriage and take their positions. The high priest barely waited for the wheels to stop turning before flinging his door open and beginning his descent toward the loose gravel below. Taken by surprise, his retainers scrambled through the opposite door of the coach, fighting to be in position to help their master, even as two coachmen came sprinting from the doorway of the Royal House. Mayhew waved away all who presumed he needed assistance as he descended the coach stairs. Upon reaching the gravel covered ground he ran... waddled actually... as quickly as he could the short distance to the portico. Climbing the few steps, he fairly burst through the tall oaken doors and into the main foyer.

The foyer was grand, as befitted the main entrance to the Royal House of Pith. To the left and right stretched halls leading to displays dedicated to past rulers and their families, along with historical plaques and artifacts from their years on the Throne. Down the hallway on the right, beyond the historical displays, were the offices of the Citadel Guard. Here there were barracks for the men, and separate rooms for their weapons and equipment, as well as an exit into the training yard behind the stables. Down the hallway to the left were the palace kitchens, where meals for all, save for the royal family, were prepared and served. With their dining hall and huge pantries, ovens and fire pits, equipment rooms, quarters for the cooks, and the livestock pens in the yard just beyond, the kitchens required as much or more room than any other single function of the Royal House, with the obvious exception of the King's quarters.

The stairs on the north and south walls of the foyer led to a second level, reserved for the offices of administrators and functionaries, such as tax collectors, printers, seamstresses, tailors and cobblers, painters, and the makers of signs, plaques, banners, and the like. Here there were quarters for those who were attached to the royal household, including minor nobles and ambassadors from neighboring lands, as well as liaisons for the separate forces of the military. Beyond this were conference and map rooms, where meetings of the heads of the military forces and tactical planning took place.

None of these things interested the Lord High Priest, who proceeded across the foyer to the Grand Staircase which extended directly to the third floor and the throne room. He vaulted the steps two at a time - for the first four steps - and then took the next six in quick chopping steps before the heaviness of his legs overcame him and he settled into a rhythmic plodding up the forty or so steps remaining. By this time his three retainers had caught up with him and jostled among themselves for the honor of helping him ascend the staircase. He waved them off heroically until, with about eight steps to go, he paused to catch his breath before extending an arm to brace himself on one or the other of his flunkies. That was, after all, why they were there.

Reaching the top step he paused again, exhausted, and took his time getting his breathing under control before disengaging from his man and approaching the four Citadel Guards standing before the huge double-doors of the throne room. Here he hesitated.

Even the lord high priest could not barge into an audience with the King uninvited. The probable fact this audience concerned affairs of the Temple did not support a break from the decorum of the court. Temporarily stymied, Mayhew debated whether to remain where he was until the audience concluded or proceed to his quarters to freshen up after his race through the countryside, confident one or more of his people would be along shortly to fill him in on the goings-on inside the throne room.

He decided that to wait outside the throne room would broadcast weakness to those who exited. He would go to his chambers.

As he turned to leave, Mayhew was suddenly hailed from somewhere down the long, wide corridor behind him and was surprised to see Cecil approaching at a faster pace than such girth should allow.

Cecil was still wearing his white robes with the crimson and gold trim, his head high, his face implacable, having eyes only for the most senior priest.

"Lord High Priest Mayhew," he said with a slight nod of his head instead of a bow. It seemed to Mayhew Cecil took pains to not show him his full and proper respect. "A word with you in private, if I may."

Not waiting for a response, the chief advisor turned and started back the way he had come, stopping before a door on the right-hand side, opposite the throne room. He paused, allowing Mayhew to catch up, before holding the door open for the priest and following him in.

They entered a small room containing a table and two chairs. A huge mirror stretched from the floor to about seven feet high on the wall. There was a crockery pot in one corner, marking this as a room for "discreet relief."

Cecil pulled in a lamp from the wall of the corridor and placed it on the hook above the table. He then offered a seat to the priest while he took the other. Mayhew, impatient as he was, still mustered the will to calm himself. He was curious as to the need for this much privacy. He did not expect to learn much from the chief advisor, but one never knew.

"The audience has ended." Cecil began, as he registered the surprise and disappointment on Mayhew's face. "It was brief, but quite interesting."

Mayhew knew that, with Cecil, there was no use pretending he was here for any other reason. *Hell,* he mused, *the lout probably knew of the message I was sent before I received it!* Maintaining a placid demeanor, Mayhew decided to speak plainly.

"Was this a Temple affair?"

"It was an affair of the King and the court," Cecil replied in a clipped voice, before softening his tone, "but it did concern matters of interest to the Temple."

Upon hearing Cecil's attempt to put him in his place, Mayhew lost some of his hard-won serenity. He was in no mood to fence with the minister this day.

"Then tell me plainly 'Lord Minister'," Mayhew fairly spat out the title, "who under my authority had the audacity to approach you to initiate an audience with the King without first receiving my blessing, as lord high priest?"

"It was Council Priest Jusaan," Cecil said, matter-of-factly. "I was well aware of the breach of protocol and would not have allowed it had the matter not been urgent."

Mayhew had heard enough to stoke his anger and justify his next move. He rose from his seat, a move that placed him only slightly above eye level with the still-seated Cecil, and attempted to stare down the chief advisor.

"Then there is nothing more to be accomplished here," he said. "I will summon Jusaan to my quarters and question him directly." Turning his back to Cecil, Mayhew moved toward the door. "And for his continued well-being, his explanation should include nothing short of a visit from The One Spirit himself!"

"T'was the next best thing," Cecil said, causing Mayhew to freeze in his tracks.

He turned to stare at the still-seated minister, curiosity burning in his eyes. But it was obvious Cecil would not divulge the particulars, leaving Mayhew the same option of which he had just spoken.

Turning away from Cecil again, Mayhew exited the sitting room and started toward his servants who were dutifully waiting where he had left them. Halfway there, the voice of Cecil again called out to him. Angrily, the high priest wheeled to face him.

"One more thing, Lord High Priest," Cecil said as he closed the distance between them. "His Highness, King Ammon IV, has decreed that, in this current matter, Council Priest Jusaan will answer directly to the Throne."

"What...? That is ....!" Mayhew searched for the appropriate words with which to smite this pompous...

"Further," Cecil continued calmly, "until His Highness says otherwise, this shall be the *only* matter which concerns Council Priest Jusaan."

Mayhew's anger sat frozen in his chest as he instantly realized that the words of the King had just removed Jusaan from his grasp. Oh, he could summon the priest, summon him in the most threatening and humiliating way he could imagine, but Jusaan would be within his right to ignore him, reducing the summons of the Lord High Priest to an exercise in impotence!

Inwardly fuming, but no longer wanting to give Cecil the satisfaction of playing cat to his mouse, Mayhew turned on his heel and stalked down the corridor, his lackeys following in his wake.

I will require detailed reports from my spies, he thought. *All of my spies! I will have answers! Only then can I determine how to deal with this affront.*

Chapter 9

Raymond had completed filling Hanshee in on anything he might have missed at the audience before King Ammon IV. Now they were trying to gain an understanding of what it all meant, before coming up with a plan to ensure their present safety and eventual freedom.

After returning to the temple, they had been moved a few levels below where they'd initially been housed, to quarters much more opulent. They now resided in what Raymond thought of as a suite, several times larger than the two rooms they'd previously been given.

The suite was off of the Royal House's northern hall, with a heavy door opening immediately into a foyer with a cushioned couch on one wall and a long, narrow table on the wall opposite. Beyond the foyer was the main room, spacious at about thirty feet wide by twenty feet deep. There was a fireplace on the outside wall, centered between two large windows overlooking the gardens that occupied most of the area on the northern side of the Citadel grounds.

Because their new accommodations were on the sixth floor of the Temple, they could see beyond the gardens to the Citadel walls, some four hundred feet from the Temple itself. Ray and Hanshee had gotten a glimpse of these walls on their way to the royal audience earlier in the day.

Almost as tall and thick as the city walls, they provided a second stout line of defense should any force overcome the city, while proving there was no shortage of stone in Pith. The walls were crested with merlons, between drum towers evenly spaced about one hundred feet apart between the corner towers. Only the corner towers were manned. This was considered an easy duty, as there had been no direct threat to the Citadel in all the years of its existence.

Beyond the walls were the rooftops of the shops and houses that made up the city proper, or its northern quadrant, at least. It stretched on for roughly two miles by Raymond's reckoning, ending at the city walls far off in the distance.

The suite had two bedchambers, separated by the spacious main room. The western room was set up with a single oversized plush bed, a large polished table, and several cushioned chairs. There was also a fireplace, smaller than that in the main room, on an inner wall, opposite the bed. This room was obviously a bedchamber for the visiting priest or nobility fortunate enough to merit such accommodations.

The second bed chamber held two sturdy double-wide cots, along with many chests and cabinets. This chamber was for the personal servants of the guest and for storage of clothes and valuables. Both bed chambers had large windows providing the same view as those in the main chamber, and all were draped with heavy tapestries appropriate for the winter season.

Hanshee had decided, and Raymond had agreed, that they should try as much as possible not to be separated. To this end, they chose to share the servant's chamber, with Ray choosing a cot and Hanshee taking his customary spot on the floor. This helped put Ray at ease as, in all the months he had spent in this land, Hanshee had never left his side except to forage and hunt. He had not realized how much he had come to depend on his friend's presence until they were presented with this choice of bedchambers.

Once they were situated, and Jusaan's underlings had taken their leave, the two discussed the afternoon's events and what they should make of them. By this time the sun was low in the western sky and it was almost the hour of the evening meal.

"So, what we know at this point," concluded Raymond, "is that the king is meeting with his court advisors this evening and will meet with his military commanders tomorrow, and it is all concerning you," he indicated Hanshee, "and how you relate to this 'Fourth Prophesy' of theirs. It would have been helpful if we could have gotten a look at the scroll. Maybe if we can find out where they keep it, we may be able to sneak out of this room and…"

"I will ask the priest," said Hanshee

"What?" Raymond was incredulous.

"Tomorrow I will ask the priest Jusaan to tell me of the 'Fourth Prophesy'," Hanshee stated.

He was sitting cross-legged on the floor of the servant's quarters, running a wetting stone along the edge of his knife blade, making a sharp edge even sharper. Hanshee was a man out of his element, used to being responsible for every aspect of his survival. To be in the Temple of The One as an honored guest of the Pith, with nothing to do but submit to the constant pampering afforded a priest, was beginning to affect him on only his second evening here.

Raymond could hardly believe his ears. He sat bolt upright on his cot and eyed his companion.

"You can't do that!"

"Why not?" Hanshee asked, without lifting his head from his task.

"Because, then he…might…explain it to you," Ray said, suddenly understanding the logic behind Hanshee's common-sense approach.

Hanshee looked up from the knife and smiled at his charge.

"From what you have explained about the audience, the priest Jusaan risked much in presenting me as a part of this 'Fourth Prophesy'," Hanshee said. "So much that his position, even his safety, may depend on keeping me contented. It may be he will reveal much to that end."

Raymond turned this over in his mind, marveling at the simplicity of the plan. It sure beat his plan of sneaking out of their room and past the guards, and somehow finding and stealing priceless artifacts from the Temple. He had no idea how many guards there would be, or where the artifacts were kept. In comparison, his was the plan of a child.

"How will you ask him?" Raymond asked. "Neither of us should have been able to understand what was happening today. I mean, what will you say?"

Hanshee laid the knife and whetstone aside and pondered this question. A small smile came to his lips. "With guile," he said.

Ray met his smile with a blank stare, his confusion prompting Hanshee to explain.

"I am a priest from a far land, the land the Pith referred to as the 'motherland'," he began. "They believe me to be part of a prophesy having great meaning to their priesthood, and to their King."

"Yes," Raymond said. He knew all that. "So?"

"Perhaps the priest simply has a scheme, and he plans to use me for his own gain," Hanshee continued. "But perhaps it is more. Perhaps he is a believer in this prophesy."

"I'm not sure what you mean," Ray said.

"I will be the 'warrior-priest' he claims me to be," Hanshee said. "I shall play to his belief. I will tell him that in my daily prayers I have heard from The One Spirit, and something is required of me. I will say The One Spirit tells me His servant, Jusaan, can provide the answers to my questions, so I may fulfill my role in His plans. I will say that we are both servants to His will, and I must trust His servant Jusaan."

Raymond thought this over and shook his head in admiration. "I would have never believed you so capable of deceit, Hanshee."

"Deceit is a harsh word." Hanshee shrugged. "Better to say trickery."

He met Raymond's gaze with a somber look that told him words of wisdom, words to be taken seriously, were forthcoming.

"Make no mistake, Way-mon, if deceit is what is required, it shall not be beneath us. We will do what is needed to prevail…always to prevail. Remember 'schemes within schemes', and how we must not be above schemes of our own?"

Hanshee had shared that piece of advice along the road to Pith, not so long ago, although it seemed like another lifetime to Ray.

Hanshee's resolve was evident, and Raymond took heart in knowing that this man, who had been everything to him since rescuing him from 'the River of Dreams,' continued to protect and guide him. He knew, without a doubt, he would have gone insane were it not for Hanshee, who had provided his sole anchor since he arrived in this terrible new world. And he knew, again without a doubt, that Hanshee would do what was needed to see them safely to his people. Even unto his own death, if he considered his death a guarantee of Ray's safe passage to the mountains of his birth.

Suddenly Hanshee jumped to his feet, startling Ray out of his thoughts of their predicament and of his good fortune for having such a friend.

"Rise Way-mon," Hanshee said, "and let us clear the large room. Tomorrow, if there is time…and there is always time…," he muttered, "we will begin your training."

"What training?" Raymond asked, as he rose from the cot.

"You must be trained to fight," Hanshee responded, "and if need be, to kill."

****

The Lord High Priest Mayhew sat back in his cushioned chair, more like a miniature throne really, and pondered all he had just been told. Three different spies, none knowing of the other's existence, had been separately summoned to tell their respective stories about the events of the last two days.

When the last of them had gone, Mayhew was astounded by what he'd been told.

With the first telling, he had refused to believe such a preposterous tale. He had called the man a liar and, despite his years of faithful service to the Temple of The One, had threatened his very soul. But when the second source told the same story, repeating every important detail Mayhew had already heard from the first, he knew this could not be ignored. By the time the third spy had passed on her information, Mayhew had gone from outrage to stunned silence.

Mayhew had always thought Jusaan had the potential to be an irritant in the Temple. He was too smart, too ambitious, and too manipulative. Too late, Mayhew had realized his mistake in elevating such a cunning individual to the Council of The Nine. He had thought the problem dealt with by appointing Jusaan as the military liaison with Galin and the First Expeditionary Legion. But what he had thought to be a neat and tidy solution to a potential problem had handed the priest what could be a fabled place in the long history of Pith, as well as the keys to Mayhew's own position as high priest. How could such an outrageous thing have occurred?

Mayhap he is the chosen of The One, Mayhew thought.

How else to explain how a predicament so distasteful could position Jusaan at the precise time and place to enjoy a stroke of fortune so grand that only the will of The One could adequately explain it?

Now he has this 'warrior-priest of old', along with the ear and trust of the King, thought the high priest. *And he appears to be beyond my reach, for the moment.*

That was probably the most disappointing part; though he held the preeminent religious position in the land, he was powerless to bring this underling priest to heel. In fact, by his thinking, it would now be extremely difficult to directly insert himself into these current affairs; affairs that, in the near future, could change the structure, the power, and the path, of the empire. As high priest he should be at the very center of these events, shaping them to the benefit of the Temple, and himself.

And I will be, Mayhew vowed.

It would require a more subdued approach, one easy to adopt, as even the lord high priest must kneel to the fulfillment of prophesy. He must speak with Jusaan and this 'warrior-priest', if that be what he really was. More likely the man was someone Jusaan had stumbled upon in the wilderness, someone who the wily priest calculated he could use to work his way back into the cozy warmth of the Temple.

And now that he had accomplished this, what other ambitions does the priest have? Does he think he can now come after the High Seat? Is he that deluded? Mayhew almost wished he was. Many a grand scheme had met its demise due to overreach.

Let him come for me, if he dares! thought the high priest.

Much more likely is that I will find 'Usaid reborn' but a fiction. Expose him, and I shall be rid of the priest for good. The thought brought a smile to Mayhew's face.

He could see himself ending it cleanly and quickly, exposing a fraud which would have placed the empire in peril, disposing of Jusaan in as public a way as possible, and gaining back a portion of the power and influence that had historically belonged to the Temple and the lord high priest. The power and influence that Lord Cecil, the guard dog of the royals, had worked tirelessly for decades to diminish. Now, the high priest must bow when the King stands instead of the other way around, as it had been in ages past.

That was a dream of a perfect ending, but Mayhew knew he was getting ahead of himself. The more he considered it, the more he was sure this warrior-priest must be a fraud. Exposing him, after the King appeared to have been taken in, might prove difficult. It is most likely better to forgo any long-range plans at this point. First, he must learn all he could from the Royal House. All three spies spoke of the King meeting with his advisors this night. On the morrow he planned to meet with his Council of Seven.

Mayhew decided he would await word of developments from those meetings before approaching Jusaan. Surely His Majesty would come to the realization that, even with all they currently possessed, the blessing of the lord high priest would be essential to confirm for the people that the Fourth Prophesy was on the verge of fulfillment.

The more he considered it, the better Mayhew felt.

"I can afford *some* patience," he said softly to his empty chamber. "As they see things more clearly, they will be calling for *me*."

Chapter 10

His Highness King Ammon the IV, ruler of the Empire of Pith, sat alone in the main room of the royal suite. It had taken longer than usual to dismiss his attendants, his servants, and Lord Cecil, who had felt it necessary to check in on him again after the momentous findings that had been brought forth at the audience. He had been right to do so. Through well over a thousand years of hardship and struggle, of survival against the elements, of battles won and lost in wars both big and small, of obstacles faced and overcome on their way to building what was a fledgling empire, the afternoon had produced probably the most astounding piece of news ever received in the royal court. News which, once disseminated, would shake the empire to its foundations.

The ramifications were staggering, and King Ammon had to demand that he be left in solitude so he could digest all the implications of what had been revealed this day. The decisions he would make in the coming days, be they based on acceptance or denial of what he had learned, could have far-reaching effects on his people, as well as on rival kingdoms both near and far.

Rising from his cushioned divan, which sat before a huge fireplace, he walked to an ornate table. It was made of intricately carved hardwoods and topped with polished marble. It stood beside a large, west-facing window which gave him a view of the courtyard below, the great wall of the Citadel, and the streets and rooftops of the city beyond. In light of the upcoming meeting with his advisors, he allowed himself only a small portion of spiced wine from one of the decanters on the table. He sipped the warm liquid as he strolled around this ornate chamber, pausing before one of the many tapestries adorning the stone walls. Each tapestry was a re-creation of a historic moment in the founding and building of the empire.

He often gazed at these depictions of the history of his people, the work of his ancestors now placed in his hands to be nurtured and further grown. There were times when he felt the many pressures inherent to any ruler, but a stroll around this chamber and the many others displaying similar tapestries usually served to reassure him that the bloodline which he represented had done well up to this point. He, being the latest in an unbroken line of kings, would do his part to add to the glorious history which had begun so long ago. Such were his thoughts as he made the rounds of the tapestries decorating this chamber.

He had watched his father do the same.

As a small boy, he had no awareness of the times of hardship, of the tensions that build on the eve of momentous decisions or prior to pronouncements that could change the shape and scope of the empire. He remembered watching as his father had slowly strolled from one tapestry to the next, appearing to study every detail before moving on. In this way, his sire had put the difficult situations he faced in perspective. In this way, he had focused his thoughts and steadied his nerve.

Early in his reign, without conscious thought, Ammon IV had adopted the same routine as his father, usually with the same steadying results.

But this evening was different and he cut short the 'tour of Pith' on the walls of his chamber and returned to his seat. Now he allowed his mind to take its own journey into the past and through the events that had brought his people to this place and this time.

His thoughts wandered back through the history he had been taught, back to the Miracle of Stronghold, when the earth shook with the power of The One Spirit and the course of mighty rivers were changed! The sheer walls of stone, until then a barrier to escape from the swords and arrows of the enemies of Pith, had somehow opened to accept a people on the edge of annihilation, offering a sanctuary and protection lasting until this day.

As the story goes, the forces of their enemy, an alliance of the Plains Nations led by the armies of Cantor, crashed again and again against the mighty stone walls. Each time they were driven back by the walls' impenetrable strength, aided by the spears and arrows of the Pith. After days of futile attacks, the enemy forces appeared content to make their camps some distance from the walls. There they fumed, having been deprived of victory by what they considered the fickle winds of fortune.

Beside the campfires visible in the distance to the sentries of the Pith, the forces of the enemy nightly worked themselves into a frenzy, with curses and shouts and stories of how the grand battle that never was should have played out, with the marauding Pith completely crushed under the iron might of the alliance. These stories were so vivid in their telling, so compelling in the victory they promised, that every few days smaller forces made up of anywhere from a few dozen to a few hundred would take up arms and launch themselves anew against the walls, hoping to fight through to the enemy protected within.

These often-drunken forays were always repelled and, over time, they diminished both in number and in effort. Before the allied camps eventually broke up, the would-be conquerors were reduced to marching to a place before the makeshift gates the Pith had hastily erected. There, just out of bow range, they hurled harsh curses and lewd gestures, working off their energies and hatred without endangering their lives. While all of this was going on, other parties were regularly sent out to scout the perimeter of the refuge. None ever returned with knowledge of a way to breech the natural walls forming an impenetrable defense around their foe.

Eventually the armies of Byrne and Rayine withdrew from the field. The armies of Cantor continued at their camps for several more weeks, exhausting all efforts to find a way to circumvent the walls and gain access to the Pith, before reluctantly withdrawing as well. However, they did not leave before establishing outposts that remained manned for centuries, and which eventually served to establish the first border between the Cantorese and what became the new nation of Pith.

King Ammon continued to allow his mind to wander back over what he had learned of the history of his people, taking comfort from the stories he was taught as a boy.

Having been so blessed by The One, who provided the protection of the great stone walls, the Pith now had the luxury of exploring this new land and utilizing the resources it provided to establish what they saw as a temporary home. What they discovered was something greater than any had imagined.

Just beyond the walls they found lush forests teeming with game, with clear, spring-fed lakes and streams. The forest yielded trees which were used to build shelters for the people, and to fashion formidable gates to protect the single opening in the walls surrounding them. Once they began exploring beyond the forest, the Pith discovered vast, grassy plains that sustained herds of deer and elk, and even mountain goats in the foothills of the mountains far to the north. There were few large predators here, aside from some wolf packs and rarely seen big cats. Game was plentiful and fairly easy to take, as the animals seemed to have had little experience with man.

Looking out over the plains, they saw the stone walls extending to the south, maintaining an unbroken barrier running far to the east where, from a high vantage point, the still-massive natural stone walls were barely visible in the distance.

Unknown to those early Pith, they were in what remained of a vast caldera, a roughly circular depression formed by a volcanic eruption which had occurred hundreds of thousands of years earlier. To the north were true mountains, with the highest peaks they had ever seen, higher even than the peaks of the great Blue Mountains of their homeland, or so it was said.

The walls of Stronghold, the name they eventually came to call this land, extended from the southeastern base of the mountains, running in more or less an oval until reaching the southwestern base of the same mountains. To travel the length of this valley, from the westernmost walls all the way to the easternmost, was a five or six-day journey for a man on foot. A journey from the base of the mountains in the north to the southern walls took just over three days.

For the tribe of Pith, this was plenty. There was land to hunt, land to farm, and forests to provide wood for fuel and shelter. The wandering tribe of Pith, nomads since being cast out of their ancestral home almost 200 years earlier, gave a prayer of thanks to The One Spirit and began working to make this valley their permanent home.

The next several hundred years were a time of consolidation for the people of Pith. Working and exploring the land, they managed to build a self-contained society within the Stronghold walls. The first major settlement sprang up around the original break in the walls, which had miraculously allowed them entrance. The rubble was cleared away and great wooden doors were hoisted into place, allowing those within to come and go as needed while offering protection from any forces seeking their destruction. Few took advantage of this as, with its three major rivers, and several lakes and streams, its vast forest and grasslands, and abundant wildlife, the Stronghold valley offered almost everything the Pith would need to survive and thrive.

Years passed, and their population continued to grow. The Pith gradually moved farther away from the settlement surrounding the gates and out into new parts of the valley. In the foothills of the great northern peaks, more resources were discovered: veins of ore of a quality and quantity never before seen by any of the Pith. Great deposits of iron, copper, and tin were discovered with minimal effort, in what appeared to be unlimited quantities, along with other metals in lesser quantities. Silver was also found in abundance, and there were gemstones in certain areas of the mountain. The ore removed from the mines was of such quality, such purity, as to have no known equal. The smithies of Pith happily went to work, smelting the ore and shaping the metals into all manner of useful tools, utensils, instruments, and ornaments.

But by far the most scintillating of all the finds were the veins of gold. The original tribe of Pith, though aware of gold, only knew of it as having existed in very limited quantities in their native lands. They regarded it as good for fashioning small tokens, trinkets, and decorations, but it was too soft a metal to have any practical uses. As they were forced into a nomadic existence, the Pith came into contact with, and conquered, many other tribal people. They absorbed these people, as well as some of their customs, as they moved from place to place. In this way, they became aware of the great value placed upon gold by other cultures which they readily assimilated into their own.

For centuries the Pith remained unmolested, building a self-sustaining agrarian society of farmers, miners, craftsmen and artisans, whose skill and creativity soon produced some of the finest implements, composed of some of the finest metals, ever seen.

Through this period of growth and expansion across the Stronghold plain, they still maintained a military presence at and around the gates. Though the years of peace proved blissful and rewarding, the Pith worked diligently to keep their history alive, so none would forget the years of hardship and struggle that had brought them to this miraculous valley. Nor was it possible to forget the enemy who still maintained watch towers on the plains to the west.

The Miracle of Stronghold became a part of their history and religion: the fulfillment of the Third Prophesy. With tangible evidence of the power and goodness of their god at which to point, the priesthood of The One Spirit grew strong, prosperous, and ever more influential in the lives of the people of Pith.

It was at this time that a second pathway into the valley of Stronghold was discovered, or rather revealed, to the Pith.

The capital city was under construction on the far eastern side of the valley. There were a good many outlying camps that would eventually become towns and villages between it and the major settlement surrounding the gates. Craftsmen of all kinds, from carpenters to stonemasons, architects and engineers, smelters, smithies, woodsmen and all the various professions it would take to build a fortress and the city that would surround it, were in demand. To support the needs of these workers were cobblers, weavers, tailors, leather workers, cooks, herdsmen, and farmers. All were needed, as work on what would come to be called the Citadel proceeded in a time of peace and security.

One day, without warning, a small tribe of strangers appeared as if from nowhere. They were discovered early one morning, moving down the slopes that descended from the Stronghold walls several miles to the southeast, above the proposed location of the Citadel.

Those who first laid eyes upon them stared in open-mouthed wonder at the group of approximately forty unkempt men, women and children, clothed in little more than skins and raw leather. Many were barefoot. The men carried rudimentary weapons and the heavier bundles. The women and children carried bundles also, smaller than those carried by the men, with the children leading and herding an assortment of animals, mostly goats, down from the hills and into the valley proper.

In their poverty and disarray, they could hardly have been mistaken for any sort of hostile invasion, but the Pith had not dealt with any outsiders for well over 150 years. They were nonplussed, not only by the presence of the strangers, but by the mystery of where they had come from.

An alarm was raised, and the workers came forward in great numbers, brandishing weapons and anything that could be used as a weapon. Their intent was clear: to fall upon and dispatch these strangers who had somehow found their way, undetected and undeterred, into their midst.

It was fortunate for the strangers that the newly recognized High Priest Cassius, well-known and influential throughout Stronghold, arrived before the slaughter had begun in earnest. He called a halt to the impending massacre, resulting in only two of the strangers having been killed. On his orders, the Pithians confiscated anything in the strangers' possession that could be utilized as a weapon, before herding them before Cassius. Under different circumstances there would have been no interference to save the strangers, but the high priest was an intelligent man. He realized the very presence of these people this deep into Stronghold meant there were many questions needing answers.

High Priest Cassius met with the leaders of the ragged band over a period of several days, providing them with food, water, and protection while attempting to find a means of communicating with them. After many stops and starts, rudimentary communication was first established based on gestures and drawings made in the dirt. Eventually some mutually understood words and phrases allowed Cassius to piece together some of the recent history of the group.

As he understood it, these people were all that remained of a small tribe of farmers and herdsmen once inhabiting the eastern foothills of the mountain range that lay to the south of Stronghold. There were many tribes residing in and around this mountain range, called the Ursal Mountains by its inhabitants. These tribes were constantly competing for resources, and these competitions sometimes escalated into feuds or even open warfare. Seldom were these conflicts of a prolonged nature. The hard lives these tribes lived meant that strong, able-bodied men were at a premium. The loss of two or three on each side usually had their leaders ready to look for less-lethal solutions to their conflicts.

If a tribe allowed itself to be embroiled in battles over long periods of time, the resulting loss of life would most likely leave them severely weakened. Even if they eventually emerged victorious, they could present a tempting target to some other tribe looking to expand its land and resources.

The tribe of the Wanderers, as the strangers were referred to by the Pith, had the misfortune of somehow angering a stronger neighbor. Ordinarily this would not have led to open conflict, except for the fact of an alliance with a still-stronger tribe, whose leader desired the wife of the chief's son. She had yet to bear the chief's son any children, and may well have been barren, so the shrewd chief used this opportunity as a means to achieve his goal.

Exaggerating her worth to the leader of the stronger tribe, the chief told him an agreement could still be reached by which his daughter-in-law could grace the leader's bed. They only had to join their forces and eliminate the neighboring tribe with which the chief had a minor disagreement. He convinced his son to go along by promising him his pick of two of the finest women from among the tribe to be conquered.

The tribe of the Wanderers, completely outmatched, went down quickly. Two-thirds of their number were either captured or killed. The other third managed to escape with whatever they could grab, gathering some of their flocks from distant pastures before making their way west, then north, away from the lands now claimed by the two allied tribes.

Their journey took them through lands already under claim by other tribes, leaving them unable to find a suitable place to settle. If fortunate, they were simply encouraged to move swiftly through these lands. They did so under the watchful eyes of those who claimed them, lest they be tempted to linger. Other times they were set upon by the owners of the land. In these instances, they lost either members of their tribe or a portion of their livestock; sometimes both. This became a recurring theme as they made their way from one hostile territory to the next, and their numbers steadily dwindled.

It was while pushing through the forest, just ahead of a small raiding party out to steal their livestock, that they came upon the great southern wall of Stronghold. Trapped against the high walls and fearing the imminent arrival of those in pursuit, they raced along its base, knowing their only hope lay in outdistancing their pursuers. Eventually, they came upon a depression in the rock wall. Succumbing to weariness, they took shelter inside in the hope of using the confined space to defend what little they had left.

Once inside, they found it to be a cave large enough to hide all the remaining Wanderers and their stock. Further exploration revealed a rear wall that was not solid rock, but what appeared to be the remnants of a collapse from long ago. Still fearing for their lives, the men began working frantically to clear the rocks and rubble, expecting that the pursuing warriors could emerge from the forest to plunder and kill at any moment. Unknown to the Wanderers, the chase had long ago been abandoned. But in their haste to outdistance the nonexistent pursuit, the Wanderers had managed to clear a hole through the wall large enough to provide a path of escape to whatever lay on the other side.

They pushed the last goat through the hole sometime after sundown. Then the bone-weary party barricaded the escape route with rocks and dirt, before making camp at the base of the northern face of the wall.

Early the next morning, they opened their eyes and beheld a continuation of the forest they had left on the other side of the high rock walls. They spent the first hours after dawn pushing through this new forest, emerging in the early morning at the top of a slope overlooking a great valley. It was not long after descending into this valley that they were discovered by those laboring to build the Citadel.

High Priest Cassius was intrigued by many of the passages in this account. He continued to care for the Wanderers for several months, learning their language and teaching them the language of the Pith. He had some of his followers build them shelters, seeing to it they were treated better than they had been at any time since being forced from their village.

In the evenings he would sit among them, learning ever more about what lay on the other side of the southern wall of Stronghold. He had their leader take him and a few of his followers back up the slope to find the cave from which they had emerged into the valley. The high priest found it to be as he had been told, even down to the remnants of the overnight camp beside the wall.

Having earned their trust and learned much more than he had anticipated, Cassius led the Wanderers across the valley, a journey of three days, to the foothills of the northern mountains. Once there, he told their leader that one of his followers would lead them up into the mountains to a place of forested meadows. There would be fresh water, trees and grasses for building shelters, grazing for their goats, and game for their hunters.

Cassius had tools provided for them: knives and axes, farming implements and arrowheads, all made from good Pithian iron. He provided them with seeds so they could grow many of the crops the Pith grew; crops which had kept them fed for the past several months. He provided all of these things and provided instruction on their uses.

The Lord High Priest also arranged for supplies to be delivered to them at intervals until they had established their own harvests. He assured them the seeds and the tools were theirs to keep with no repayment necessary, and the lands were to be their new home forever.

He then spoke his blessing over them in the name of The One Spirit.

High Priest Cassius eventually departed, but not before being showered with love and adoration from the Wanderers. Despite being told the provisions were gifts, the tribe pledged to repay the debt of kindness bestowed upon them by the goodness of this "One Spirit", by the hands of His servant, Cassius.

Upon his return to the settlements, Cassius conferred with the elders of the Pith. He shared with them a good portion of the information he had gleaned from the Wanderers, but not all. What he shared was enough to stoke their curiosity about the lands lying to the south, and how they could be exploited for the benefit of the Pith. Over the years, this curiosity would slowly blossom into action.

At the urging of the priesthood, one of the first official actions of the newly established King was to authorize an excavation of the cavern that had led the Wanderers into the valley. This became the southern gateway out of Stronghold.

Once this work was completed and the passage secured, Pithian explorers - young, intelligent, vigorous men who craved adventure - were dispatched into the lands beyond. They were tasked with learning about the land and its inhabitants, hopefully by living among them and learning their languages and customs. They were to return to Stronghold at intervals of no longer than three years, to report on what they had learned and to compare notes with others of their ilk. In this way, the Pith developed rudimentary maps of the lands to the south, profiles of the tribes inhabiting them, understanding of the territorial lines applying to each tribe, and how the tribes interacted with one another. When the time came to institute a program of conquest, the armies of Pith were well aware of what to expect from the southern tribes, and had strategies in place on how best to deal with each.

The campaigns of conquest were waged over a period of several decades and provided the Pith a new education in the ways of war. This was sorely needed after so many years of peaceful expansion inside the secure confines of Stronghold.

The various tribes they encountered were never a match for the Pith, either technologically or numerically. Nevertheless, they fought with a fierceness unknown to the inexperienced soldiers who were first sent against them. Despite superiority in manpower, weapons, and armor, there were many battles where the Pith barely eked out a victory. In a few cases, where the embattled tribes had the foresight to join forces against the invaders from the north, the armies of Pith suffered a rare defeat.

It was said in the capital that, if the Southlands could have produced one or two charismatic leaders who could forge and hold alliances so that the various tribes would fight as one, the Pith may have been relegated to the lands inside Stronghold. Indeed, they may even have found themselves under siege from Cantor in the west and the unified tribes in the south.

But unification was not in the future for the southern tribes. Although they fought with courage, it was only a matter of time before the Pith would prevail. These campaigns were a valuable training ground for the military of Pith, its culture, and its future leaders. Many were the stories of heroism filtering northward to the people of Stronghold; stories inspiring pride, commitment, and support. The ranks of the army were never wanting, as many a lad sought to walk beside the seasoned soldiers who were spoken of glowingly as "the Heroes of Pith." They dreamed of living out the glories of battle, their youthful imaginations stoked by the tales told of and by those who had served.

By the time the majority of the southern tribes had been conquered, the Pithian military had grown up. Whether in campaigns fought in the mountain passes, or in the glens at their base, in the thickly wooded forest of the foothills, or the jungle-like denseness of the river-valleys lying farther east, the Pithian military heeded the lessons learned from battling their foes. They adapted their tactics and equipment to deal with the different terrains and conditions, eventually establishing a hard-earned and well-deserved reputation as the most formidable broken-terrain fighters in the land.

Chapter 11

King Ammon again moved over to the table by the window and replenished his spiced wine. His first pouring had managed to leave his goblet without his noticing, so caught up was he in recalling the history of his people. On the eve of important decisions, remembrances of past events in Pithian history served to calm him. Hard decisions, and the changes they brought, had always been a part of the journey of his people. It would likely always be that way.

Any man could lead a pampered existence, suckling from the breast of luxury and indulgence, and think himself a king. But Ammon always knew it was by his decisions, especially those where the stakes were the highest, did a man show himself truly possessed of royal blood...truly noble, and worthy to be called a King. And as would any true King, Ammon welcomed the challenge; the opportunity to prove his metal and direct his people down the right path at this crucial time in their history.

Smiling slightly at the hand dealt him by The One, Ammon settled into his chair and allowed his mind to wander back through the history that had produced the Pith in their present form.

****

The newfound confidence of the Pith in the strength and readiness of their military was soon to be put to the test.

Not every campaign was one of conquest. Many of the high mountain tribes held territory on both slopes of the Ursal Mountains, their eastern lands being at such elevations as to have no real value to the Pith. Their interest in these tribes lay more in pacification. There were some pitched battles between them, and in these the Pith showed they had the strength and the ruthlessness to push forward to total conquest if need be. But they were more concerned with protecting their flanks while fighting other tribes in the mountain valleys and lower elevations. In most cases, the high mountain tribes, having had a taste of the military strength of the Pith, were more than happy to enter into agreements, some would say alliances, with these hardened fighters from the north.

The typical agreement allowed the tribes to continue in their daily lives as if nothing had changed. They maintained their lands just as they had before the arrival of the Pith, and all decisions concerning their tribes and lands remained in their hands. There were only two obligations.

The first obligation was for each tribe to deliver a yearly tribute to the Citadel, to be placed at the feet of the King. The amount was a paltry sum by the standards of the Pith, but the payment itself, and the manner by which it was to be paid, was calculated to bind the tribe by thought and action to their new overlords.

The second obligation was that, in times of war and upon receipt of a formal request, each was to be bound to come to the defense of the other. This was to be respected at all times, unless two warring tribes each held alliances with the Pith, in which case the tribes could not expect the Pith to choose a side. It had already been noted by the Pith that, except for their own recent forays into the high passes, the tribes had only ever taken up arms against each other.

By reaching this agreement of alliance with several of the high mountain tribes, the Pith were assured that they would not be engaged on a second front, and from higher ground, while fighting against the other tribes of the Ursals. Under the wording of the agreement, the Pith had the right to petition the high mountain tribes to join with them in any actions against other Ursal mountain tribes. This was not their intention when proposing the alliance, and the Pith retained too much pride and greed to make ever such a petition.

The surprise came one day when envoys from an alliance of high mountain tribes arrived at Stronghold. Their stated purpose was to petition the King of the Pith to honor their agreement to fight alongside one another when formally called upon.

The tribal envoys were escorted before the Pithian King, where they explained their western borders were under pressure from the armies of Rayine, the nation on the southern border of Cantor. Rayine had been instrumental in the alliance that almost wiped out the Pith before the Miracle at Stronghold.

For several decades, it had been recognized that the purest metals and the finest forged implements flowed out of Pith. Trade had even been established by some of the merchant houses of the Great Inland Sea. These merchants regularly made their way north along the trade road running from the port cities of Durr and Maestell, northwest between the southernmost peaks of the Ursal Mountains and the Great Swamp. The road then turned north along the western Ursal foothills into the nations of Rayine and Cantor, before ending somewhere above the Plains Nations, in the vast northlands.

Having heard talk of a new settlement in the high country east of Cantor, one of the most enterprising of the merchants thought the rumors worth investigating. What he discovered at the end of his search was a fledgling nation rich with the largest ore deposits currently known. They were producing the finest quality of iron, copper, tin, and silver. Their artisans and smithies were turning these high-quality metals into some of the finest and most detailed ornaments and implements ever seen. The quality of their weaponry was unmatched anywhere in the known world.

It was not long after the initial foray that merchant caravans began arriving at regular intervals at the gates of Stronghold. The Pith soon enjoyed a reputation among the nations for producing the best metal and the finest implements, be they for farming or fighting, that could be purchased anywhere. Soon genuine Pithian blades were coveted by the upper echelon of every military along the great trade routes, including the Cantorese, who nonetheless did everything in their power, short of launching an attack, to minimize the trade coming out of Pith.

Those in Rayine were not as hostile toward Pith as their neighbors to the north, but felt obligated by their long relationship with Cantor to maintain an aggressive posture.

At some point, the Rayine decided the Pith should not hold a monopoly within the nations as the only producer of high-quality ores and metal implements. Mistakenly thinking the Pith were mining the eastern foothills of the Ursals for their deposits, the Rayine sent wave after wave of prospectors, under the protection of the Rayine military, into the western foothills, hoping to find deposits of similar size and quality. Their plan was to undercut the Pith with comparable ore and implements that, due to their location, were much more attainable than those of their neighbor to the northeast.

In implementing their strategy, the Rayine prospectors eventually began routinely trespassing onto lands historically belonging to the high mountain tribes. The Rayine military found themselves in almost constant skirmishes with one or another of the tribes, over prospectors who had been harassed or killed for trespassing. It eventually reached a point where the leadership of Rayine had determined to launch an all-out attack on the mountain tribes to secure the resources of the western Ursals for their benefit alone.

The tribal leaders, seeing that the Rayine had begun the process of amassing their military on the plain adjacent to the mountains, with the apparent goal of forcibly seizing all the land previously acknowledged as belonging to the tribes, turned to the Pith to fight beside them in defense of their homes. This was, after all, the centerpiece of the agreement of alliance entered into by both parties.

To say that this turn of events was a surprise was an understatement of epic proportion. When the agreements were originally proposed, the Pith never imagined it would be the tribes petitioning for their support in war. And against the Rayine, no less.

Despite the obligations demanded by the alliances proposed by they themselves, the initial reaction among the nobles and military of the Pith, was to ignore the petition for aid. This would have been both arrogant and dishonest, but hardly unheard of when agreements are reached between parties of unequal stature.

But there was a small contingent in the Pithian hierarchy who saw this as an opportunity.

The armies of Pith had already succeeded in subjugating, more or less, the greatest part of the opposition of the southeastern tribes. They could afford to redeploy their battle-hardened troops from the eastern foothills of the Ursals to the western slopes without compromising their gains of land and prestige. Refusal to do so would have the effect of injecting hostility into the relationship with the high mountain tribes where none currently existed. They might then turn their attention away from the Rayine and onto the Pith, who had deceived and insulted them.

Open warfare with the mountain tribes was winnable, of course, but it could have the effect of unifying and emboldening the southern tribes who continued in their resistance. Pith would then be involved in a two-front war. It would most likely drain their treasury and manpower, and delay their final victory for years to come. This alone was enough for certain of his advisors to urge the King to acknowledge the alliances and send troops to the aid of the tribes. After all, if treasure was to be spent, it was best spent defeating old enemies rather than creating new ones.

There was yet another reason many wanted to honor the agreement.

The Pith were flush with the newfound potency of their military. They now had a significant army of battle-tested, battle-hardened men. They had a full armory stocked with what was acknowledged to be the finest in bladed weaponry, arrowheads, light armor, and anything else made of metal and meant for war. They were feeling full of themselves, and many saw an alliance with the tribes as an opportunity to test their mettle, not against a foe a few steps removed from fighting with rocks and clubs, but against one they could regard as an equal. They felt sure their army could handle one of the three who had almost brought their journey to an end so long ago, and they wanted to prove it.

There was a small contingent in the Pithian hierarchy holding this view. Among them was the King.

When word went forth stating the Pith were prepared to honor their word and fight alongside the high mountain tribes, the reaction was as swift as it was surprising.

There were specific tribes with which the Pith had entered into agreement. They were usually those whose territory placed them in position to interfere with Pithian plans for some other tribe that had been targeted. Every high mountain tribe did not fit this definition, and most were not included in the alliances hammered out by the Pith. This did not hinder tribes from up and down the length of the Ursals from sending representatives to make known their willingness to fight alongside their native brothers and the army of the Pith. Each new offer of support was greeted with appreciation and respect from those who had petitioned the Pith. Even if the contingent sent to fight consisted of merely a handful of men, all were welcomed. From an initial contingent representing three tribes, fighters from seventeen greater or lesser tribes stood assembled on the day when the soldiers of Pith were scheduled to arrive.

They arrived with the fanfare of a young nation having newly discovered its strength.

The efforts still underway in the eastern foothills had been curbed to provide experienced fighters for the campaign against the Rayine. Having also received word of the historic alliance, the tribes in the eastern foothills seemed content to pull their warriors back, maintaining a state of readiness, while watching the goings-on in the high plains. This meant the newly established garrisons in the foothills could be minimally staffed, the majority of those fighters ordered to march west to meet up with columns advancing from Stronghold's gates.

The combined forces were given two days to rest and reorganize. Weapons were edged and repaired. Where needed, new weapons were distributed even as old clothing was discarded for new. The armories had nearly been emptied for this historic endeavor and pains were taken to see that every soldier was fully equipped with weapons and wearing colors marking them as a soldier of the nation of Pith.

For these two days, food and drink were plentiful, and a festive atmosphere reigned as the great army encamped on the high plains made its final preparations. The men were held in check to a degree; no one wanted frivolous horseplay to lead to unneeded injuries or deaths. Hard drinking was prohibited and watered-down wine was the strongest drink available.

The men were encouraged to enjoy themselves. Those arriving from the garrisons were told to recuperate from their tours and to eat, drink, rest, and have any nagging injuries or wounds tended to. Among the fresh troops, competitions sprang up between the different commands. Archery, knife and axe throwing, foot races, and other activities kept the men in high spirits.

On the morning of the third day the companies formed up. Standards were raised, and horns were sounded. Officers on horseback were resplendent in light armor, their breastplates, shin and arm guards, and helmets all polished until they shone like silver and gold. Each had a crimson robe draped across his shoulders, matching the crimson crest adorning many of their helmets. Underneath they wore tunics of crimson or light gray, depending on their rank and placement in the army.

The common soldiers wore tunics of wool or leather, some with heavier molded leather covering their chests and backs. Their helmets were also made of hardened leather. Now and then a soldier was spied wearing light mail under his tunic, or a light metal helmet covered in leather. These were rare, as not all families could afford to outfit their sons in the latest protective gear. All the men marched in sandals tied up their calf. Around each waist was a sash of crimson trimmed in gold, the colors of Pith.

As for weapons, they were divided into two camps: archers and infantry.

Each archer marched with a short, recurved bow. Each had a quiver half-filled with arrows. The supply wagons that followed were heavily laden with arrows, new bows, bowstrings, and any other equipment the archers may carry, such as short swords and a dagger-like knife worn at the waist.

The infantry relied mostly on longer, heavier swords, and battle axes with handles up to two feet long. These axes had heads smaller and much lighter than a woodsman's axe. The long handles meant they could be swung with amazing speed and force. The iron heads were sharpened to a razor's edge on one side, and many had six-inch sharpened spikes on the other. They also carried heavy knives made for close-quarter fighting. These were only slightly smaller than short swords, but carried only a third of the heft. Wagons followed in their wake also, carrying replacement weapons of various types, along with shields.

Together the officers and their men made an impressive sight as they marched in formation toward the eastern mountain pass the leaders of the three tribes had designated as the place they would gather.

On the day they would meet, the tribal leaders stood on high ground, surrounded by their fighters. A distant blast of trumpets told them the soldiers of Pith would soon be in sight. The rumble of their footsteps was heard just before they rounded the last outcropping of rock and came into view. As the tribal leaders looked on, row after row of soldiers marched before them to take up positions across the high mountain plain chosen for their first meeting. It took over an hour for all the Pithian soldiers, their support wagons and officers, to take up their positions. They stood tall and proud, looking into the eyes of the multitude of native warriors gathered there to witness their arrival.

Many of these men had faced each other as enemies not long ago, and there was fierceness in the eyes of each that spoke of intense combat remembered, and of friends and comrades on both sides who were slain in battles past. There was also a respect for the prowess of a former adversary. Each hoped their new allies would fight the Rayine with the same fire and fury they had displayed when fighting against each other.

After ceremonies were performed and introductions made, the men of Pith were allowed to make camp. The warriors of the tribes, hesitant at first, soon began to mingle on the outskirts of the encampment, curious about their new allies. Until this day, the two sides had only been this close in battle. The warriors observed the Pith closely, talking quietly among themselves about the ways of their onetime enemy, occasionally calling attention to some strange or amusing sight by pointing and sometimes laughing.

The soldiers of Pith had been given their orders. Upon pain of death, in absolutely no way were they to antagonize the warriors of the tribes. Any and all hostilities were to be buried pending the successful completion of this alliance. Surprisingly, the men had little trouble obeying these orders. Those who showed signs of having difficulty keeping their hostility in check were banished to tents in the center of the camp.

Many of the Pith, especially those from the garrisons, had learned some of the tribal languages. Being just as curious about the warriors as the warriors were about them, conversations began to spring up. Slowly at first, but more and more as time passed, some of the Pith and some of the tribal warriors mingled there on the plains and seeds of understanding began to germinate.

While the rank-and-file soldiers from both sides continued their evaluations of their onetime enemies, the officers were meeting with the leaders of the tribes to plan strategies and deployment. The Pith had map-makers present and they worked feverishly to draw maps of the western slopes, based on rapid-fire descriptions coming from the war leaders of the tribes. The warriors were intimately familiar with the land, but none of the Pith had ever ventured onto the western slopes of the Ursal Mountains. The hastily drawn maps were invaluable in preparing the Pith for the new terrain and the conditions of the upcoming campaign.

Once familiar with the land, decisions had to be hammered out concerning strategies and tactics. How and where to deploy the fighters and how best to blend the different forces into cohesive fighting units were difficult questions, and called for prolonged debates shifting from benign to intense. Such was the nature of military planning, and the leaders on both sides were meticulous in these preparations. Once agreement was reached and the preparations concluded, the leaders of each fighting force emerged with new respect for their onetime foes.

The time of planning was different for the rank and file.

Warriors from the tribes quickly found ways to amuse themselves with games and competitions that seemed strange and foreign to the soldiers of Pith. They looked on with interested amusement as the warriors played a game centered on a tightly wound ball of leather that could only be advanced through opposing players using the legs and feet. The agility displayed by the warriors in this difficult effort kept the soldiers of Pith mesmerized. One of them asked if he could try and, emboldened by his example, others also came forward. The chaos resulting from the efforts of the inexperienced Pith had the warriors of the tribes rolling on the ground in laughter. At first the Pith bristled, thinking they were being ridiculed, but the sight of two of their own crashing headlong into each other in pursuit of the leather ball, which rolled untouched between them, caused them to burst into laughter too.

After that, the two camps joined the games in earnest, with many of the Pith determined to learn the finer points of this kicking around of a leather ball, while tribal warriors happily joined the Pith in contests of speed, strength and skill, as well as various games of chance.

Conflicts were few, as each side had been made to recognize the importance of maintaining good relations during these crucial times. The few who chose to push the issue were treated to public humiliation; naked paddling on the bottom, or being made to walk around the camp clothed in the garb of an infant, signifying an inability to exercise self-control. This was usually enough to both entertain the others, and dissuade them from similar outbursts.

The officers in charge of the camp were overjoyed as the mixing of the two forces, a potential powder keg even absent the history of hostility, had evolved into what looked much like bonding and camaraderie. This was seen as a good omen with regard to the upcoming battle with the Rayine.

After six days all plans were set and all commanders of both sides knew their positions and their roles. The camp was disassembled and the men prepared for the final leg of the journey that would take them through the high mountain passes and down into the wooded slopes of the western Ursals.

A different Pith emerged for this journey.

Gone was the officers' gleaming armor, bright tunics and resplendent crimson robes. They were replaced by more rugged wear, much like the garments worn by the rank and file; tunics of wool with hardened leather breast plates, and leather-covered shin and arm guards. The shining, crested helmets were set aside for those of dull metal, hardened leather, or none at all. Only their ornate personal weapons, and the markings inlaid into the breastplates and arm guards marked them as officers.

The rank-and-file soldiers were garbed the same as when they arrived, save for the absence of the crimson and gold sashes around each waist. A full complement of weapons had been distributed to all, and the archers' quivers now bristled with arrows.

The tribal warriors, understandably concerned upon first seeing the colorful and shiny Pith, now nodded their heads in acknowledgment. These were the enemies they remembered; once awkward and ill-equipped soldiers who had quickly learned from their mistakes and were now able to move through, and melt into, the heavy brush where much of the fighting would take place.

With everyone now well equipped, their skills honed, their placements known, and their strategies understood, the time to fight had arrived. Soon the combined forces were moving farther up into the mountain passes, where they crossed over from the east and eventually disappeared into the forests and glades of the western slopes of the Ursal Mountains.

Chapter 12

The evening meal had come and gone. King Ammon, still deep in his thoughts and memories of lessons learned and passed down through the history of his people, had chosen to dine alone. It was an indulgence in which he seldom partook. The smallest divergence from his usual habits was enough to send his aides scurrying through the Royal House, searching for something; medicine or mirth; priestly assurances, or the ministrations of a comely woman, anything to break the malaise of their King.

He smiled as he thought of how his subjects, those responsible for his well-being, worried ceaselessly over the minutia of his everyday life. If only he were so fortunate as to have the comfort of one man as his only concern! But Ammon was an intelligent man, wise in the ways of ruling, yet not above understanding the rigors of the common man. Long ago his father had taught him that every life has its challenges, its burdens and its struggles, the weight of which bent the back of every man to one degree or another.

Words of mirth brought forth laughter from both the king and the commoner, and who is to say which enjoyed his laugh the most? Was it the king surrounded by wealth and luxury, to which a good laugh may be only a passing thing, quickly forgotten between bouts of fine food and drink, fawning company, and pampering by all who surrounded him? Or was it the commoner, to whom a bout of genuine mirth could be a balm to his soul after long days filled with toil and sweat, where all things seemed to work against him, and only by the labor of his own callused hands did he and his family get to enjoy the simple reward of having bread to break, and a roof under which to break it, in the quiet of the evening?

Ammon knew the answer to this riddle: it was both, and neither. For it was not the weight of a man's purse that determined his happiness, but the size of his burdens and whether he had the strength and the will to carry them, both for himself and for those who depended upon him.

The life of a king was filled with wealth and luxury. And so, it was fitting that the burdens of a king; the secrets he must keep, the decisions he must make, be enough to sometimes reduce the luxury and wealth to so much ash in his mouth.

The reality of the Fourth Prophesy was just such a burden. With it would come decisions that would make this king...or any king...long for the life of the smithy who labored daily at his forge, or the farmer doing the same in his fields; the life, the burdens, and the decisions, of the common man.

His young nation...this fledgling empire called Pith...had come a far distance in a comparatively short time. Now, as its King, Ammon would have the honor of making the decision that, on the one hand, would spit in the face of the god who had cared for them, nurtured them, saved them, and brought them to their present glory. A decision that, on the other hand, would require he and his people to willingly walk away from everything for which generations of Pith had, apparently with the blessing of The One Spirit, worked and fought and bled and died to create.

Thoughts of this nature, of the challenges faced and sacrifices made by his people, prompted his mind to drift back to his earlier ruminations. His thoughts returned to the first alliance in their history, an alliance with the mountain tribes against the

Rayine, who in years past had conspired with the nation of Cantor to wipe out the Pith.

****

On the eve of battle, their plans were judged to be sound and the placement of their forces well thought out.

The Rayine had tired of the tribes of the Western Ursals causing mischief as their prospectors sought the rich deposits of ore they suspected were waiting in the recesses of the mountains. They were tired of skirmishes and had determined an invasion of the land, to wipe out all native opposition to their plans, was the only way to proceed.

To this end, they had spent the last forty days amassing their troops and preparing them to enter the forest with a force calculated to overwhelm the paltry numbers of mountain tribe fighters they suspected resided there. They awaited only word from their scouts that the natives had again struck at their mining operations, so they would know where to concentrate their efforts. There was, however, a thin thread of concern winding through their forces that all of their extensive preparation had been for naught. This was because, since the gathering of the Rayine troops had begun, all had been quiet in the mountains.

That was about to change

They began to arrive in the evening; scouts, lookouts, and survivors staggering down from the mountains just as the sun was setting. They brought with them horrifying tales of conflict, ambushes and surprise attacks, resulting in the killing and wounding of many Rayine.

In all cases, the stories were similar. Small groups of fierce warriors took the miners and their guards by surprise. The fighting was fast and furious. Usually the guards, and the miners who fought alongside them, were driven away. Their equipment was broken and their camps were ransacked. Anything of worth was taken by the invaders. This scenario had played out simultaneously at six different mining camps spread out across the western slopes.

With the arrival of the survivors, a sense of excitement ran through the soldiers encamped at the foot of the mountains. They saw an opportunity for the action they had been anticipating since the order to gather at the base of the mountains had come down. Word moved swiftly through the ranks; come sunrise, the fighting men of Rayine would be on the move!

Their battle plan was simple. They would march east into the wooded hills of the Ursals and crush any resistance they found there. The different locations of the native strikes meant the forces of the Rayine would be spread along a front at least a league in length, but they had been gathered together in such numbers as to be ready for any and all contingencies. They were confident they had manpower sufficient to lay waste to the warriors of the tribes.

They were wrong.

The following morning the Rayine entered a tree line still cast in deep shadow, as the rising sun was still nestled behind the Ursal Mountains. From there they began to slowly worked their way up into the hills. Heavy weapons and armor, made for fighting on flat terrain, proved a hindrance to their movement through the thick brush, but the soldiers pressed on. By the time they finally reached the ruined mining camps, the sun had long since crested the mountain and they were hot, thirsty, and tired.

As expected, the camps were deserted. The battle the Rayine anticipated lay farther up the slopes. This meant an additional climb of undetermined distance. It was decided a late-morning rest would be appropriate before again forming up to advance on the higher elevations. Word was passed down the line, and many Rayine sought relief by removing their breastplates and helmets, laying them aside to enjoy a sip of warm water and a bite or two from their food pouches.

They were in the midst of this respite when the first volley of arrows struck.

With their comrades dropping around them, the soldiers of Rayine struggled back into their protective gear, formed up, and charged into the brush from where the arrows had come. There they found sign left by a foe who had released several volleys and retreated farther up into the mountains. Their pride stung by the sneak attack, the Rayine moved quickly to follow the tracks and bring the natives to heel.

This scenario played out all across the lines of the Rayine offensive. The heavily outfitted soldiers ventured farther and farther up the slopes, onto unfamiliar terrain for which they were poorly equipped to wage a campaign. Each time they stopped to rest, another volley of arrows spurred them to continue the chase. When the Rayine finally wised up, and the arrows no longer caught them by surprise nor laid many low, the tribal warriors changed strategies and engaged the Rayine directly. Not in mass, but in small groups able to rush in, strike a blow, and retreat into the brush. These tactics served to further enrage the Rayine, who pressed on in pursuit of the small bands, secure in their ability to destroy them, if they could only catch them.

Just past the noon hour, the Rayine were hot, hungry, thirsty, and exhausted. They were aware their lines were broken but, in the dense trees and brush, they had no way to accurately gauge their flanks. They had been able to engage the natives just often enough to see a few of them fall, further whetting their appetite for an all-out battle. Even in their current exhausted state, they felt compelled to press forward whenever an opportunity for pursuit presented itself.

It was mid-afternoon when the Rayine heard the horns. The whole of the forest fell eerily silent except for the blasts that came from everywhere and nowhere. The first horn blast was answered by others a short distance away. These were answered by those further in the distance, until the repeated sound was so faint that it may have been only imagined. After the last echo of the horns had died, the Rayine stood frozen in tense anticipation.

The heat of the afternoon, the weight of their armor and weapons, the exertions of the day, these things merged with the quiet after the blaring of the horns and seemed to make the confines of the high forest close in on the soldiers. They felt it pressing against their flesh and causing the fears and concerns, pushed aside in their urgency to engage with the enemy, to rise up and take hold in their conscious minds.

Then all hell broke loose!

Without warning, the Rayine found themselves engaged by fighters seemingly as numerous as the trees surrounding them. Having long ago been separated from their lines, many quickly discovered they were under attack from at least three sides. And those who attacked were not just native warriors. Many appeared to be soldiers such as themselves, though not as heavily armed and so not slowed by the weight of their armor and gear. While the Rayine had endured the long hot trek up the mountain and the repetition of fighting through the brush - fighting with the natives - an all too brief rest - and more of the same, these new fighters appeared to be fresh and ready for battle.

And they fought like demons!

Their strikes were quick and powerful, the hard, sharp spikes on the end of their axes easily penetrating the armor of the Rayine when wielded with a full swing. When attacking with blades their aim was precise. Not always striking to kill, many warriors felled Rayine by hamstringing them. Some slashed at the tendon in the armpit to render their broadswords, already too big and cumbersome for combat in the confines of the forest, even more useless.

Then the horns again sounded and, as one, every enemy warrior dropped to the ground, lying as flat as the terrain would allow. The Rayine were startled at this tactic, but before they could take advantage, they were hit with a wall of arrows. Most were deflected by their armor, but the arrows were fired in such numbers that few of the standing Rayine escaped without at least one arrow finding a soft spot or a joint where the armor did not quite meet. After the clang of the last arrow, the prone warriors sprang to their feet and flailed anew at their tired and stricken enemy.

It was then that the ranks of the Rayine finally broke. All across their front Rayine soldiers turned and fled, stripping off their armor and discarding useless weapons in an attempt to coax more speed from their battered and broken bodies. Tripping and stumbling, falling and getting back up and running even harder, the hapless soldiers of Rayine were in a mad dash to flee the wooded hills that had proven to be the death of their pride and their ambitions.

For many it was simply their death.

It was said those finally emerging from the tree line in the late afternoon and early evening numbered roughly half of those who had entered early that morning. There was no attempt to regroup, form up ranks and return to the fray; the *fray* had pursued them down the mountain. The Rayine survivors tore through their encampment at the base of the mountain without slowing down, leaving a cloud of dust to mark their progress as they ran for all they were worth toward their capital of Wroughtmire.

The pursuing alliance of the high mountain tribes and Pith spent the next several days pillaging the encampment, eating Rayine food and drinking Rayine wine; taking anything they deemed of value and burning the rest.

It was said the defeated Rayine watched the black smoke rising from their former encampment from distant perches atop the walls of Wroughtmire.

****

Ammon let a satisfied sigh escape his lips.

Ever a student of the history of his people, the story of the Battle of the Western Ursals had always been one of his favorites. It marked the first steps of the Pith down a path which had forever changed them.

The treaties with the high mountain tribes are remembered by the historians of Pith as their very first act of true diplomacy.

The agreements to fight beside them, promises kept only due to the pressure applied by a few far-sighted and powerful individuals, are held up as the first alliances formed by the Pith in their new home.

The defeat of the Rayine, not an overmatched tribe of native warriors, but a long-established fixture in this new world, was the first victory of its kind for the Pith since leaving the motherland.

This achievement was remembered in the annals of Pithian history as marking the period in time when the Pith, long a strong and proud clan from the prairies west of the Blue Mountains, first *behaved* as a nation and thus *became* a nation.

Ammon rose from his chair and stretched his legs, which tended to become stiff should he hold one position for too long. He expected the council of his advisors to arrive at any minute and decided to freshen up a bit. A king must always maintain an appearance of strength and control, especially among those who are constantly measuring, constantly testing, and constantly scheming.

He moved through quarters filled with intricately carved furniture, its beautiful tapestries and thick carpets woven of the finest wool and silk. The rich appointments, carvings, paintings and statuary were the very best to be had in the fledgling empire. All of these things went unnoticed by the King. As he approached the basin holding fresh water for washing, his thoughts again drifted back to the time of his nation's emergence.

****

As with any youngster, the quick and relatively easy victory in the Western Ursals gave the army of Pith a false impression of its prowess. This impression was corrected when a division of the army of Cantor arrived in support of their neighbor to the south.

The Pith had become accomplished fighters in rough mountain terrain and the thick woods of the slopes and foothills. But in battle on an open field, they were soundly beaten by a force of Cantor regulars little more than half their number. After taking heavy casualties, the Pith and their allies were forced to retreat back to the foothills of the Ursals.

The soldiers of Cantor, much wiser than their allies from Rayine, had the good sense not to follow them there.

The victory over the Rayine was preserved and another painful lesson was learned. In the coming years the Pith would again adapt, holding on to their strengths while working to eliminate their weaknesses. Decades later, when next they met the nation of Cantor on the field of battle, they were able to fight them to a standstill. Had the war run its course, it was likely Cantor would have ultimately prevailed, but outside pressures brought the war to a premature end with no clear victor.

But that is a story for another time.

****

Having cleansed himself, Ammon summoned the servants who had been eagerly waiting just beyond the heavy oaken door of his personal chamber. In they rushed with fresh robes, perfumes, and fresh wine. He allowed himself to be pampered as a king must, all the while thinking of the blacksmith who would never experience luxury such as this, but who would never know the burden of possibly tearing his beloved nation apart.

Chapter 13

King Ammon IV watched as his council of advisors filed from the room.

Cecil has done his job too well, he thought, recalling how useless these nobles had been.

Each had tried tirelessly to peer into his mind and give him the advice they thought he most wanted to hear, and Ammon's assessment referred only to those courageous enough to offer an opinion on a matter of such magnitude as this. Many offered no council at all. Over the years they had been so cowed by the Chief Advisor, in the name of the Throne of course, that all they had become good at was seeking the Kings favor and undermining their peers.

Ammon watched as Cecil closed the door behind the last of the advisors before turning to face him. Heaving a sigh rich with disappointment, the Chief Advisor moved his bulk toward a table in the corner of the room on which sat an assortment of decanters. Choosing a tall dark container, he filled two glasses to their half mark and, after carefully closing the seal, carried the drinks over to his King who had taken a chair by the fireside.

"Strong drink, Your Highness," said Cecil, proffering a glass, "for these times will require strength, and we will be hard-pressed to find it among those on the council."

He handed the King a glass, tipped his own in salute, and took a sip, his face contorting from the bittersweet taste.

"I think you have moved in the past with too heavy a hand, Cecil," said Ammon, "and the current council of advisors is the result. Those men, though noble born, lack the courage to speak their minds. Their sole concern appears to be securing their place on the court, and the Prophesy be damned!"

Ammon then took a sip from his cup, his face showing no effects. "Just what have you done to them in my name?"

"In your name, My Liege, I have striven to keep them awake and alert. I have seen a royal court become too comfortable a place, and comfort breeds mischief for such as those. Presently you have a court absent of schemes against the Throne, your rule secure and unquestioned."

"I have a court absent of wise council, as those who should be among my best cower for fear of losing their titles, their lands, and their influence," the King said, irritation growing in his voice. "A certain level of comfort and security allows room for thoughts of other matters besides one's personal well-being. Your methods are good, if securing the authority and power of the Throne is the ultimate aim. But in times such as these, it is a benefit to not have to rely solely on oneself!"

Taking a breath and softening his tone, the King continued.

"What wisdom allowed us by The One Spirit is seldom contained in a single man, though he be a King."

Cecil nodded his head in response to the truth of the words.

"I may have been a bit harsh in my manipulations," he conceded. "Perhaps my concerns have been too narrow. I have always had faith in your noble blood, as in your father's and his father before him; faith that you would lead well the people of Pith so long as your Throne was secure."

"I know, Cecil," Ammon gave a tired sigh. "Virtue - an unflagging loyalty to the throne - be the root of your sins." He met his Chief Advisors eyes, a half-smile playing across his lips. "That is why I find it so difficult to punish your 'enthusiasms'."

"To see your disappointment is punishment enough, my liege," said Cecil. "Though it be too late for me, I will strive to pass on these lessons to my successor, whoever you choose that to be."

"You'll get no sympathy from me, old man!" Ammon laughed. "You serve your third King, and judging by your wit and your stride, I think you covet serving a fourth!"

Both men laughed at this, and then the room became silent as they looked into their respective glasses, both deep in thought. King Ammon broke the silence.

"In truth, I can give no thought to my disappointment in my advisors. I knew my course before I called for them." Again, he sought Cecil's eyes, and held them by the force of the fire reflected in his own.

"When prophesy be the mover of events," he said, "what choice does a King really have? Either I bow to the will of The One, if this be His will and His destiny for our people, or I trust to my own judgement, my own desires. Which is the greater risk to the future of Pith?"

Cecil answered in the only way he could.

"If this be His will, there be no choice," the Chief Advisor said, the finality of his statement echoing through the King's mind long after the sound of the words had died.

After a while, Cecil spoke again.

"How shall I prepare for the Council of Seven, my liege?"

"Thankfully," began the King, "they are not so cowed as my court advisors," he smiled briefly, "but I don't seek their advice so much as their cooperation. Hold them together until all have arrived. Feed them but lightly, and no strong drink. They must be alert and in their right minds when they are told of my plans. There will be questions, but it is doubtful any would stand openly against the Throne in times such as these. Galin is the key, as it will be he and his forces that will lead in whatever plans are made. When I am prepared, I will send a messenger and you will move them into the map chamber. I will join them there."

Cecil made a formal bow.

"It will be as you direct, my liege."

Chapter 14

Galin enjoyed an advantage over his fellow commanders in that he was the only one of the Council of Seven with firsthand knowledge of the events of the last two days. This allowed him to engage in an informed speculation as to the purpose of this gathering. The conclusions he had reached had done little to ease his worry.

His attendance at the royal audience gave him a base of information from which to work. What he had learned there was that Jusaan did indeed have schemes afoot, and they centered on the two prisoners taken on the southeast slopes of the Ursal Mountains who the priest had somehow transformed into honored guests. In achieving this Jusaan had risked much, placing himself in line for the wrath of both the lord high priest and the King. This told Galin that whatever was afoot was not of minor significance.

Unfortunately, Galin had been excused from the session prior to its conclusion. But like many others, he had trusted members of the royal court who would bestow upon him tidbits of information when needed. This is how he had learned all of the past day's events somehow linked this "warrior-priest" to the Fourth Prophesy.

Galin was never one to delve to deeply into the world of the priesthood, instead preferring to keep his feet planted on the firm ground of the here and now. Who really knew if the mysteries the priest ascribed to were not creations of their own minds? Prophesies and miracles and the like; it made his head hurt to contemplate them for any length of time. This was why, though exposed to extensive religious study as the son of nobility, he much preferred military history; weapons, tactics and strategies. Swords and armor; axes, lances and arrows; cavalry and infantry and siege engines and fighting men; these were the tools of his chosen trade and he understood them. Facing a flesh and blood enemy on a field of battle, be it mountains or plains or any terrain in between; these were the challenges to which he could most readily relate.

Not that his study of the military history of his people was not spiced with what many referred to as miracles. The greatest miracle of all was the First Siege of Stronghold, a battle that, by all rights, should have wiped the Pith from the face of the earth.

As the battle had progressed, their enemies had them outnumbered and surrounded on three sides. The Pith were pressed so tightly against a wall of solid rock that there was no room to form a defensive line or to maneuver in any way. When only a miracle could save them, they felt the ground heave and rumble, and watched as it opened up and swallowed a quarter of those massed against them. That same heaving of the earth opened a passage in the rock wall behind them, allowing the women and children, and finally their fighting forces, to escape. Their warriors then regrouped in the gap, and stood strong as their disaster-addled enemy threw themselves against them, again, and again to no avail.

Almost 900 years later it sounded preposterous, but Galin knew it to be true. He had studied it as a boy and taken trips to the deep trench which still contained thousands of broken weapons mixed with the bones of oxen and horses, and of the men of three nations that were amassed against the Pith. It was real, for he had seen it. And the passage that had appeared in the stone wall that day? That passage had been widened and was now shielded by gargantuan wooden doors; doors so massive as to need teams of oxen just to open them. They opened inward, into the lush valley of Stronghold, center of the Pithian Empire.

This, he had been taught, was the Third Prophesy come to fruition.

Galin reflected on this history and had to accept that maybe miracles were real. Maybe the priests knew of which they spoke. This worried him anew, for the one thing he did know about prophesy was that, if true, the future would most certainly be different from what he was used to. Change, massive change, was the jealous suitor to prophesy, and followed her everywhere she reared her head.

It was not so much the Prophesy, but the change accompanying it, that Galin feared. It was difficult to prepare for the unknown, especially for a soldier; one used to exerting some level of influence over time, terrain, men and equipment; the variables of military success.

"…and if he stands to himself, so deep in thought he cannot hear his own name being called, could be we *all* have cause for worry."

"Wha…?" Galin was caught off guard, unsure if the words he heard were directed at him. He raised his head and saw several of the commanders looking towards him as if expecting a response.

"I'm sorry," Galin said, and directed his gaze to Aubree, commander of the First Stronghold Legion, who watched him with his eyebrows raised. If any in that group spoke, it was surely him. "I did not hear all that you said."

"Because your head has been buried in your mug of wine since our platters were removed," said Aubree.

He stood up from his chair in the midst of three of his fellows and rounded the table so as to approach Galin, and be better heard by his audience

"You are the loudest, the brashest," Aubree said, "the most arrogant in a room full of loud, brash, and arrogant men. You also have the ear of the King, more so than any man here. Yet you stand apart, silent, your eyes lost in the bottom of your wine." He came to a stop before Galin and peered into his face as if searching for a clue to his mood.

"What do you know that the rest of us..." he waved a meaty arm to include all those assembled, "...don't? What is it that has the commander of the First Expeditionary Legion so reserved this fine morn?"

Aubree was a stout man of over fifty years, neither short nor tall, but wide and solid, like a block of stone cut loose from the mountain and shaped into a man. His stature fit his command perfectly, as he always bragged that his infantrymen, once established, were "unmovable, like a wall of stone," daring the enemy to come and break themselves upon their pikes and shields. He feared nothing, and with a personality almost as large as Galin's, he enjoyed poking the bear many looked upon as the pampered favorite of the Royal House.

Galin knew what Aubree thought of him, but he also knew he had the older man's respect. "Pampered favorite" was but one of the descriptions whispered behind his back. The others included, "detailed strategist", "brilliant tactician", "keen of mind", "fierce and deadly combatant", and "natural leader." These attributes, along with Galin's outsized personality, were why even as he poked at him, Aubree looked to him for reassurance concerning the call by King Ammon IV to meet with them this morning.

Galin first met the eyes of Aubree and then raised his head to survey the room. The group that Aubree was entertaining; Rudin, Commander of the Second Stronghold Legion, Bruchi, Commander of the First Legion Cavalry, and Hailee, Commander of the Second Legion Cavalry, were all staring at him. Galin looked beyond them to one of the far corners of the room to see that Callmus, Commander of the Second Expeditionary Legion, and Colevant, Commander of the Garrison of Pith, had paused in their conversation to peer in his direction as well.

Galin turned back to Aubree with a slight smile.

"No need for you to be so worried," he said, grasping Aubree's shoulder. "Whatever the future holds, know ye the First Expeditionary Legion will always be there to save your infantry from utter defeat!"

Galin followed this with a laugh, and everyone joined in, even Aubree. Galin knew this break in the tension was only temporary and that those assembled would be looking for real answers as to why couriers had been dispatched, requiring the presence of The Seven on such short notice.

Galin turned to Rudin, who had traveled the farthest, arriving just that morning from the gates of Stronghold in a fast carriage that several teams of horses had pulled through the night.

"Lord Rudin," he said, stepping past Aubree before the brash commander could once more focus the attention of the room upon him. "What word from the expedition into the Southern Mountains? Had they reached the gates of Stronghold before you took your leave?"

Rudin, an older, portlier version of Aubree, looked down into his cup as he replied. "Word has them about a day out from the gates," he said, before raising his eyes to Galin in question. "I was surprised to see you already here, Lord Galin. Word also held that you led the expedition. If true, you should have arrived well after me."

"Your spies keep you ever a day behind, Rudin!" Galin replied, setting off another bout of laughter from all in the room. Whenever a secret slipped loose in the Royal House, Galin had visions of the skies above the Citadel darkening with the wings of messenger pigeons loosed by all the different loyalties lurking within. Through it all, one could be assured that Rudin would more than likely be the last to know.

Just as the laughter was dying down, the door swung open and a Citadel Guard, resplendent in crimson and gold, entered the room. Assuming a position beside the open door, he stood at formal attention to announce the arrival of the King.

"His Royal Highness, King Ammon IV, approaches!"

All eyes had turned to the guard in curiosity as soon as he entered, but now those gathered in the room adopted a more formal posture. All put down their drinks. Those who were seated stood to receive the King. Those who were standing stood straighter. Moments later, King Ammon IV strode through the door, his avian eyes seeking out and hungrily meeting the gaze of each of his commanders. Each man bowed his fealty, some more than once. Nodding his head in acknowledgement, Ammon IV was followed closely by Lord Cecil, High Minister and Chief Advisor. The King took up a position at the head of the heavy oak table.

With the seal of Pith, a crimson sun encircled by golden rays, emblazoned on the wall behind him and framing his personage, he waited for his commanders to take their positions around the table. Once everyone was standing behind their seats, the King sat and, with a nod of his head, signaled those around him that they also may be seated.

Attendants fluttered around, placing clean goblets before each person seated at the table, and pouring cool watered wine into each. The attendants left several containers of watered wine on the table before taking their leave. Finally, after all of their needs were addressed and the servants had left the room, a pregnant silence descended.

Ammon took the time to study each man who sat around the table. They were all hard men, able and experienced. Some had attained their commands due primarily to their noble birth. Others had begun as lowly foot soldiers and worked their way through the ranks to their current positions of authority. All had seen violent campaigns and acquitted themselves as befit soldiers and leaders of the Pith. Ammon nodded in satisfaction at the men through whom he controlled his empire. More than ever before, he would need their wisdom, their experience, their patience, and their unquestioning loyalty, for he knew he was about to ask of them what had never before been required of soldiers of Pith by their King.

"Lords commanders," Ammon began. "You have all served the empire well. For some here, I am the third King to call upon your skills and you have ever answered the call with honor, passion, and faithfulness. I salute you, commanders of Pith!"

He raised his goblet in recognition of those seated before him. The commanders, following his lead, raised their goblets and gave short exclamations, before downing generous swigs of watered wine. Then quiet again descended on the room.

"What I have brought you together to ask of you," Ammon continued, "is nothing less than your duty; your duty to the empire and your duty to The One Spirit, by whose decree our ascent as a people was ordained."

He paused to let his words sink in. It was unusual for their god to be referenced regarding a military campaign. Those around the table took note, exchanging glances.

Ammon went on, "There have recently been occurrences of which many of you are not aware. Without hesitation, I refer to these occurrences as *miraculous*."

This pronouncement brought forth furrowed brows and anxious stares from all seated around the table.

"Lords commander," Ammon said, looking around the table gravely. "I have recently been in consultation with the priesthood, and I am now convinced that the time of the Fourth Prophesy is upon us."

King Ammon expected his commanders to be shocked by his words. Maybe they would be struck dumb by the weight his pronouncement carried. Or maybe they would be moved to lift their voices with astonished questions as to the how and why of it all. What he did not expect were the looks of confusion greeting him from nearly every face. Even Galin seemed not to grasp what he had said, and he had been present at the audience of the previous day.

Now, himself confused, Ammon looked to Cecil, whose questioning visage gave no answers to this strange response, before both their eyes were drawn to Galin, who apparently had found his tongue and was preparing to speak. Ammon waited patiently for his favorite commander to put an end to the state of confusion that had engulfed the table.

"My Liege," he began, "at our heart we are but humble soldiers who are sworn to, by your word, give our lives in defense of the empire and its ideals. A soldier's head is filled with thoughts foreign to most, and that is by necessity, as a soldier must be prepared to do things in defense of the realm that bear no relationship to the godly. The realm of the priest is as separate from the realm of the soldier as the liquid dreams of the night are separate from the harsh truth of the day. Prophesy plays little, if any, role in a soldier's thinking. It is for this reason, not any disrespect toward the Crown or the Temple, that you see confusion in our eyes."

There was a moment of silence as Ammon considered these words.

"So, none here are familiar with the Fourth Prophesy?" he asked.

After a pause, Hailee, commander of the Second Cavalry Force, rose from his seat. Easily the oldest of the assembled Commanders, Hailee was also the most devout.

As an orphaned child, Hailee had been raised in the Temple of his village by the Vestals bound thereto, and had received a temple education, heavy in the teachings of The One Spirit, and the many Truths and Prophesies by which the Pith were bound to their god. As a Young man he had considered a life in the temple, until a lapse in judgment with a local girl. The vicious beating he received from the Priest led him to leave the only home he had ever known in the dead of night.

First wandering from village to village, he eventually found employment with the garrison of a small town and, in soldiering, found a new focus for the energies he had devoted to the temple. He rose steadily through the ranks proving himself as possessing the discipline and ferocity required of a soldier, as well as the many attributes required as a leader of men. Even so, he continued to hold fast to the many lessons he had learned from the vestals, and was well versed in many of the Truths, and each of the Four Prophesies.

"Your highness, if I may?" Hailee began, as the eyes of all present turned to regard him.

With a nod of his head, King Ammon gave permission for the elderly commander to speak.

"Priests and scholars have long debated the details of the Fourth Prophesy," Hailee began, "the only prophesy of the four given Usaid that has not yet come to pass, and the only prophesy for which there is considerable doubt. It speaks of our return to our Motherland, a worthy goal during the time of Usaid, when our people were wanderers without a home, but a questionable goal for an established empire as we have now become."

At this point, Hailee should have seen a change in his King; a narrowing of the eyes, a furrowing of his brow, and a scowl creeping in where once had been a look of curiosity. But Hailee did not notice, and so continued on with his explanation.

"Even with the obvious difficulty of convincing our people to forsake all they have built in order to pursue a prophesied destiny, there is still the problem of how the Fourth Prophesy would be fulfilled."

Here Hailee paused, awaiting the obvious question which would give him leave to continue with a lengthy explanation.

But, though all eyes held fast to him, no lips moved in question. Finally, he plowed ahead with the answer to the unasked query.

"According to the ancient scrolls, the people would know the time of this prophesy was upon us when old Usaid shook the dirt off and came back himself to lead us to the motherland!"

Hailee looked around the room, chuckling at the absurdity of the ancient priest returning to the Pith after a thousand years dead, but the laughter froze in his chest when he saw the visage of his king.

King Ammon IV looked down on his most ancient of commanders with a look of pure disdain, as would a High Priest poised to punish a blasphemer, and those who had begun to laugh along with Hailee found the air sucked from their lungs at the obvious displeasure displayed by the Royal Personage. Ammon tore his eyes from Hailee, allowing him to regain his breath, and surveyed those around the table. Once again in total command, he turned back to the old warrior and spoke.

"You make a mockery of one of our most sacred texts," Ammon said softly, his gaze reaching new levels of hardness. "Do you believe your King has assembled his commanders to regale them with jokes?"

"No, my liege," Hailee whispered with bowed head and immediately retook his seat.

"STAND!" the King bellowed, with a rage that caused the very teeth in their assembled heads to shake! "I've granted you leave to speak and, by my Sword of Judgment, you will speak until I say enough!"

His old knees cracking with the effort, Hailee fairly launched himself out of his seat and to a standing position, prepared to endure the Kings displeasure.

Again, the room fell silent, as Ammon regained his composure. One breath…then another…until he was again ready to speak.

"I take it from your mocking tone that you do not believe in the Prophesy, nor do you fear The One Spirit," the King said, cutting a sharp eye at Hailee lest he dare to offer up a defense. The commander neither opened his mouth nor dared to twitch under the glare of his King.

"We all know of your upbringing, Lord Hailee," Ammon continued, "and your knowledge of the sacred texts. Perhaps you can share with us the nature of the *debates* between the priest and the scholars."

"My liege," Hailee bowed his assent, then spoke quickly, relieved to be on firmer ground.

"Since the first through the third Prophesies have been fulfilled as they had been literally given, it was the position of the scholars that the Fourth Prophesy was not genuine since Usaid could not literally return from the dead."

Hailee looked around the room, as if seeking confirmation from those assembled that people who died tended to stay dead, before continuing.

"Thus, the scholars spoke of the Fourth as a false prophesy, written at a later date by one of Usaid's acolytes who was no doubt homesick for the motherland and without knowledge of the glory awaiting our people.

"This was notable because it is the priesthood who usually supported a literal interpretation of any Truth or Prophesy. However, in this one instance, the priesthood has chosen to interpret the Fourth Prophecy as requiring a 'reincarnation of the spirit' of Usaid, returned to fulfill his promised role and lead his people home to the motherland in triumph."

Finishing his explanation, Hailee began to sink into his seat before catching himself and again standing ramrod straight before his King.

Hearing the complete explanation, King Ammon nodded his head in assent before again questioning the old soldier.

"If the spirit of Usaid were to present itself to you...to us," the King waved his arm to encompass the room, "and the Fourth Prophesy were upon us, what would you do?"

At this question, the Commander of the Second Cavalry stood tall and responded with a fierce pride. "I would do my duty, My Liege, whatever the Crown decided that to be!"

These words brought a grim smile to Ammon's lips, which in turn brought relief to the Commander's mind.

"And you, Rudin," the King continued, addressing the commander of the Second Stronghold Force who was seated beside Hailee. "What would you do?"

Rudin sprang to his feet. "No less than he!" he bellowed, motioning toward Hailee.

So it was that King Ammon went around the table, questioning each commander as to his loyalty and intentions. Each swore to follow the will of the Crown, whatever it might be.

Lord Galin was the last to take the pledge and, being the boldest, dared pose a question after swearing his loyalty.

"My liege," Galin began, "you said earlier that the time of the Fourth Prophesy may be upon us. Now that you have our renewed pledges of fealty, would His Majesty share what he knows with these servants of the Crown gathered before him?"

For yet another time the room grew silent while the King considered the insolence of his favorite commander, and Galin's fellows braced themselves for the renewed anger of the King. When Ammon IV broke the silence, he surprised the gathered commanders by the calmness of his words.

"First, I shall meet with the lord high priest and The Council of the Nine. Only then will we know what the future holds."

Chapter 15

Mayhew did not have long to wait before the King's courier arrived. It was midmorning, yet the high priest appeared tired, most likely due to his fitful sleep the night before. Still, he was quick to receive the royal messenger, who brought an invitation from the King for the lord to take the noon meal with him. This was even quicker than Mayhew had expected, the King having met with his advisors just last evening and having not yet met with his Council of Seven.

Ammon seems to have come to his senses much earlier than I anticipated, he thought.

After sending his acceptance back with the messenger, he sat to ponder his position and how best to handle the King in this delicate situation. He knew he must not present a threat, or Ammon would not allow him access to Jusaan and this warrior-priest. Would the King move against him? That would be a risky move, at best. Although the power of the high priest had been diminished, Mayhew believed his position was still beyond the reach of the King. Only the Council of Nine, acting unanimously, could remove a high priest before his death. The likelihood of that happening was almost equal to that of a Prophesy being fulfilled. The high priest could only be replaced by one of the Council of Nine and, though ambition flowed through that group like a lowland river during a spring thaw, their ambition was his protection. None would be willing to vote for any but himself, thus ensuring the position of the reigning high priest would remain secure.

Had the King made the necessary inroads into the council to be able to bend The Nine to his will? Mayhew thought it unlikely.

But the threat now posed by Jusaan as the handler, so to speak, of this warrior-priest could not be ignored. If the council saw him as the legitimate manifestation of the spirit of Usaid, and the harbinger of the Fourth Prophesy, then Mayhew could easily imagine the council uniting behind Jusaan, the King's choice, and deposing him.

Yes, Mayhew thought, *that is the real threat here.*

But he had doubts His Highness had already planned that far along, else he would not be asked to join him in the midday meal. This was Ammon's opportunity to feel the high priest out; to find out where he stood on the fulfillment of the Fourth Prophesy and the steps that lay beyond. This being the case, Mayhew saw his first priority was to put the King's mind at ease. He would stand ready, after the necessary hemming and hawing, to support His Majesty even to the point of elevating Jusaan, so long as he remained subordinate to the lord high priest.

Mayhew felt, in this instance, he could handle the demands of King Ammon. What game was afoot with Jusaan was another thing. He must remain vigilant, ready to slap the priest down should he appear to overreach, or undercut his superior. No matter what, Jusaan must be watched, his whereabouts accounted for at all times.

Mayhew now realized he may have underestimated Jusaan. He hoped it was not too late to rectify that mistake.

****

King Ammon IV greeted Lord High Priest Mayhew with cool aloofness. This demeanor was mirrored by the lord high priest. If each could see into the other's mind, they would be surprised to learn they had similar thoughts; both had much to learn and little time in which to learn it. Even so, propriety must be kept, and so they were both seated with haste, but with appropriate ceremony, for the midday meal. Ammon had requested his best; roast pheasant, new potatoes, assorted greens, and a pudding made with several varieties of preserved fruit. This was accompanied by spiced wine and hot spiced tea. After the last course was served, Ammon waved away the servants so that he and Mayhew could enjoy their pudding and tea while conversing in private.

"So, Lord Mayhew," Ammon began, using the most familiar form in addressing the high priest. "What have you heard of the goings-on in your absence?"

Mayhew took time to gather his thoughts, wiping at imaginary sauce on his mouth as a pretense.

"Let me first compliment His Highness on the quality of this meal," he began, folding the napkin neatly and placing it on his lap before continuing.

"What I have heard is both inspiring and troubling, Your Highness," the high priest said, "for obvious reasons. To be present at the beginning of the fulfillment of the Fourth Prophesy... to witness the will of The One unfolding in my lifetime... it is more than any high priest could openly pray for."

Mayhew paused, allowing a look of dreamy contentment to wash over his face. Then he continued. "But a wise man knows that to accept all he encounters at face value is a recipe for disaster, and I fear the consequences should this 'warrior-priest' be a clever ruse, or a dupe."

Mayhew watched carefully, though discreetly, to see what effect this statement had on his King. For his part, Ammon showed no sign of being disappointed with the high priest's words, and instead seized upon them to move the conversation to where he wanted it to go.

"It is only natural I share your exhilaration, Your Grace," the King said. "We may truly live in a wonderful time. But I also share your concerns. We two both know what it means if the spirit of Usaid does truly walk among us once more. To be entrusted by The One with a holy campaign of such ambition...of such magnitude..."

Ammon reached out and clutched Mayhew's hand in his own, this breach of protocol, as well as his iron grip, surprising the high priest and drawing his eyes first to his hand and then to the King's grim visage.

"...we must be sure!"

Ammon's fierce whisper pierced Mayhew's ears as clearly as the bell that sounded the call to Temple. He knew he could not break his King's grip, so did not try. Instead, he looked deeply into Ammon's eyes, holding him with a look of equal intensity.

"To that end, Your Majesty, I must speak to this warrior-priest," Mayhew said, "and to Council Priest Jusaan."

"And you shall," said Ammon, releasing the high priest's hand and leaning back in his ornate chair. "I have asked Jusaan to present Hanshee...that is his name, 'Hanshee'... to the Council of The Nine this very day. Of course, he agreed, but he insisted you be there to preside over any questioning that will take place."

So, he has planned that far along, thought Mayhew.

"Your powers of discernment will be needed to ferret out any deceit on the part of this warrior-priest," Ammon continued, "or any duplicity on the part of one of the Nine."

"And what of Council Priest Jusaan?" asked Mayhew. "Do my powers of discernment extend to his character as well?"

King Ammon IV leveled a hard gaze at the High Priest and Mayhew feared that, with this question, he had advanced a step too far. But then the King turned from him to stare out of the open window.

"Council Priest Jusaan risked much to bring this man to the attention of the Throne," he said. "He has risked my wrath," the King now turned back to the High Priest, "and yours as well. Why... he risks his *very soul* should he be the perpetrator of treachery of this magnitude!"

Ammon again looked out of the open window before finishing. "Council Priest Jusaan has my trust...for now."

Mayhew found it difficult to hold his tongue, but knew it to be the wisest course of action. He hated to have to debase himself before the King, as if his title were meaningless. He hated to have to hold back his impulse to crush under foot those he knew to be working against him. But he understood that only patience would win the day in this matter. He must bear this current indignity so that, when the time was right, he could bring to bear a power and influence of which the Throne had no clue the Temple possessed. He would endure so that one day soon he could set things right again.

These thoughts passed through Mayhew's consciousness in an instant. He leaned back in his seat and looked to be contemplating his position. Then he turned to face his King.

"And so, my liege," he said. "You have called *my* council to meet and have established their boundaries. Pray tell, what time am I permitted to preside over them?" Mayhew asked sarcastically.

King Ammon smiled.

"I knew this would stick in your craw," he said. "Will you refuse my request?"

Knowing that he had given the King the resistance that had been expected, Mayhew completed his capitulation.

"It seems the situation leaves me...leaves us...no choice," he said.

Recalling the earlier words of Lord Cecil, the King responded.

"Where the will of The One is concerned, there is seldom a choice. They will expect you within the hour."

Chapter 16

Despite the cool air that poured through the windows on both sides of the fireplace, Hanshee and Raymond were both covered in sweat. The heavy tapestries had been tied back to provide a draft into the main room, which they had cleared of all furnishings to provide more space for Hanshee's "training".

Raymond had been athletic all of his life. He had taken up boxing early on, giving it up for karate which lasted into his early teens. Add high school and a year of small college football, and his current workout regimen, and it was easy to see why he had always thought himself to be in shape. But since he had been with Hanshee, his body had become more lean and hard. He had dropped about twenty pounds just by living and eating off the land, and had found he now possessed more useful strength and more stamina. He was quicker, faster, and more alert. It was his opinion that at this moment, he was in the best shape of his life.

Why was it then, that his legs felt like rubber; his chest heaving in the attempt to bring in more air; the sweat literally pouring off of him? He cast his eyes toward Hanshee, who was also sweating, but his breathing was normal and his legs appeared strong and steady. Hanshee looked Raymond over but showed no sign of approval, leaving Ray to wonder whether he had performed up to Hanshee's expectations in his first training session.

"You may rest now, Way-mon," Hanshee said, taking pity on him.

Raymond rose from his half-squat position to stand fully erect, relief evident on his face. Bending at the waist, he rubbed his thighs in an attempt to stimulate circulation while Hanshee smiled at him from across the room.

When Hanshee had proposed to train him to fight, he was at first taken aback. Even among the very best fighters he had seen and trained with, he had never witnessed such speed and power as Hanshee had demonstrated. He had seen Hanshee fight, and when Hanshee fought, it was no game; it was for survival. "Impressive" hardly described the sight. Words like "brutal", "bloody", and "merciless" painted a better picture, at least of the result.

Raymond had never been close to a life-or-death fight before. All of his fighting had been in the controlled setting of a boxing ring or a dojo. A part of him was scared, but another part of him wanted to learn so that, maybe, he could protect himself and others the way Hanshee had protected him over the months they had travelled together. He now believed he was fully aware of the cold brutality of this world, and realized that when Hanshee told him he must learn to fight, and to kill, it was not said for effect.

Logic told Ray that to learn now meant he might have the tools needed to survive at some future time, and so he steeled his nerve and prepared himself for the controlled violence that was to come.

Now, after two straight hours of stance work, with his knees constantly bent, he thought he had reached his limit of effort and pain.

"All true power comes from a strong foundation," Hanshee had said. "Though you think your legs strong, they can be made much stronger still."

Their movements had been slow and deliberate. Their steps were precise. Once they achieved a strong stance, Hanshee would hold it, sometimes until Raymond's legs were visibly shaking. Then Hanshee would slowly, deliberately, and precisely, lead his charge into another painful position, expecting Ray to find relief in the transition.

While Raymond continued to try to rub feeling back into his legs, Hanshee walked over to the large tub filled with water. Scooping some out with a bowl, he used a cloth to wash away the sweat from head to toe. Besides being a formidable fighter, Hanshee was a stickler for cleanliness.

"How did I do?" Raymond asked.

"You did as you were asked," replied Hanshee.

"But did I do it well?" Ray pressed. "Are you satisfied with my first lesson?"

"You followed instructions. Your movements were correct. You did not collapse," Hanshee replied, looking askew at Ray.

"Is that good?" Ray continued to press.

"It is good not to collapse," said Hanshee, and this time he lay down his cloth and faced Raymond. "What do you seek, Way-mon?

"I don't know...," Ray began, "... actually, I DO know. My people call it 'positive feedback'. When asked to learn a task, my people like to be told how they are progressing. It motivates us. It gives us a reason to continue."

"I see," said Hanshee thoughtfully. He approached Raymond and placed a hand on his shoulder, looking into his eyes. "You wish to know if I am pleased with you."

Ray felt sheepish under Hanshee's intense stare. "Yeah... I guess you could put it like that," he said.

Hanshee continued to hold his gaze until Ray could no longer meet his eyes and turned away.

"You must understand," Hanshee said, "that my pleasure is not enough. If you fight to please me, you will die. If you fight for any reason but for life... your life... the life of those you care for... you will die. To fight in the manner that you must, no outside force can push you, or sustain you, or give you victory. All must come from within you. It must be your own approval you seek. If you seek it faithfully and give it sparingly, then when the time comes and your life hangs in the balance, you *may* live."

"Now," Hanshee continued, "were *you* pleased with your effort?"

Ray gave this question some thought before responding.

"I was," he said.

And with that, Hanshee turned and walked away.

Ray staggered over to the tub and, mimicking Hanshee, began to wash the sweat from his body. As he struggled to cool down, the tepid water and cold air coming through the windows combined to send a pleasant chill through him; the kind that felt good after a hard workout and a good sweat. After finishing washing, he began to dress. It was then that he heard a knock on the door. Startled, he looked up at Hanshee, who returned his questioning look before going to the door. He reached it just as it began to open.

Hanshee blocked the door with his sandaled foot after it had opened only a few inches and waited quietly for whoever was there to announce themselves. After a moment, a high-pitched voice spoke.

"Council Priest Jusaan wishes to speak with those within," said the nameless underling.

The words weren't spoken in the ancient tongue. Hanshee had no clue as to what had been said, but he recognized the name of Jusaan. He looked to Ray, who quickly nodded his head, letting Hanshee know to let Jusaan enter. Hanshee removed his foot, allowing the underling to stumble clumsily against the opening door. Regaining his balance, he moved aside, allowing Jusaan to enter.

Wearing thick crimson and gray robes against the midmorning cold, Jusaan looked around the room and noticed there was no fire in the fireplace. Hugging himself and looking crossly at Ray, who had just finished dressing and come out of the small bedchamber, he turned to Hanshee and spoke.

"Greetings, my brother," he said in the ancient tongue. "I have come to assure myself of your comfort. I see your acolyte has yet to start your morning fire. Would you like my man to see to it?" He turned to his man, who was still standing in the open doorway.

"No," replied Hanshee. "I find the morning cold..." He paused, considering the right word, "...pleasing."

Jusaan arched his eyebrows in disbelief. He then revealed the real reason for his visit.

"It has been made known to me that the Council of The Nine, of which I am a member, is called to meet in the hour after the midday meal. We expect the presence of the Lord High Priest, Mayhew, and all would like you to attend. You will wear your native garb."

"I will accompany you," Hanshee responded, "Way-mon will accompany me."

"This is permitted," said Jusaan. "I will come for you both after the midday meal." He looked at the cold fireplace and then at Raymond. Clutching his robes about him in an exaggerated fashion, he left the room, followed closely by the underling.

Closing the door securely, Hanshee approached Raymond, in order to discuss this new development.

They had been expecting something like this. The servants, Laretha and Meesha, had explained much about the Temple, about its purpose and how it was governed. Hanshee and Raymond decided this would be a good opportunity to see, firsthand, the Temple hierarchy and how the council worked. Maybe they'd find out more about this "Fourth Prophesy" that seemed to have everyone so excited, and how Hanshee was connected to it.

Raymond had just finished building a fire in the large stone fireplace when a knock on the door announced more visitors. This time, it was Laretha and Meesha with the midday meal. They smiled brightly as they entered, Laretha carrying a tray laden with good things to eat; hot bread, fresh from the ovens, with butter and honey; succulent meat; dried fruit, and a wedge of cheese. Meesha followed with two cool jugs of watered wine and various spices and utensils that might be needed.

Hanshee and Raymond made the room ready, moving the large table to a comfortable distance in front of the fire, and placing four chairs around it. The women arranged everything on one end of the table, allowing ample room for the four of them to eat at the other end. After all was made ready, Laretha and Meesha waved Ray and Hanshee to their seats and placed platters laden with food before them. After pouring each a goblet of watered wine, the women were free to make plates for themselves and join them.

This arrangement had been decided upon earlier that morning, when Raymond had insisted they all take the midday meal together, rather than the women serving him and Hanshee and then leaving to have their own meal separately.

As the four of them ate, they settled into a conversation made slightly awkward by the fact of three different languages being spoken around the table. If Hanshee had a question for either of the women, he must first speak it to Raymond who, if the question were for Laretha, could then ask her directly. If the question was for Meesha, Laretha would translate the question and the response. Raymond could then translate her response for Hanshee. This was done in reverse if Meesha had a query of Hanshee. This method of communication led to a little confusion and a lot of laughter.

At a point about halfway through the meal, Raymond suddenly turned to Hanshee and stared wordlessly with a huge grin on his face. At first puzzled, Hanshee then mirrored the grin, realizing Ray's "special gift" had kicked in and he now understood what the women said to each other. Laretha and Meesha had no clue as to why these two large men were beaming at each other. Their looks of confusion caused both Hanshee and Raymond to burst into laughter. The laughter proved contagious, and for a while the food and drink were forgotten as all those around the table were consumed with snorts and bellows of laughter.

"These two are so strange!" Raymond heard Meesha say to Laretha, after she was able to catch her breath. "Strange and funny!"

"They remind me of my older brothers," replied Laretha. "They are so close. They share a bond; you can tell."

"It is good to work only for them," continued Laretha. "Serving two is so much easier than running here and there, fetching and carrying and cleaning up behind priests, acolytes, visitors, and everyone in the temple!"

"Yes," agreed Meesha, "and it is pleasant to sit and eat such good food, and not the leavings of others." She poured herself more watered wine. "We must serve them well, for they have truly saved us!"

The women giggled, thanking the fates that this new priest, so strange yet so important, had requested them to see to his needs, and those of his acolyte, thus freeing them from the constant drudgery that was the day-to-day life of a servant.

Raymond kept his head down, taking in every word, smiling inwardly with the knowledge that their presence had made the women's lives easier. What he heard next nearly caused him to choke, and he coughed as he reached for his wine goblet.

"And would you serve them further?" Laretha asked Meesha, a playful smile on her lips. Both women appraised Ray as he reached for his wine and tried to recover his breath. Then they turned to back each other.

"For some, it is expected," said Meesha, looking down at her plate of food, "but they have not made it known. Perhaps they prefer the company of each other."

"Nonsense!" exclaimed Laretha. "Did you not say how you felt the acolyte's response to your touch when you first bathed him? I certainly felt the priests!"

"You reached for the priests!" said Meesha, and again the two girls erupted in a fit of giggles.

Raymond glanced sideways at Hanshee, who was staring at him, a question in his eyes. Ray just smiled and shook his head as he went back to eating. Saving an explanation for later was probably best.

After he had finished his meal, Hanshee had a request for Raymond.

"Way-mon, tell them of our summons by the Council of The Nine. Ask of them if there is anything we should know about these priests that would be helpful."

Raymond posed the question to Laretha, careful not to confuse the tongue in which he addressed her. She turned to Meesha and the two of them shared a quick conversation, the gist of which was that they knew little about the inner workings of the priests' council. Judging by the women's worried expressions, it was no small thing to be called before the council.

Presently, Laretha turned to Raymond. "Seldom are outsiders called before the council," she said. "Meesha says it has never happened in her time here, nor has it happened in mine. For ones such as us, I would be concerned, but Hanchee..." she nodded toward Hanshee "...is very important to Council Priest Jusaan. I do not think you have anything to fear."

"What do you know of the Fourth Prophesy?" Raymond asked. Again, Laretha turned to Meesha and translated the question. "He is asking about the Fourth Prophecy."

Upon hearing this, Meesha sat up straighter. Focusing her eyes in the distance, she spoke as if reciting a lesson learned long ago.

"The Fourth Prophesy is the prophesy of redemption, when we will return to the motherland and be again accepted among our original people."

"How do you know this?" cried Laretha, clearly astonished by this revelation.

"It was taught to me as a young girl, by my grandmother," Meesha said. "She had been a vestal at the temple of my village. After serving her allotted years she was released to marry. She chose my grandfather, a common man, rather than the elderly nobleman under whose care the village had been placed. He was her only noble choice, as he had no male heir who wished to betroth her."

Laretha looked at her friend with a new understanding, before turning to Raymond and repeating what Meesha had told her. Ray, true to his ruse, waited patiently while Laretha completed her explanation, then turned to Hanshee and passed on the story.

"This is quite interesting," said Hanshee. "'Redemption'…and return to their 'original people'."

Raymond asked Laretha, "Do you know where this 'motherland' is, and who these 'original people' are?"

This time, Laretha answered without consulting Meesha.

"I have been told the Pith come from a land far, far away to the west, beyond the Blue Mountains, which are the highest in the world," she said. "My people are from the south, and though we call ourselves Pith, there is very little Pithian blood in our veins. I have been told the original Pith were a darker people, more like you, or him." She nodded at Ray and pointed to Hanshee.

Raymond relayed this information to Hanshee, who nodded in understanding.

Hanshee had known something of this, from the clues Jusaan had dropped since their capture in the mountains to the south. But this was the first he had heard of a desire by the Pith to return to the land of their origins. Considering the reasons behind their long-ago departure from their homeland, and the militaristic society he had observed since encountering them, Hanshee wondered what a "return to the motherland" would look like. He doubted it would be peaceful.

It had grown quiet around the table, the revelation of the call before the council having snuffed out the earlier atmosphere of levity. The women began clearing away the platters and goblets, making small talk between themselves. Ray barely paid attention, deep in thoughts of the upcoming meeting.

Hanshee went into the smaller of the two bedchambers and donned his original garb, what Ray thought of as a soft leather jockstrap, covered by a leather loincloth. A sword hung from a leather harness on his back, while his knife hung from the front. He finished by donning his pouch over one shoulder, a pouch from which Ray had seen him extract spices and potions, medicines, and gold coins.

As Meesha and Laretha were about to leave, there came a loud knock on the door. Ray opened it to reveal two Citadel Guards, who had come to escort them to the council chambers. The women took their leave, and one of the guards locked and secured the door. Then Hanshee and Ray fell into step behind them, on their way to another audience before another local authority and what they hoped would be another piece of the puzzle.

****

The council chambers were sparsely furnished, containing nothing beyond seating for ten. There were nine council seats, each atop its own dais and arranged in a semi-circle, as well as a tenth seat, a throne really, set upon the highest dais, and facing the nine seats. This tenth seat was available if the lord high priest deigned to present himself.

All of the council, including the high priest, had been seated by the time Hanshee and Ray were allowed in. Jusaan had come forward to lead them before the council. He stood beside Hanshee the way a proud owner would stand beside a champion stallion. Ray, in accordance with his role as a loyal acolyte, assumed a deferential position behind and to the right of Hanshee.

"Your Grace," Jusaan began, bowing toward the lord high priest, "fellow members of the Council of The Nine and brothers in The One Spirit. You have no doubt heard of the great discovery bestowed upon your humble servant while encamped in the wilderness of the Southern Ursal Mountains. It was the will of The One that one of The True be present to correctly interpret His sign and thus, prevent a rash execution by our military; an action which would have surely brought His wrath down upon a people who so callously discarded the instrument of His will."

Jusaan paused so that all could digest his pronouncement and gaze upon Hanshee. The sacred scroll had been displayed prior to Hanshee and Raymond's arrival. All present had seen the illustration representing the great warrior-priest Usaid, of whom Hanshee was the living image. Jusaan was aware of the effect the sight of Hanshee would have on those assembled, and had sought to reinforce it by requiring him to wear his traditional garb.

"It is written," he continued, "in the Fourth Prophesy, that the great warrior-priest, Usaid, would return to lead us on a pilgrimage back to our native land…triumphant! Blessed am I to be chosen by The One Spirit to escort His instrument before you and set in motion the events that will lead to the divine redemption of the Pith!"

The council members held their tongues until well after the echo of Jusaan's pronouncement had died. Then, with a slight nod from Lord High Priest Mayhew, one of the assembled priests stood. He was Council Priest Brumard, one of the senior members of the council, thought by all to be the most likely to ascend to the High Seat should, heaven forbid, something terrible befall Lord High Priest Mayhew.

Having reached his full height, he paused to look around the room at his fellows, before locking his gaze on Jusaan.

"Do you stand before us today," Brumard asked incredulously, "and claim that this man is the great warrior-priest Usaid?"

There was scorn in the question, a scorn Jusaan was obliged to ignore, yet in his response he let a portion of his irritation show through.

"Though priests and scholars have debated the point for generations, surely only the irrational believe the prophesy speaks of Usaid returning to us in the flesh." Jusaan countered.

After waiting for the snickering to die down, he continued.

"My contention, my brothers, and dare I say the current position of the Throne, is that this man, Hanshee, embodies the very spirit of the great warrior-priest Usaid."

"And why would you first approach the Throne with a matter of the Temple?" Brumard almost spat the question, feeling the sting of Jusaan's subtle rebuke.

"This is a matter of both the secular and the divine." Jusaan smoothly responded. "You know the duty that would fall upon the Throne, should the Fourth Prophesy come to pass. To hold these developments from His Majesty would be akin to blasphemy."

"In the absence of the lord high priest," Jusaan continued, less forcefully, "I felt it my duty to approach the Throne directly. His Majesty is aware of protocol and tradition, and would have reacted most harshly should he have considered the purpose of my request trivial. Thankfully, in his wisdom, His Majesty agreed with the need for my haste and has extended his authority even unto these proceedings."

Jusaan was aware of the effect of this pronouncement, just as he knew Brumard's question was really asked, by proxy, by the Lord High Priest Mayhew. His response was a way of telling all those present, especially Mayhew, that he, Jusaan, was now a force to be reckoned with, and that the hierarchy of authority had been changed, quite possibly for good.

Mayhew, a seasoned politician, maintained his composure through the low buzzing of conversation that enveloped the room. After a moment, he raised a hand in a bid for silence, and the room quieted down.

"Your position is clear," said Mayhew, speaking for the first time, "as is the position of the Throne, should we come to an agreement that the Fourth Prophesy is in play. I take it that... Hanshee?... is prepared to be questioned by the assemblage?"

"At your discretion, Your Grace," said Jusaan, "and in the ancient tongue. To my knowledge, he only speaks the ancient tongue."

The room exploded in the whispered voices of the assembled priests, if such a thing could be imagined. What Jusaan just said, if true, marked the man standing before them as authentic and, nearly of itself, made the case for the Fourth Prophesy!

Again, Lord High Priest Mayhew allowed the Council Priests to vent their surprise before calling for quiet. Then, with a nod of his head, he gave his permission for the questioning to begin.

The priest seated to the far left slowly stood and addressed Hanshee, hesitantly asking a question in the old tongue.

"Who are you, and where are you from?"

The silence in the council chamber was absolute as the assembled priests leaned forward, barely breathing, waiting to hear how this man would respond.

Hanshee understood the value of a dramatic pause. Rather than instantly respond, he took the time to look from face to face in the room, thus letting all present know that, even as they weighed him, they were being weighed. Then, he brought his gaze back to his far left, to the priest who posed the question, answering in language both swift and precise.

"I am Hanshee, of the People of the Earth. I am of clan Dula. My people inhabit a land far to the west, beyond this place of cities, beyond the great desert, and beyond what you know as the Blue Mountains."

Now the priests abandoned their whispers, reacting in astonishment with voices that, at first, drowned out any calls for order from Mayhew. Hanshee continued to look around as if nothing out of the ordinary had occurred. Lord High Priest Mayhew had to rise from his seat to establish order in the chamber once more.

After quieting the room, Mayhew remained standing, staring intently at Hanshee as the warrior-priest continued to survey the room. Hanshee watched as the assembled priests regained their composure and then, as if feeling the eyes upon his back, he slowly turned until he faced the Lord High Priest, meeting his gaze without compromise.

It had been Mayhew's plan to let his councilmen interrogate the stranger while he sat back and evaluated everything from his tone, to his posture, to the responses he offered. But the lord high priest now felt that things had changed and, perhaps, he needed to take a hand in the questioning in a way that would either expose an imposter, or confirm a prophesy.

Never looking away as he again assumed his seat, Mayhew allowed a half smile, almost a sneer, to form on his lips as he spoke.

"Tell me," Mayhew said in a voice of supreme calm. "What know you of the Pith?"

To those assembled, this innocuous request was wielded as a stiletto sliding noiselessly between two ribs and into the heart. It was a question Jusaan had never thought to ask, the answer of which would reveal the true origins of this man. Did he know nothing of the Pith? Had he been coached to present a tale that could be easily picked apart by someone with real knowledge? Or were the Pith a true part of the history of his people?

Jusaan fought to keep the anxiety he suddenly felt from showing on his face.

Hanshee never diverted his gaze, meeting the high priest's eyes as he began to recount, with all the passion but only a fraction of the venom, excerpts from the same history he had recounted to Ray on a cool autumn night spent as a captive under hardwood trees and a clear, starry sky.

Careful to leave out details casting the Pith in too villainous a light, Hanshee nevertheless remained true to the history. When he had finished his tale of honor and duty, of conflict and victory, of treachery fomented and treachery punished, the look on the lord high priest's face was all the confirmation any of the others needed. The Fourth Prophesy, and all that it represented, was indeed upon them!

****

The King's response was swift, and soon his Council of Seven was again seated around the big oak table of the map room. This time, they were joined by Lord High Priest Mayhew and Council Priest Jusaan, as confirmation that the warrior-priest, Hanshee, was indeed the harbinger of Prophesy.

His Majesty, King Ammon IV stared every man down before he spoke.

"I remind you of your pledge of loyalty and duty," the King said, "given in this very chamber on this very morning. I understand your pride makes this reminder unnecessary, but what your King, and your Temple, are about to ask of you is unprecedented in the history of our people."

He paused to survey the faces before him. Satisfied his commanders were resolute, he continued. "The first and Second Expeditionary Forces, the Second Stronghold Force, and the Second Cavalry Force, will begin both individual and joint training immediately. These forces will be augmented by one-half of the city garrison, to be commissioned evenly between them, the members to be chosen at the discretion of their commander, Lord Commander Colevant. The remaining forces will unite to form a cohesive defensive force for the continued protection of Stronghold and the Citadel."

With the fires of destiny burning brightly in his eyes for all to see, the King continued.

"Those forces that were first named will form a single force under the command of Lord Commander Galin that, come the spring thaw, and having been well trained, well equipped, and fully supplied, will be prepared to march west. Our destination will be the Blue Mountains and beyond, into what the sacred writings of the Fourth Prophesy refer to as the Motherland!

Chapter 17

Some said the snows came earlier and more often this year than in any other winter in memory and the thick fluffy blanket of white that seemed to be replenished every other day, gave credence to those with this point of view. Still, the day-to-day grind of empire must continue, and there was as much activity around the royal compound, referred to as The Citadel, as in the warmth of summer.

Those who paid attention could see the deployment and rotation of the Royal Guard had been changed. Longer shifts in the more easily accessed quarters had become normal. Guards had much less of a presence on the periphery and in the obscure corners of the compound than they had in the past. There was a sprinkling of old and new faces here and there, as men not long retired from service were lured back to augment a Royal Guard whose numbers had been thinned to augment the Citadel Garrison.

Few in the Royal House knew the reasons for these changes and, because the important areas of the compound were still well covered, had little curiosity as to why. Almost no one suspected the part played by the military in these changes as the Commanders, under order from the King, kept the knowledge of the Fourth Prophesy between themselves and the Council of Nine. General knowledge of the reason behind the changes could have an unpredictable effect on the masses, and the less they knew the better for the planning and execution that must take place.

Of course, there were rumors. There were always rumors of one sort or another. But few believed them, and more believable scenarios were always easily substituted for speculation about scripture and prophesy.

These mid-winter days would have been extremely easy for Raymond, if not for Hanshee. Since it was their official duty to enjoy the perks of being guests of the Temple, with all the pampering the designation implied, on most days there was literally nothing they were required to do. Imagining his own level of readiness beginning to wane due to easy living, and seeing the need for his comrade to learn to defend himself, Hanshee continued the daily training regimen designed to provide intense instruction to Ray, and exercise for himself.

To Raymond's mind, the activity was brutal. Hanshee asked Ray to keep up with him for as long as possible, and he pushed his student harder with each passing day. Ray had never trained to this degree before; had never experienced anything close to it. Every day he lasted a little longer than the day before, yet every day ended the same: with his body succumbing to pain and exhaustion, leaving him lying on the floor, spent.

It was at these times, when Ray felt he could barely move, that he focused on Hanshee. Unencumbered by his student, Hanshee poured himself into conditioning in ways Ray never imagined. Hanshee would use the same movements that had defeated Ray and take them to different and higher levels, punishing his body with calisthenics, stretches, and continuous forms similar to the kata Ray had learned in martial arts, but more intricate and much more intense. The performance of these forms left Hanshee gasping for air, and Raymond breathless with the realization of what the human body could be made to do.

The speed, the power, the agility, the fluidity, and the grace of Hanshee in motion, if just in training, was to Raymond one of the wonders of the natural world. Add to this an almost supernatural precision and focus, a focus needed to fully control what was unleashed in his moving body, and Raymond was ready to believe Hanshee could literally become "the Panther", as the soldiers had taken to calling him; a mythic combination of beast and man.

The demeanor of the Royal Guard had changed since the return of the First Expeditionary Force. Though mostly stationed in and around the Stronghold wall, some of the men had filtered the forty or so leagues to the Citadel, or to places in between. Doing what soldiers do when given enough time, goblets were lifted, drink was quaffed, and stories were told. One of the favorite stories was about a happening one cool fall morning on the high plains of the southeastern Ursal Mountains when Botha, a legendary figure throughout both Expeditionary Forces, met a mystery warrior and his own demise.

According to the most reliable version making the rounds, Botha was taken apart, piece by piece, by an unknown warrior who had been captured in the forest. The stranger had been handed over to Botha, a known sadist who enjoyed nothing more than inflicting pain, for the amusement of the troops. It was said this unknown warrior first taunted the giant, and then slowly broke him down, striking, blocking, and countering with a speed, power, and precision never before witnessed by those who were present. By the time the stranger finally dispatched Botha, after literally beating him to his knees in total submission, the only marks on his own body were made by the blood of his victim.

To many the story sounded unbelievable; another tall tale told by men who regularly trafficked in tall tales. But many who told it swore to have been there, and could point to others who supported their story word for word. It was not until this mystery warrior was described that a few soldiers, Royal Guards transferred to the garrison, found their memory jogged and related stories of a recent guest of the Temple fitting the description of 'The Panther', as the witnesses were calling him.

As the stories spread and more Guards realized just who might be a guest in the Temple, they began to see the warrior-priest in a different light. Now they watched his every move as he walked past, searching for telltale signs of the awesome power, speed and grace of the stories. Some appeared to take his measure as if hoping to one day challenge this 'Panther' to combat. Others stood taller and straighter when he appeared, so as not to be found wanting in comparison.

Raymond took notice, and so did Hanshee, though he never said a word.

They still had Laretha and Meesha to see to their needs, and over time those relationships also changed. The physical attraction only hinted at in the beginning had since led to more. As Hanshee and Raymond were their only responsibility, Laretha and Meesha had the time and the excuse to spend many nights in their quarters. Many mornings the young women were late in arriving at the kitchen to prepare the morning meal for the honored guests of the Temple. They were fortunate Hanshee's burgeoning reputation, unproven but believed nonetheless, was such that by the time they arrived, the kitchen help had already prepared a platter for "the Panther" and his acolyte plentiful enough to feed several others. Laretha and Meesha were always gracious, sometimes thanking the workers who made the platters with a peck on the cheek, before taking the morning meal up to their charges.

On one of these mornings, a particularly cold morning, Raymond lay in his cot warmed by the sleeping body of Laretha beside him. Always excited by the prospect of female company, but not one for random or casual flings, Raymond found himself drawn more and more to the young servant woman for reasons besides the bed. He was developing feelings for her and, whether real or needed to fill a void within, he had come to enjoy them, and her, just the same.

But at this moment he felt trapped.

He felt trapped because he had to take an epic morning wiz, but to do so he would have to leave the warmth of the body sleeping peacefully beside him and brave the chilled air and cold stone of the morning. He would surely get relief, but in doing so would awaken Laretha and lose his 'cloak' against the cold.

Considering his situation, he knew there was really but one course of action. The need to take an epic morning wiz, like death, could only be postponed for so long. Reluctantly he eased his body from the bed, striving mightily not to awaken the sleeping form beside him but, alas, it just was not meant to be. She stirred, and he froze, hoping she would simply roll over. He froze, and the need to take an epic morning wiz seemed to grow exponentially! He involuntarily twitched, from the strain of holding it in, and Laretha opened one eye, saw the early morning light framing the tapestry hanging over the window, and launched herself from the bed, cursing him in her native tongue for not waking her up.

As the covers flew back, Ray was assaulted by the cold, but cold becomes meaningless when an epic morning wiz is calling. He staggered up from his bed, searching for the clay pot that was in the corner right over there… except it wasn't. As she threw on her robes and woke up the still sleeping Meesha, Ray was seriously considering pulling back the window coverings and greeting the morning with a golden stream.

Then he spied Hanshee, who had probably risen an hour earlier, and so quietly Meesha never knew she was alone under their covers. Hanshee was smiling the jokers smile he sometimes smiled with his whole face and Raymond knew, as surely as the sun rises in the east, that Hanshee had the clay pot hidden somewhere in the room. Hanshee must have seen the realization dawn on Ray's face because he burst into laughter and rolled on his side, revealing the coveted clay pot in the corner behind him.

Raymond was furious!

But fury, much like the cold, becomes meaningless when an epic morning wiz is calling. Ray staggered over to the corner and reached over Hanshee's prone body to snatch up the clay pot.

Sweet relief!

And now he was ready to release his full unfettered fury on 'The Joker' but, at that very moment, a gust of wind blew the tapestry inward and he was struck by an icy blast of winter! Raymond found himself floundering back toward his bed where he tried to bury himself under the still warm covers. His full unfettered fury would have to wait until Hanshee had stoked the fireplace.

Soon Hanshee had the fire in the large fireplace blazing, and had brought a bucket of burning wood and coal into the sleeping chamber as amends to Raymond for the trick with the clay pot. Ray had to forgive him and soon he was up washed and dressed in heavy woolen robes which would ward off the cold until the quarters had heated up sufficiently. The table and chairs had been set up before the fireplace and now Raymond waited with Hanshee for the arrival of the girls and the morning meal. As they waited, they spoke more about what they did and didn't know about their predicament.

It had been about twenty days since they had been called before the Council of Nine. That meeting had proved fortunate as, in their questioning, the council priests had let slip clues as to why Hanshee and Raymond were there, and what plans were in store for them.

The Pith, having assimilated many cultures during their time as fighting nomads, and even after establishing themselves in the valley they'd come to call Stronghold, had become a civilized nation. They were far different culturally, and even physically, from when they were driven from the land of their birth. Because of his skin tone, his features, his clothing and his language, the priests likened Hanshee to Usaid, the legendary warrior-priest who had led their forefathers, first in a war of conquest, then in a ruinous attempt at governing an empire and, lastly, on the long and arduous journey of exile from the lands west of the Blue Mountains.

Raymond and Hanshee had heard, first from Laretha, and later from Jusaan when he addressed the Council of the Nine, that the Pith believed they would one day return to the land from which their ancestors had originally come. Jusaan had clearly said he believed Hanshee embodied the spirit of Usaid, and had presented Hanshee to the Council of The Nine as such.

Putting all of this together, Raymond and Hanshee thought they had a fairly good idea of what the Fourth Prophesy entailed and how it related to Hanshee. How Hanshee's presence had set this prophesy into motion was understood. How it was to be accomplished, his leading the Pith back to his homeland, was where their understanding broke down.

Raymond envisioned a caravan winding for many miles through the countryside, the people of Pith and all their possessions, like a giant parade with Hanshee at its head, marching toward the Blue Mountains. Or maybe Hanshee would be expected to lead a delegation made up of nobles, merchants, diplomats and such, in an attempt to negotiate with their former brethren a peaceful repatriation by the Pith. Once an agreement had been reached, word could be sent to the bulk of the populace, and the return could commence.

Although the latter seemed more likely, neither scenario answered some pressing questions for Raymond, such as why a major nation would give up all they had attained over 1,000 years - their entire civilization and their dreams of empire - to be reunited with their brethren of old in a faraway land which none of them had ever even seen.

And the logistics of such a move!

The more he thought about it, the more Ray believed this Fourth Prophesy was somewhat of a fairy tale, a beautiful story of two peoples separated by treachery and strife again reuniting as one. He could see this story being passed down from generation to generation as a happy ending to their ugly truth of being cast out into the wilderness by their brethren.

Following the meeting with the council, Jusaan's visits had decreased in frequency and duration. Apparently, having accomplished whatever his initial goals had been with respect to their presence, his only concern now was keeping them healthy and happy. Every few days he would briefly drop by to check up on his special guests, making sure their physical needs were being met. This was always as he was hurrying one place or another, and these times had proven inopportune for Hanshee's plan of simply asking Jusaan to explain the Fourth Prophesy. Until such an opportunity presented itself, the pair was relegated to continuing to collect clues here and there, in an attempt to further piece the mystery together.

They were still in the midst of their discussions when Laretha and Meesha arrived from the kitchen with the morning meal. This was now a sight so common that they barely looked up, so did not notice right away something was amiss. It was not until Meesha dropped the platter heavily onto the foyer table, almost spilling its contents, that both their heads whipped around in surprise.

At first, they were puzzled by what they saw.

Laretha, having propped the door open for Meesha to enter, stared wide eyed as her companion leaned over the platter she had just dropped to the wooden surface. After appearing to force herself upright, Meesha started toward the table where Raymond and Hanshee sat staring at her. Her first step was erratic, as if she was unsure if she could remain upright. Her second step was worse, and by her third step she found herself reaching out toward the two as she dropped to her knees onto the carpeted floor. As she fell, her mouth came open as if to call for help, but no sound came out, and she toppled further, falling onto one hand, her other still outstretched in the direction of the table.

Hanshee flew from his seat, moving fast enough to catch Meesha before she fell completely to the floor. Raymond was right behind him as Hanshee spun her until her back was to the floor and then gently lowered her, keeping her head slightly elevated while he looked into her eyes. Without looking up, he spoke to Ray.

"Ask Laretha what happened. Quickly!"

Ray complied, quickly turning toward Laretha and asking what had happened to Meesha to put her in the state she was in. Laretha only stared at him wide eyed, as if not understanding what she saw, or what she heard.

"Speak woman!" Ray shouted to her again. "Do you know what happened?!"

A look of stunned surprise still on her face, Laretha finally found her voice.

"You…you can speak the Pithian tongue?" she asked as if in a daze.

Raymond sprang to his feet and covered the distance between them in two giant strides.

"Yes, I can!" he said forcefully, grabbing her by the shoulders and locking his eyes onto hers. "Now tell me…do you know what happened to Meesha?"

This brought Laretha briefly out of her state of shock and she managed to stammer a reply.

"I…don't know," she said, looking down at her friend, who was glassy-eyed, foam dribbling from the corner of her mouth. "She was fine… I don't know…she was…she had some wine…she said she was thirsty after coming up the stairs…she had some…a little wine to quench her thirst…but she was fine…"

"She has been poisoned," Hanshee said flatly. He laid Meesha down on the carpet and sprinted to the bedchamber for his pouch.

Raymond released Laretha. Going to Meesha, he leaned over her in time to see her eyes slowly roll up into her head until only a hint of pupil remained.

Moving swiftly, Hanshee pushed past Raymond and knelt beside the stricken woman. Cradling her head with one strong hand, he wiped away the foam around her mouth before placing a pinch of white powder on her tongue.

"Water!" he demanded, glancing at Raymond, who lurched to the table, poured some water into a goblet, and placed it in Hanshee's outstretched hand.

Hanshee brought it to Meesha's lips and slowly poured a little water into her open mouth, hoping to elicit an automatic swallow response before pouring more.

It never happened, and Meesha died there on the floor, her head still cradled in Hanshee's gentle hand.

As Hanshee slowly lowered Meesha's head to the carpet, Laretha finally registered what had happened. Her arms slowly went limp, threatening to drop the two pitchers she was carrying, one of water and one of watered wine, to the floor. Ray had turned to her again to question her and, seeing her strength start to wane, proved quick enough to catch her hands and guide them to the table, where she was able to release the jugs without spilling the contents.

Then she screamed.

With her eyes focused on nothing, Laretha screamed loud and long, and it seemed her soul would leave her body with the force and emotion of her scream. Thankfully, her scream brought the guards, whom Jusaan had ordered to never be far from Hanshee. They peered through the portal and saw the hysterical Laretha. They looked further and saw the body of Meesha stretched out on the floor, more foam having formed around her mouth and nostrils. Words were quickly exchanged between them and one remained while the other sprinted to find his captain and Council Priest Jusaan.

Chapter 18

As Jusaan trod the empty temple halls, his mind again rehashed the events of the early morning.

He recalled his irritation at having a most sumptuous morning meal disturbed by insistent pounding on his outer door. He remembered his displeasure turning to shock at the announcement there had been a death in the Temple, in the quarters of his honored guest. He remembered running, as fast as his legs could carry him, through the halls and down three flights of stairs, to the sixth level and to the very door of the guest quarters. He remembered his relief as, having pushed through the guards surrounding the portal, he was greeted with the sight of Hanshee, still alive and uninjured, standing as if on guard over the lifeless body of a woman.

Then came the questions; who was the woman? What caused her death? How did this happen? Was there treachery? The story told by the other servant woman led the guard captain to suspect poisoned wine. Was this a simple accident or an attempt on the life of the Harbinger of Prophesy, an attempt to undermine the will of The One Spirit? If so, who could be responsible for a blasphemy such as this?

There had been a quick investigation. A search of the kitchens was done and the kitchen boy, a young lad who had gone to the barrels to fetch the water and wine for Meesha, was also found dead. He too had ingested poison, by his look the same poison to which Laretha had succumbed, leaving open the question of whether this was a terrible accident, or an intentional act. Others had consumed wine from the same barrel without incident, which was proof of nothing.

Lost in his musings, Jusaan had by now crossed the bridge on the seventh level, connecting the temple with the Royal House, and was met in the foyer by the fierce continence of Lord Cecil. Two guards accompanied him and, for a moment, Jusaan wondered if they were there for him. To be dragged in chains before His Majesty would be the ultimate indignation and probably the precursor to a swift execution.

Jusaan quickly dismissed these thoughts from his mind. One servant girl was dead; an inconvenience but not a tragedy. There were others to take her place. Though the circumstances begged many questions, the fact remained that the warrior-priest Hanshee was unscathed, and the Pith were free to move forward toward their destiny.

Summoning his composure, Jusaan ignored Cecil's stern visage.

"Lord Cecil," the priest said, bowing his head slightly.

"Council Priest Jusaan," Cecil responded, with a slight inclination of his head. "It is so good of you to be prompt."

"In times such as these, Lord Cecil," the priest replied, "when even the most innocent of events must be viewed with suspicion, being prompt is among the least of our sacrifices."

"So, you have already confirmed the innocence of the servant's death?" Cecil asked. "His Majesty will be happy to learn of your conclusion, and curious as to how it was reached."

"It was not terribly difficult," said Jusaan. "If there was an attempt on the life of the Harbinger, it was a clumsy one, taking instead the lives of two nondescript underlings. It was most probably the accident that it appears."

"You are probably correct," said Cecil, pursing his lips as he appeared to consider the council priest's conclusion. "Maybe it was an accidental poisoning. But maybe it was an assassination attempt so cleverly laid that, though it failed, no witnesses or clues remain to point to the identity of those behind it."

Jusaan bristled at the accusation.

"Do you think me incompetent, Cecil?" he asked. "I'm sure His Highness has heard from the captain of the Royal Guard, and thus knows all that I know. I look forward to his sharing his conclusions with me."

"His Highness has other matters to attend to," said Cecil. "He has sent me to perform that function."

This statement, spoken nonchalantly, caught Jusaan by surprise; he had been certain he was on his way to be interrogated by Ammon himself.

Cecil watched as Jusaan's look of surprise dissipated, to be replaced by one of cautious curiosity.

"So, Cecil," Jusaan said, "what conclusions did the King reach?"

"His Majesty has additional questions," said the Chief Advisor, "such as; to what type of poison did the victims succumb? Where did this poison originate? Was there any poison, of any kind, found in the Kitchen? And, why haven't these basic questions been answered?"

"Why... I...," Jusaan stammered, caught completely off guard and searching for an acceptable response. "I am but a humble priest of The One! How am I to be held responsible for answering such questions? These are not matters with which the Temple regularly concerns itself!"

"Which brings us to His Majesties conclusion," said Cecil, his eyes bearing down on the now visibly frightened priest. "He has concluded that the safety of the Harbinger cannot be assured in the Temple, a Temple which does not "concern itself" with matters of treachery conducted under its very nose. He has further concluded that, in defense of the Faith, and for the protection of the Harbinger, he and his acolyte will be moved into the Royal House without delay."

"That is not possible!" Jusaan almost shouted.

Cecil was quick to pounce.

"You do not approve of the Kings reasoning?" the Lord Chief Advisor asked. "Would you like the opportunity to press your case before His Highness?"

"No," Jusaan said, checking his impulsive outburst. "It is just… their proximity to my quarters in the Temple ensures my ability to see to their needs and…"

"Considering the poisoned corpse of a servant found in their quarters," Cecil said with obvious disdain, "it is questionable as to how adequately *you* have seen to their needs. However, your point is valid, which is why you will be moving into the Royal House as well. You will be moved this very day, and will be allowed two servants to aid with your personal needs. The Royal House will provide servants for the needs of the Harbinger and his acolyte. Please have your servants prepare for your departure."

"What?" Jusaan could barely contain his outrage. "Why am I required to leave my quarters?"

"For their comfort," said Cecil. "You have been their guide through all of their experiences in Pith. The Harbinger has grown to trust you. I am sure they will turn to you to help them adjust to any future… situations."

Cecil turned to leave, but turned back to further address the priest.

"And please do not forget, as His Majesty has not forgotten," Cecil said, tossing the priest a crumb, "you are The Chosen of The One, blessed to have brought the Harbinger into our midst. As such, your place, be it in the Temple or the Royal House, is assured."

****

The shadowy figure moved easily down the torch lit back street, a heavy hooded cloak providing concealment as well as protection against the cold. He was at home in these back streets and alleys, having frequented them, and the taverns backed up to them, many times in the past.

He was a tall man and his stature, along with the confident way he moved, gave pause to any who at first glance might have thought him prey. A second glance and they pulled their own hoods close around wary faces and, if needed, made way as he strode by. Though he may appear a stranger, they knew a predator when they saw one.

He had just left his third tavern of the night, having enjoyed a goblet of hot spiced wine at each, never planning to stay for too long unless he was blessed to encounter unusual... talent. But even that exception would not have halted his progress, and as he approached the intersection of the alley and the main street, he spied what had pulled him from the warmth of his apartments and into the bowels of the city.

It was a nondescript coach, showing signs of neglect here and there, and stained so dark a shade of brown as to appear black in the sparse light of lamps and torches. The coachman sat motionless atop his seat, the reins dangling from his gloved hands undisturbed in the stillness of the cold night. Even the horses stood as statues, with only the slowly rising steam of their breath marking them as living things.

The coach stood at the agreed upon location, with shades drawn, as the hooded stranger cavalierly sauntered up to the door. Without hesitation he snatched it open. Effortlessly he eased himself inside, his considerable frame immediately swallowed by the blackness therein. As he settled himself onto the rear seat, two taps were heard from the darkness before him, and the carriage slowly began to move down the street.

It took a few moments for his eyes to adjust to the darkness, but soon he could make out a figure sitting opposite him, similarly hooded but not of his stature.

The air inside the carriage was quite a bit warmer than outside due to a pot filled with hot coals which had been set into the floor beneath a metal grate. Because of this, the stranger felt comfortable pushing back his hood and running a hand through the loose curls of his close-cropped hair. He looked across at his companion who, aside from having tapped twice on the ceiling to alert the coachman to proceed, had not moved. Usually not a patient man, it irked the stranger to have to sit quietly and wait for his host to break the silence. Therefore, he didn't.

"Interesting news from the temple this morning," he began in a taunting tone. "There were two deaths by poison, but not the two one might have expected. What say you to this, Lord Mayhew?"

At the sound of his name, Mayhew's head jerked involuntarily. A long sigh emerged from under his hood, and the lord high priest found his voice.

"Mistakes were made," he began. "There were…"

"I was assured there would be none," the stranger snapped.

"When working through others…"

"Your handpicked 'others'," reminded the stranger.

"Damn you, Galin! It may be we work against the very will of The One Spirit!" the high priest spat, unaccustomed to being questioned by any save the King himself.

"Don't hide behind the name of your god!" Galin countered. "If your belief is so strong, why then do you attempt to alter His will? Why attempt to thwart prophesy?"

Again, a long sigh preceded the high priest's response.

"I don't believe this savage is the harbinger of prophesy…no more so than do you." said Mayhew. "But the fact others do… that His Majesty does… throws everything into question."

Feeling he had adequately rebuked the lord high priest, Galin allowed his tone to become slightly less confrontational.

"The future of our people hangs in the balance, no doubt… but the solution to this problem is obvious and easily handled, or so you said."

The two dark figures found themselves leaning to the side as the carriage rounded a corner.

"To *handle* a situation such as this with the proper finesse…"

"You have tried and failed," spat Galin, dismissing Mayhew's attempt at an explanation. "Probably a bit too much *finesse*, if you ask me. And in doing so, you have made our task all the more difficult by placing your 'savage' under the direct protection of the Royal House. I doubt your influence extends to their kitchens, eh, priest?"

Mayhew chose to remain silent, unable to defend his obvious failure.

"You have placed us at far greater risk," Galin continued, "and the opportunity for a solution both quick and clean may have passed."

Galin locked eyes with those inside the dark hood of Mayhew.

"I'll have my turn now, priest," he said. "Though I admit, my methods may not be as subtle as those of the Temple."

"You would launch an assault on the Royal House?" Mayhew could not hide his astonishment.

"A surgical strike, if it comes to that," said Galin, with impatience for one not versed in the military arts. "And you need not worry; our hands will remain clean, though it may be that certain quarters inside the Royal House will run red."

This pronouncement produced the shudder from the high priest Galin had sought, and he chuckled as he twice rapped his knuckles on the roof of the carriage, signaling the driver to bring them to a halt. As he reached for the carriage door, Mayhew weakly grasped at his extended arm, causing him to pause.

"When will you move?" the high priest asked in a horse whisper.

Galin smiled at the troubled face under the hood, barely visible in the light of a torch hanging from the wall before which they had stopped.

"Patience, priest," he said. "Matters such as these take time."

"I only wish to know so that…"

"So that you can arrange to be away from the Citadel, and thus escape any stench of suspicion, eh?" Galin said, finishing what he knew to be the high priest's thoughts. "Know this much, priest; none will know the day nor the hour, so none can raise an alarm."

With that, Galin stepped from the carriage and into the cold of the dimly lit street. He melted into the nearby shadows before turning to watch as the dark carriage moved down the street and rounded a corner. He continued to listen until the rhythmic hoof beats of the horses faded into the other night sounds. Then, looking around to get his bearings, he proceeded in the direction he knew would take him to the nearest tavern.

Chapter 19

Ray marveled at the opulence of their new quarters.

The apartments they now inhabited were deep inside the Royal House and had been originally intended to house the children of the King. Their current dwelling represented a fraction of the entire complex yet was twice the size of their former accommodations.

Before them was one large room, divided not by walls or columns, but by the different furnishings defining its many uses. The main entrance was a large door made from dark and light woods, inlaid with silver and polished stones to form a beautiful portrait of the Royal House against a backdrop of mountains. To the right, as you entered, was a large table comprised of a granite slab polished to a high gloss nestled atop five ornate wooden pedestals. Four chairs were currently situated around the table, though there was room for many more.

On the opposite side of the entrance were furnishings meant to hold various bowls and vessels, more chairs, and several mirrors. This corner was set up as a place for washing and personal cleanliness.

Further into the room there was a small fireplace on the inner wall, the western wall, before which were set up two beds, one large and one slightly smaller, in respect for the 'greater' and 'lesser' relationship between the 'Harbinger', the latest designation given Hanshee as "the harbinger of the Fourth

Prophesy", and his disciple. A larger fireplace graced the eastern wall, an outer wall some thirty feet distant and directly across from the smaller fireplace. Two chairs had been placed before the large fireplace, again one larger than the other, as well as a low table and several cushions. Beyond this, on the far northern wall of the room, was storage space for the few possessions accompanying them, as well as trunks and armoires filled with cloaks, robes, shirts, tunics, undergarments, boots, almost any type of clothing they might require during winter and spring in the mountains of Stronghold.

All of these furnishings were positioned atop rugs and carpets which left little bare floor visible. The walls were adorned with tapestries, paintings, carvings, and artifacts, the central theme of which was, as was typical of the décor of the Royal House, the power and majesty of Pith.

Beside the fireplace on the outer wall was a pair of tall doors inlaid with panes of glass from bottom to top; a rare thing, even in a nation with the riches of Pith. The doors opened onto a balcony as large, if not larger, than the room. Built from white and gray polished stone gleaming in the afternoon sun, and surrounded by a low stone wall, it looked out over a private courtyard, with a granite walkway surrounding a field of dormant grass. There were various wooden constructs at its edges that could be moved into position to facilitate play for younger children. Other wooden structures were intended for older children to use for exercise and weapons training.

This courtyard could only be accessed by a stone staircase, the bottom of which was just visible from the right-hand corner of the balcony, the access door located outside the room that served as quarters for the new guests.

Beyond the courtyard were the mountains, the far eastern part of the stone walls of Pith. These were the natural walls of stone that, along with the northern mountain range, completely surrounded the huge valley that was the center of the Pithian empire. Though the stone from the nearer outcroppings showed signs of having been quarried, the mountain walls farther out appeared untouched by human hands. They rose sharply toward the sky, a daunting obstacle seemingly impossible to scale.

Raymond opened the wood-framed glass double doors and strode across marble tiles, joining Hanshee who stood before the low wall which surrounded the balcony. He was looking out over the courtyard directly below and up to the tops of the mountain walls in the distance.

"This is beautiful, isn't it?" Ray asked as he approached his friend. "Just look at that view."

The midday sun was a few hours past its zenith. Its warmth was the perfect contrast to the clean, cool breezes sweeping down off the snowcapped mountains far to the northwest. Hanshee allowed his eyes to linger upon the mountain peaks before turning to Raymond with a bemused expression.

"Yes, Way-mon," he replied. "There is much beauty here." He shifted his gaze back to the peaks. "There is always much beauty in mountains."

Raymond was confused by the look Hanshee had given him, and found himself pondering its meaning.

"You weren't just admiring the mountains," he finally said. "You were checking to see if we are safe here. You were looking for a way in."

"And a way out," said Hanshee, still, surveying the rocks in the distance.

Raymond could not help but feel a little pride in correctly reading Hanshee. The fact his own mind went so quickly to their safety meant at least some of what his mentor was trying to teach him was finding a home in his thoughts. Of course, he would never want to be so obsessed with safety that he became paranoid, unmoved by the beauty to be found around him but, looking at Hanshee, he knew there could be room for both.

The sound of someone knocking on the outer door brought Raymond out of his musings, and both he and Hanshee left the balcony and reentered the main room. There Hanshee stopped while Raymond, fulfilling his role as acolyte to Hanshee's role as warrior-priest, proceed to the door. After first looking back at Hanshee to be sure he was prepared, Raymond opened it to reveal Laretha holding a tray heavy with platters of beef, fowl, and fresh baked bread, the steam still rising from all. There were also bowls of steamed vegetables and dried fruit, the total so bounteous Ray felt compelled to rush forward and relieve the young woman of her burden before its weight overcame her.

Standing beside Laretha, and obviously the one who had knocked on the door, was another female servant unknown to Ray. She entered with two large pitchers, one of cool water, the other of watered wine. She placed them on the table to Ray's left, then reached into the pouch of her smock and produced two goblets, placing them beside the pitchers.

This new servant was an older woman, probably in her mid-fifties and Raymond watched as she shuffled across the room to the small fireplace, where she retrieved a teapot which she filled with water before returning it to its spot before the fire to heat.

Watching her go about her business, Raymond couldn't help but think of Meesha, who had succumbed to poison just yesterday and was, to his mind, the reason they had been moved to quarters inside the Royal House. It was never said that her death was an attempt on their lives - actually Hanshee's life, as only he was central to the Fourth Prophesy - but even in this world, two plus two still equaled four. Hanshee's increased vigilance, if such could actually increase, pointed to the same thing; yesterday someone had made an attempt on their lives.

And Meesha had died as a result.

Raymond wasn't as close to Meesha as he was to Laretha. He and Laretha had been first to communicate, and it was through her the four of them found voice, one with another. Hanshee had been much closer to Meesha, eventually sharing his bed with her. He had tried his best to save her and, in the intensity of his effort, showed he also cared deeply for her. Whether there was true affection between them Ray couldn't say, for once her death was established and her body removed, Hanshee gave no indication - not by his words, not by his actions, not by his demeanor - she had ever been there.

Laretha had stayed with them in their move to the Royal House because it was known they preferred her to see to their needs and they had developed somewhat of a rapport even though they were thought to be unable to speak a common language. They had developed trust in her and, once she was cleared as the would-be assassin, she was reassigned to the Royal House with them.

As the older servant exited the room, Raymond turned to watch as Laretha placed the various dishes on the table and set places for him and Hanshee to eat their somewhat late midday meal. She kept her head down while preforming her tasks and, when finished, quickly turned to leave. As she walked by him, Raymond reached out and took hold of the sleeve of her robe. She stopped, her head still lowered, apparently unwilling to look into his face.

Raymond paused, unsure if he was doing the right thing, unsure what he would see if she raised her head. Would there be anger at the loss of her friend, anger at Hanshee and him for being the targets of an assassination attempt that killed Meesha instead? He would understand if that were so. Would there be guilt on her part for being spared the death that had come for her friend? Raymond had heard of this in soldiers who had lost comrades in the wars of his world. Often when they returned home, they were consumed with the guilt of having survived when so many deserving of life had fallen.

Hesitantly, he turned her body to face his, and lifted a hand to her chin. Ever so gently, he raised her head until her eyes met his. She did not resist and when their eyes met, he saw not anger but a fierce strength, a strength that remained even as her eyes swelled with tears. As he watched, the tears overflowed, running down her high cheekbones and over her cinnamon cheeks.

Her strength remained even as he wiped the tears from her cheeks and, failing to stem their flow, reached for her and embraced her. She came willingly into his arms and, once nestled against his chest, allowed herself to sob silently in remembrance of her friend.

Ray held her and felt her sobs… and then felt his own, as they stood and embraced. He did his best to comfort her, and after a while it became Laretha comforting him as he sobbed not just for an innocent life lost, but for all the misery and confusion and anger and pain and hopelessness he had felt ever since he awoke on the banks of the River of Dreams.

He was not sure how long they stood there, but eventually they both felt replenished and gently released their embrace. They again looked into each other's eyes, into eyes reddened by the shedding of tears, but also softened by the comfort that sharing a burden can bring.

Hanshee stood back and watched as they slowly broke their embrace and, with red eyes and a half-smile playing across her lips, Laretha took up the empty tray and left the room. Raymond followed and gently closed the door behind her. Continuing to stare at the door for a few moments, Ray slowly turned an embarrassed grin toward Hanshee.

"I guess it just needed to come out," he said, referring to his tears.

Hanshee approached and placed both hands on Raymond's shoulders.

"I have been told," he said, "a good woman allows a man to unburden himself in a way his companions cannot. What you did here, you needed to do… for some time. And having done so, you must now, as always, focus on the challenges of living."

Raymond wanted to respond but no words would form in his head. He felt he was on the verge of tearing up once again and thought how embarrassed he would feel if Hanshee…

"Let us eat!" said Hanshee, releasing Ray and striding purposefully toward the table of still steaming food.

****

There were times when Raymond thought that, under different circumstances, he could come to enjoy this life, or certain aspects of it.

As a guest of the Royal House, he was treated almost as an extension of the royal family. His every need was taken care of, either by Laretha, or by a host of other servants who waited breathlessly to assist the Harbinger and his acolyte in any way they could.

Jusaan came to them on the evening of the first day in their new quarters, accompanied by Lord Cecil, Chief Advisor to the Throne. Speaking through Jusaan, Cecil extended to them the formal welcome of His Majesty and explained that, as guests of the Crown, all the amenities of the compound were available to them, with the exclusion of the royal suites and the map room. Otherwise, they had but to make a request through Council Priest Jusaan as their official interpreter, for the palace staff to present itself at their service.

Jusaan hated this arrangement. Out of concern for the needs of their guests, it required him to be at their beck and call at all hours of the day and night. And he a council priest! It was humiliating. Thus, his relief was tremendous when the servant, Laretha, confided that the acolyte could speak the tongue of her father's people who were from Aggipoor, a city near the foothills of the southeastern mountain range. This revelation was to

Jusaan as water to a man dying of thirst. He immediately promoted Laretha, putting her in charge of the staff he had been given to see to the needs of the Harbinger, freeing himself from such mundane tasks as arranging for their meals and baths, ensuring there was enough wood for the fires, and seeing to the emptying of the waste pots.

For Laretha, the promotion meant more coin and less hands-on work. Now she stayed in communication with her charges, discerning their needs, and delegating anything involving physical labor to someone beneath her current station.

Except the baths.

Hanshee and Raymond were quite capable of bathing themselves, and had done so whenever the opportunity arose before being captured in the Southern Ursal Mountains. But every so often it was felt the royal guests required a personal touch when it came to grooming.

No longer living in the wilderness, Hanshee had no opportunity to replenish the powders and potions in his "magic pouch," so he sought to conserve what remained of them. This meant he was required to shave now, both his head and his face, to maintain his appearance. Raymond also decided to dispense with the hair on his head to match his clean face, and so mimicked the look of his "master." This became part of the ritual they shared every third or fourth day.

On evenings of their choosing, tubs of steaming water, along with fragrant soaps and oils, would be brought to their quarters by hulking manservants. They were followed by other servants carrying platters of seasonal treats and pastries, along with steaming pots of spiced wine and tea. Last would come Laretha and a young woman named Aleria, of about her age, who Laretha had hand-picked to wait on Hanshee.

After shooing the others from the apartment, the women helped their charges out of their robes and into the hot baths. There they soaked while the four of them enjoyed delicacies and drinks. Then Hanshee and Ray were given a thorough shaving of their head, face and neck. After that, the women used both hard and soft-bristled brushes to deliver a thorough scrubbing of the royal guests. Full-body massages with hot oils completed the ritual, or at least the part pertaining to grooming.

Residing in the Royal House, amid the sculptures, paintings, and tapestries which mostly depicted scenes of battle and conquest, made Raymond and Hanshee curious about Pithian history. Fortunately, there were plenty of resources available on the subject. Besides a library, there were chambers housing relics from as far back as The Crossing and beyond.

"The Crossing" was how the Pith referred to the period when their ancestors migrated from the plains and foothills west of the Blue Mountains and passed through a southern gap in the mountain range into a harsh, arid land inhabited by cave-dwelling savages. It was through this east-west passage that Usaid successfully led the remnants of Clan Pith.

There were hallways in the Royal House devoted to portraits of earlier rulers, along with artifacts from their times on the throne. Several of the long-term staff proved helpful in discussing this history and its significance; some even recognized ancient implements and could describe their uses. Those who were ex-military were knowledgeable about the battles depicted on the tapestries adorning almost every wall in the complex. Hanshee and Raymond spent much of their time on tours of these exhibits, learning more about the people of Pith; who they were, how they came to be in this place at this time, and what motivates them to build an empire and to challenge all other cities and nations they come into contact with.

Regardless of who led these educational forays, Laretha accompanied them as an interpreter, faithfully relaying information from the guide to Raymond, who then translated for Hanshee. Ray continued to keep his ears open for any other information that might float his way, either from the guides or by listening to conversations of random people who passed them in the halls. No one but Hanshee and Laretha knew he could speak the Pithian tongue, and Laretha remained unaware of the true extent of Raymond's linguistic gifts.

It was on one of these "field trips," as Raymond had taken to calling them, that they found themselves at the southeast corner of the Royal House. Here the building's wall, and the rear of the stables, provided two sides of the boundary of the yard in which the Citadel Guard and the City Garrison took their training. The former weapons master, a crusty old officer with a pronounced limp, served as their guide. He spoke to Hanshee, through Laretha and Raymond, about many of the ancient artifacts on display. Some were the weapons of their enemies, captured in battle and displayed as trophies. Others were weapons of their own making, usually with a storied past making them worthy of interest.

During the time spent in the passage leading to the barracks and training yard, many guards passed them. By this time, the story of "the Panther" had spread from the gates of Stronghold to the barracks and latrines of the garrison, and all who passed suspected who Hanshee was. Most tried not to stare openly, preferring a quick look or a sideways glance. Others stared boldly, as if wanting to be noticed by the legendary slayer of Botha.

Of course, there were some who were not satisfied just to look, but stared upon Hanshee with open challenge in their eyes. Some even spoke aloud, not directly to Hanshee mind you, though they all doubted he knew their tongue, but it was obvious by their volume and tone what their intentions were, even without Hanshee understanding the words.

When this first began, Laretha cast nervous glances at Raymond. She hoped he would not convey to the Harbinger the jeers and insults being cast their way. Raymond forced himself to appear unruffled. This once-difficult task had become easier with practice, and now he showed no sign of distress, regardless of the graphic descriptions wafting toward them concerning just what this or that warrior would do if the Panther were to somehow summon the courage to face them in combat.

On this day they had worked their way to the weapons room of the Citadel Guard. Hanshee, being well-versed in all of the standard weaponry used by the Pith, would now and then heft a sword or a spear to gauge its balance or potential for lethality. Old Tyrus, the former weapons master, had given his permission, and noted with a practiced eye this "warrior-priest" might just be more warrior than priest.

When Ray heard a voice from the yard behind them shout, "Tyrus, best not to let them play with the tools of men; they might cut themselves!" he was not surprised. What surprised him was Tyrus, as the weapons master turned to face the resulting chorus of laughter, and replied.

"I've got a quick eye, lads, the good one I have left, and I would say 'the Panther' knows how to handle not only himself, but every weapon on this wall," he said, waving an arm at the wall of weapons behind him.

This brought a chorus of taunting replies from the growing group of men in the yard. What began as two or three who were curious about their guest had grown to seven or eight, with more soldiers approaching, curious to see what the shouting was all about.

Hanshee and Raymond pretended not to notice the commotion, but Hanshee managed to moved slightly closer to Ray. Holding up a long knife as if pointing out a curiosity, he spoke.

"I feel the restlessness from the soldiers behind us," he said, as he intently examined the weapon.

"They have all heard tales of your fight with Botha," replied Raymond, while pointing to some obscure detail on the blade. "They are growing restless and some, egged on by their brethren, are growing bold and hurling insults our way. Maybe we should…"

Just then Raymond heard Tyrus, who had turned to Laretha with a question.

"My pardons, miss," the old warrior said, "but would you ask our guest if he would be willing to take part in some training with the men? They've all heard stories about that Botha thing and would like to see for themselves what The Pan…Hanshee, is it? … what Hanshee can do. I'd be interested in seeing for myself."

Laretha looked worried, but she dutifully turned to Raymond and repeated what Tyrus had requested.

Ray already knew, having understood every word that had been said, but he listened intently before turning to Hanshee and relaying the situation as he saw it.

"I don't like the sounds of these men, Hanshee," he said. "Some even claim friendship with Botha and may want a chance at revenge, or maybe to use you to gain a reputation of their own."

Hanshee said nothing, continuing to make a circuit of the room, appearing to appraise the weapons and tools lining the walls. He stopped when he reached the portal leading to the training yard and let his eyes wander over the men who had gathered there. They were an assortment of City Garrison and Citadel Guard, all hoping to either test him or see him tested.

As Hanshee stood there, one of the soldiers, a tall, lean sort, reached beside him to a stand holding practice weapons. These were wooden swords and knives carved to form and weighted to simulate lethal iron blades. He chose a short sword and paused, making a show of examining it for defects and to feel its weight and balance. Then, without warning, he tossed it to Hanshee.

Hanshee easily plucked it out of the air by its hilt and flowed effortlessly into several practice slices, spinning full circle as he carved the air around him before suddenly stopping, frozen in a front guard position amid murmurs from the group who had gathered to watch. Holding this position and never taking his eyes from the man who had tossed him the weapon, Hanshee tilted his head in Ray's direction and spoke a few words. Raymond relayed the message to Laretha, who turned to the gathered soldiers and translated.

"Lord Hanshee says he does not 'engage' for sport or entertainment," she said. With that, Hanshee casually tossed the training implement back to the soldier who had thrown it to him. The soldier caught the weapon by its grip, as Hanshee had, launching it into an awkward looking spin before stopping in a poor imitation of 'front guard'.

It was then that one of his companions, the second of the three who were at the core of the group, stepped forward and addressed Laretha in her native tongue.

"Countrywoman, we have heard tall tales of all sorts about how this 'Panther' defeated Botha," he said, gesturing at Hanshee, "More than that, he broke Botha before slaying him, or so the story has been told. Maybe this priest is not 'the Panther'," the man spat the words, "but we have been told he is and, seeing the savage here and now, we don't believe any of the lies we have heard."

For reasons he could not fathom, the soldier's pronouncement had the effect of angering Ray and he found himself leaving Hanshee's side and stepping out into the practice yard, where he addressed the man in the language of Aggipoor.

"My master has no need to prove himself to you," Raymond said, pointing at the accuser. "He has no need to prove himself to any of you!" He made a sweeping gesture that included everyone who stood in the yard. "He is not a savage, nor will he fight for amusement, be it yours or the King himself!"

"Then maybe it is you who is 'the Panther'," the man replied. Waving his comrades forward, they quickly surrounded Ray, the original three now joined by a fourth.

Only then did Raymond realize how the situation had changed simply by his leaving the protection of Hanshee's side. He quickly looked around, confirming he had a soldier on every side with nothing between them should they decide to continue to push this situation into open conflict. He knew there was no way he could face even one of these hardened warriors armed with weapons, even practice weapons, they had wielded all of their lives but that he had never even held. Already he could feel his breath quickening, his pulse racing, and the panic growing as his head turned from one warrior to another, unable to watch them all at the same time and unwilling to give any of them the chance to strike at him from behind.

Suddenly, Hanshee was in the circle of would-be attackers with him, and it seemed his very presence gave them pause. He moved around Ray, slowly and deliberately, facing first one warrior and then another with a wide-eyed stare that made him look to be on the edge of madness. This look, as crazy as it seemed, froze the warriors in their tracks and even made one or two take a step back. The looks of bewilderment on their faces were a stark contrast to the smug aggression they had reflected just moments before.

Once he saw the men were sufficiently cowed, Hanshee pointed Raymond toward the portal leading into the weapons room. With a slight shove, he sent him on his way. Raymond stumbled, then regained his footing. Slipping between two of the warriors whose attention remained glued to Hanshee, he rejoined Laretha and Tyrus who were standing near the doorway.

Turning to thank Hanshee, he was stunned to see him still standing in the center of the circle, his wide-eyed stare darting from man to man. Only when he saw Raymond reach the safety of the threshold, did Hanshee allow his expression to return to normal. Turning, he started to follow Ray between the two warriors closest to the door.

Raymond couldn't guess what motivated the man, the tall, thin one who had thrown Hanshee the practice sword. He may have been angry at Ray having been allowed to escape the circle so easily, or embarrassed at how Hanshee had stopped four warriors in their tracks with just a look. Whatever it was that had gotten under his skin, he made up his mind that one of the two strangers would be made to stand and prove to him and his comrades that the legend of the Panther wasn't the lie they suspected it was.

So it was that the unnamed warrior stepped in front of Hanshee, blocking his retreat into the weapons room. Hanshee came to a dead stop before the man and stood there, hands down, face placid, but completely focused on the warrior before him. Raymond watched from safety, standing near the entrance to the weapons room as Hanshee faced the warrior, neither moving forward nor retreating. The other three warriors could have disappeared in the wind for all the attention they garnered. Hanshee had eyes only for the one standing before him.

"Well?" spoke one of the other three, obviously anxious to see if the reputation of the Panther was justified or just a tale. "There he stands, right before ye."

The tall, lean warrior, slightly taller than Hanshee, licked nervously at his lips while letting his eyes seek the faces of his three companions. The others looked on with anxious stares, nodding their heads in encouragement for their comrade to commence with the attack. Satisfied they stood with him, and taking courage from this, the warrior fixed what he thought was a confident grin on his face and threw a vicious left fist at Hanshee's head.

Hanshee remained the picture of calm as he leaned his body back slightly while bringing up his right hand to parry the punch in the direction it was already going. Then, using the same hand, he hooked the warrior's wrist and redirected the spent punch, pulling the arm to the outside and away from his body. The warrior was baffled at how all of his power had been negated and redirected without very much effort from this savage priest and he instinctively let fly with a looping right fist at least as powerful as the left.

Hanshee, still controlling his assailants left arm with his right hand, stepped into this new attack, blocking it sharply with the snapping edge of his left hand, which he then allowed to slide down to the warrior's right wrist where he applied an iron grip and yanked, pulling the warrior forward and off balance. Simultaneously Hanshee stepped in and across with his right foot and pivoted to his left. The result was that the warrior was pulled into a perfect hip throw which sent him crashing onto his back, in the dust of the practice yard, between his three comrades.

What happened next etched itself into Ray's mind:

Even as the warrior fell, Hanshee followed him to the ground in a squat and applied an arm bar to the right arm that he had never released. A loud pop, the sound of the dislocating right elbow, reverberated through the yard, and the hapless warrior threw his head back to scream in pain... a scream cut off before it began, for Hanshee had brought a hammer fist down on his exposed throat, crushing his windpipe and silencing all but the gasping and gurgling of a man now struggling to breathe.

While still watching his assailant fight for his breath, and thus his life, Hanshee effortlessly rose from his squat. Slowly raising his head, he looked from one face to the other, wordlessly asking which of the three would be next to challenge him. Frozen to the spots on which they stood, they all dropped their gaze to their stricken comrade, unable or unwilling to meet the eyes of this warrior-priest who brought death in an instant.

Hanshee remained standing among the three guardsmen until he was satisfied his point was made. He then turned and walked back toward the weapons room, his face, Ray noted, never having changed expression from when the doomed warrior had first stepped into his path.

Raymond continued to stand in the portal, shocked by the speed and decisiveness Hanshee displayed. Free of Hanshee's presence, the three warriors rushed to their fallen comrade, but there was nothing for them to do. Raymond watched briefly as they frantically attempted to administer some type of aid, then he too turned away. It was clear the guardsman had breathed his last.

Hanshee stood quietly beside him, his face placid, as if he were watching the quite surface of a pond. Old Tyrus just stared at him, open-mouthed. Laretha didn't seem to know where to look, staring first at the dying warrior, then at Raymond, then at Hanshee, then back to the dying warrior.

Raymond finally took control of the situation, taking Laretha by the shoulders and instructing her to tell Tyrus the royal guests would like to return to their quarters.

"Of course, my lords" Tyrus said, coming out of his stupor and offering a slight bow to his guests. "I'll have two of the guards…" his words trailed off awkwardly as he again allowed his gaze to rest on the fallen guardsman and his companions.

"I know the way," Laretha replied curtly. Ushering Hanshee and Raymond before her, they started out of the weapons room, out of the barracks, and down the long hallway where the portraits of great Kings and commanders of Pithian history looked down as the Panther strode past.

Chapter 20

The message arrived late in the evening, at a time when most had retired for the night. Galin had been expecting something like this, considering the open contempt he had shown the lord high priest at their last meeting.

He had left his apartments in the Royal House, a perk enjoyed by each of the Council of Seven, with a grin and a wink to the guards on duty, letting them know his companion for the night would not be happy if their rendezvous was delayed. The two guardsmen shared a lecherous grin at the thought of the commander meeting this night with the wife or daughter of some high-ranking noble.

Galin made his way past the guard to a seldom-used stairwell in the rear of the Royal House. Two levels down was a back way into the cellars, to the level just above the dungeons where unrepentant enemies of the Crown historically disappeared. Though the cellar door seldom saw use, the hinges were well oiled and the door made nary a sound when Galin placed his shoulder to it and gave a good push. Closing it securely behind him, Galin paused and used his flint and iron to strike fire to the small torch he carried under his robe.

The dancing light from the torch cast eerie shadows upon the crates and barrels surrounding him. Whatever rested within these containers had, as told by the thick spiderwebs running around and between them, been forgotten long ago. Allowing his vision to adjust to the torchlight, Galin noticed footprints in the dust of the floor that appeared to lead to, and then away from, the door he had just come through. Pulling the hood of his robe up to conceal his face and keeping his eyes down, he followed the footprints through the maze of containers, broken chairs, and old furnishings, through gray veils of cobwebs and past the many stout pillars supporting the structure above.

Finally, the footprints led him to another door. This one was in the same condition of disrepair as the one he had used to gain entry, but the dust on the floor before it suggested it had been opened recently. Galin looked around the cellar, more from habit than from any real belief he might not be alone. Then he gave three evenly spaced, quiet, yet insistent, knocks.

Immediately following the third knock, the door swung silently toward him, forcing him to step out of its path. In the open doorway stood an old man, a servant of the Temple for many decades and highly trusted by the lord high priest. The old servant stepped aside to allow the commander to pass and, while Galin waited, closed and secured the door. Satisfied, he took up a torch flickering in a metal bracket on the wall. Silently, he led Galin to the base of a stairwell which appeared not to have been used in living memory.

Here the old man spoke: "You must go up this stairwell m'lord," he said, "but have a care. At every landing there will be a door. Each door has been sealed and walled from the other side so none on that side know a door is there. Go to the eighth landing and upon that door you will knock, exactly as you knocked on the cellar door."

With this instruction, the old man stepped aside and allowed Galin to begin his ascent.

Galin climbed the stairs warily. He noticed that, although dust and cobwebs marked the stairwell as seldom-used, the smoothed edges of the stones of the stairs bore witness to centuries of wear. His only light was from the torch he still carried and there were no openings in the exterior wall that would mark the location of this secret stairwell from the outside.

He reached the landing serving as the halfway, turned, and continued up to the first door. Here he stopped to examine the ancient oak door, still sturdy for all of its years. The hinges, he noticed, hung on the outside and were well oiled. He wondered what part of the Temple lay beyond the threshold, as he turned to continue his climb.

Galin climbed past six more doors, each identical to the last, and each hanging on well-oiled hinges. When he finally reached the eighth door, he paused before knocking in the same sequence he had used on the cellar door below. A moment passed…then another, and then he heard a faint scraping coming from the other side. There was a click, as of a latch being thrown, and then the door shuddered and began to open outward onto the landing. Once again Galin had to retreat from an opening door, but this time the opened door revealed a well-lit foyer.

Galin did not recognize the slim, middle-aged man standing before him. The personal butler of the high priest was rarely seen outside the temple. He greeted Galin with a deep bow and, with a wave of his arm, stepped aside to allow him entrance.

"If it pleases m'lord, you won't need a torch in the chambers of the lord high priest," the butler said, extending his hand.

Galin passed him the torch, which the butler extinguished before hanging from a bracket on a tall cabinet beside the now-closed door. Looking back at the door he had just come through, Galin found it was no longer there. In its place was a section of paneled wall, nearly indistinguishable from the rest of the paneling making up the interior of the room. Only a practiced eye would notice the slight rise in the height of the surrounding molding, giving the only hint a doorway was there.

Looking at the floor in front of the now-hidden door, Galin could see that something had been recently moved from that spot. He was sure that if he were to enter this foyer from any of the other doors he spied in the room, the tall cabinet would be positioned directly in front of the hidden door.

"This way, m'lord," said the butler, leading him through a portal opposite the hidden door and into a small library.

The library walls were lined with rows of shelves and cabinets containing both books and scrolls. There was a buffet to one side, on which rested several decanters containing an assortment of wines and liqueurs, as well as the goblets and chalices used for their consumption. In the center of the room was a round table about six feet in diameter, the top of which appeared to be carved from a single piece of honey-colored hardwood. There were two chairs at the table, the larger of which was occupied by the Lord High Priest Mayhew.

Galin paused upon seeing him and Mayhew met his gaze with unconcealed confidence. Simultaneously raising his glass and nodding his head, he sent a wordless greeting to Galin, then motioned toward the empty chair across the table from his. Galin glanced at the chair, unsure if he did not want to remain standing for what he suspected was to come. He then acquiesced as the butler pulled the seat out for him.

"What will you be drinking, m'lord?" the butler asked.

"Brandy," replied Galin curtly, never shifting his gaze away from Mayhew, who now wore an arrogant smile. Once the brandy was poured and placed before Galin, the butler bowed and took his leave. All the while Galin and Mayhew continued to lock eyes.

Galin sat erect, hands on his knees, facing the high priest while trying to hide his impatience. Mayhew delicately sipped from his chalice, his smile growing ever larger.

Finally, he spoke.

"You really should enjoy your brandy, Commander. Few have had the opportunity to sit in that chair and enjoy the very finest from the fields and vineyards of the Temple. Why, I doubt Ammon himself has ever sampled a brandy as exquisite."

"So, you brought me here to sample your brandy?" Galin asked, a little too quickly.

"I brought you here to discuss your failure," Mayhew stated flatly, correctly sensing the commander was on edge.

Seeking to exercise greater control, Galin slowly reached for the goblet in front of him. He examined the dark amber elixir as he swirled it around the glass. Then he brought it to his lips and, after a dramatic pause, downed it in one gulp, causing Mayhew to shudder that so fine a beverage should be consumed as if it were a flagon of ale.

Galin saw this and smiled in satisfaction as he placed the empty goblet back on the table.

"Of what failure do you speak, priest?" he asked.

Mayhew gazed at him steadily, a hint of amusement in the slight upturn of the corners of his mouth.

"This very morning, at the training grounds," the high priest began, "it seems some of your...agents...accosted the Harbinger. I hear the most courageous died at his hands, while the others failed to engage him, preferring instead to soak their loins in fear."

At these words Galin's demeanor instantly changed, the cold descending in waves from his next words.

"You...would dare...speak to me of courage and fear?" he growled. "You, who have never faced so much as a rodent without calling for your butlers and little gelding priest boys to kill it for you? And now you would pretend to know what lives in a warrior's heart at the moment he is called upon to put himself to the test?"

Galin rose so suddenly from the chair that he nearly sent the heavy antique crashing to the floor. Then he leaned his frame as far as it would go across the table toward his host, whose eyes now reflected apprehension in place of arrogance. With teeth tightly clenched and eyes ablaze, he spat out his next words.

"What lives in your heart, priest? When have you ever filled your hand with iron and fought for anything? What have you ever risked?!"

Mayhew was motionless under Galin's cold stare, and remained so as the anger slowly ebbed from the commander's eyes.

Presently Galin straightened and stared silently down at the priest, allowing the last of his fury to subside. Then he turned to the buffet behind him and, grabbing the decanter of brandy, filled his goblet to the rim. He downed half of its liquid contents in one swallow before returning to his seat where he placed both his goblet and the decanter on the table before him. He then turned his attention back to his host.

"With regard to whatever occurred in the training grounds this morning, I had nothing to do with it," he lied.

Mayhew regarded Galin through narrowed eyes. Did the commander think his bluster and bravado would dull the senses of the High Priest? Leaning back in his chair, more of a miniature throne really, he appraised the situation before further pressing Galin.

"Then I must ask again," Mayhew said, "as I have in the past: when and how do you intend to strike?"

"What difference the 'when' and 'how' to you, priest? It's not as if you have much choice but to await my actions. That is, unless you want to again try your cowardly poisons and risk killing half the court in the attempt."

Now it was Mayhew's turn to become angry and he fairly launched himself from his seat.

"We of the Temple have ways beyond anything you could imagine!" he said, his face contorted in momentary anger. "If blood and fire is all that you respect, ..." Mayhew caught himself in mid-sentence.

Galin stared wide-eyed at the fat, angry high priest. His mind worked furiously, taking in what had just been said, as well as what had been left unsaid. Ever since he was a child, he had heard bits and pieces of stories... legends... but no. That is all they were, just stories and legends. This time when he spoke, he allowed a calm to come to his voice.

"The training goes well, priest," he sighed, referring to the additional training ordered by the King in preparation for the return to the motherland in the spring. "Too well, in fact, so the sooner it be done, the sooner we can abandon this idea of prophesy before it takes on a life of its own. But with the Harbinger under the protection of the Royal House it will require planning, detail, and the right man, or men."

"So?" Mayhew wondered where Galin was going with this.

"Soon, priest," the commander said. "It will be soon. That is all you need to know."

They exchanged stares for a moment more before the High Priest, realizing he would get neither an admission of failure nor more insight into the commander's plans, called for his butler to see him back through the secret passageway.

Long after Galin had gone, Mayhew sat alone and pondered the events leading to their present dilemma. The commander was right in that it would take extraordinary skill and planning to execute an assassination while the Harbinger was residing in the Royal House. After the servant's death by poisoning, Ammon would never allow the Harbinger or his disciple to reside anywhere else.

Patience.

Patience was the key at this point. He would allow the commander his chance. If Galin could succeed without further involvement of the Temple, then so much the better, but Mayhew had real doubts about Galin and his resources. This was not direct and open battle, a field on which he was sure Galin excelled. Assassination should be a subtle and delicate thing, even when achieved by violent means.

It is only prudent, Mayhew thought, *to have a contingency plan prepared.*

Chapter 21

For the remainder of the day following the incident in the training yard, Raymond remained uncharacteristically silent. If Hanshee noticed, he did not let on. He was prone to stretches of silence himself. But, being Hanshee, he *had* noticed and was waiting patiently for Raymond to approach him with whatever was troubling his mind.

The next morning, as Laretha and Aleria were clearing away the residue of the morning meal, Raymond pulled Hanshee out onto the balcony overlooking the private terrace.

As usual, the morning was cold, but the stillness of the air made the cold bearable. Hanshee followed Raymond out to the very edge of the balcony, where he waited patiently while his charge gazed into the distance, searching the sheer rock walls and the distant mountain peaks for the right words with which to express his thoughts. After a while, Raymond turned to Hanshee and spoke, his expression reflecting the depth of his concern.

"Hanshee my friend, I find it difficult to place into words what you have meant to me over the last six or so moons. You have saved my life more times than I might even know. From the day you pulled me from the river of dreams," he smiled, "and nursed me back to life, you have been my protector and provider and defender. I know it is due only to your efforts that I stand here now."

Hanshee remained silent as Ray paused to gather his thoughts before continuing.

"I call you 'friend' because it is the only word I know that describes what you have been to me, and yet, it does not go far enough."

Again, Raymond allowed his gaze to drift to the distant peaks as he steeled himself to express what was on his mind. Hanshee waited patiently for Raymond to continue.

Allowing himself a huge sigh, Raymond again turned to Hanshee, meeting his attentive gaze and resolving to get to the crux of his concerns.

"Hanshee, I have seen you confront eight men in single combat. With only one exception, each of those men are now dead." Raymond paused, waiting for some reaction, but Hanshee's steady gaze never changed as he waited for Ray to continue.

"I know the men you have killed were most likely not good men, and some of it may have even been necessary, but..." At this point Raymond appeared to lose the thread of what he wanted to say, and his eyes pleaded with Hanshee to understand what he found so difficult to convey.

Sensing how distraught his friend had become, Hanshee spoke up. He did not attempt to defend his actions, but rather to draw from Raymond the words he could not find.

"What would you have had me do?" Hanshee asked in a soft and slightly puzzled voice, the vapor of his breath rising in the stillness of the morning air.

"I don't know, but it seems there should have been other ways...other means of dealing with those men. I am starting to wonder... and I am ashamed to say this as you have been more than a friend to me... but when I see you take life so casually, it makes me wonder." Raymond steeled himself to say what was on his mind. "I wonder will it always be this way... and am I truly safe with you? Could you one day kill even me with such ease?"

Raymond searched Hanshee's face for the answers to his questions, but found none in that stoic gaze. He shivered, whether from the cold or from the thought that what he imagined the future to hold could come true, he did not know.

Seeing his friends' distress, Hanshee finally spoke.

"Way-mon," he said as he placed a comforting hand upon Ray's shoulder, "let us go inside to the fire, and I will try to answer your many questions."

Raymond allowed Hanshee to guide him toward the doors and out of the cold. The servant women had finished their cleaning and the two now had the chamber to themselves. Once inside, Hanshee immediately discarded his robe, and moved to take a seat on one of the cushions beside the large fireplace. Raymond moved toward a nearby chair, then hesitated, and chose a cushion on the floor as well. There he sat, not quite as comfortably as Hanshee, and waited for the promised words.

Hanshee first looked into the fire as his mind searched for the words he knew he needed to address the concerns…and fears… he saw growing in Ray. The dancing flames seemed to have a calming effect on his mind, allowing his thoughts first to drift, then to coalesce, into what he hoped would be the right thoughts, leading to the right words, to quell the fears he sensed in his charge.

"Since the day I pulled you from the river," Hanshee began slowly, "I knew you were different. There were no signs of man at the river. I know, because I searched up and down its banks for many days and saw none. Yet there I was compelled to wait, and there you appeared. Your dress told me you were different, from a land far away, but my thoughts went no farther and I took hold of the task then at hand, the task of saving your life. Since that time, I have tried to understand you, and help you to understand me. I feel we have an understanding in some ways, but there still remains a chasm between us, one for which there is no easy bridge.

"In the time we have spent together you have told me many things about your world." Raymond opened his mouth to question this, but was silenced by Hanshee's raised hand.

"You have told me these things, often without saying a word," Hanshee smiled, "for the way a man lives can tell his tale much more clearly than his words. Words can be confusing, or incomplete, or twisted, if there is intent to deceive.

"Where you are from, you lived a life of ease," Hanshee continued, "as is not seen in my world unless one be a king, or a priest, or a very wealthy man; a city dweller. But a life of privilege and riches, like that of a king or a priest, brings with it certain...behaviors...certain patterns of thought and beliefs. These I have not found in you and, if we had not been consumed by the task of survival, I may have given more thought to the mystery of you. Survival... the work of survival... has not been a concern since we were brought here by the Priest Jusaan, and my mind has wandered back to those early days... and to the mystery of the river and the mystery of you."

Raymond was quiet as Hanshee paused, took up the iron poker, and began to stir the embers in the fireplace while pulling his thoughts together. The shifting logs cause new flames to appear, but the heat was still comfortable on their bare skin after the time spent in the cold of the balcony. Satisfied the fire would continue to burn evenly and well, his thoughts once again focused, Hanshee put the iron down and continued.

"I was trained by my clan to be a hunter and a warrior," he said, gazing into the flames. "I surpassed my brethren in all ways and, when the need arose, was chosen for the Test." Turning once again to Raymond, Hanshee held his gaze with the intensity of his stare. "The Test is an awesome thing."

As he spoke, Hanshee's vision seemed to change focus, looking beyond Raymond, beyond these quarters and this castle and beyond this nation, to visions hidden from all eyes save his own. Then his eyes became sharp and clear as he went on with his story.

"I survived... and began my training, with the High Priests of the Blue Mountains, to be Maiyochi"

Ray knew there was much more to be said; about The Test and the training to become Maiyochi, about the Blue Mountains and the High Priests who dwelled there. But he knew if these things were to ever be discussed, it would not be at this time.

"The priests spoke of many things. They spoke of mysteries beyond my understanding," continued Hanshee. "I wondered why these mysteries were spoken of, and of what use they could be to one such as I? Those were the thoughts of a child; not a child in years, but a child in wisdom. One might say an infant in wisdom" Hanshee chuckled, "as I have come to understand with each passing day more of the reasons why the priests chose to bestow upon me stories and teachings I then thought of as the ramblings of self-important elders."

"Once, around the fire, after several difficult and dangerous days of training, when I thought myself too tired even to hold on to the thought, the priests who were present began to speak of places far different from where we dwelled. These places they spoke of, a warrior could not reach by foot, nor by boat, nor could a warrior reach these places even should he become a bird! But the priest knew these places were real, and they spoke among themselves of the wonders and mysteries one could experience there. They spoke among themselves but they spoke to me, I know now, for some knowledge is only there for those who have eyes to see and ears to hear. Since that night I have not often thought about these 'other worlds', but these memories have been finding their way back into my thoughts of late."

Hanshee regarded Raymond with as serious a look as he could as he spoke his next words.

"I believe you have come here, to this world, from one of those other worlds. I do not know of your world. In truth, I need know only that it exists. We - you and I - are here in my world. And in my world, a warrior must always be prepared to strive, to fight, and yes, to slay, if he wishes to survive into the next day.

"You have questions of me, Way-mon. You call me your friend and more, yet you fear me. I will tell you now, as I have told you in times past, you have no reason to fear me. You are my reason for being here, in this place, at this time. I would never turn against you and will not desert you in this place or any other. My duty is to return you to my people, to the priests of the Blue Mountains, because it is *your* duty to save my people. And though I first saw you as *only* a duty, time has passed. We have come far and done much. Now I wish to see you, and be seen by you, as a true friend."

Now Hanshee tried to address the root of Ray's concerns.

"As for the taking of life, you are right I have slain many men since we met, and the slaying of those men troubles you so that all you can recall is their deaths. But remember, I have faced more than I have felled. In the city of Aggipoor, the two guardsmen on horseback and the farmer of swine I did not slay. When they faced me, they did not present a threat. One guardsman was thrown from his horse and did not rise, while the other fell to his knees in surrender. As for the swine farmer," Hanshee shrugged, "he was never a threat.

"The taking of a life is serious...not a thing to be done lightly," Hanshee said. "There are reasons to take life, many reasons, but if done for the wrong reason, or for no reason, it can turn a single trouble into many; it can turn a small trouble into a mountain.

"The thieves I killed because they would have killed first you, then me. Think back! We were in a strange place and would have been judged harshly if we could not escape. We had no time for struggle. The same goes for the guard who trapped us between buildings. Do you not see this to be true?"

Hanshee paused to allow Raymond time to consider this.

"You are right Hanshee," he said slowly. "As I look back on those deaths, as shocking as they were for me, you really had no choice if we were to escape. It is just …you are right, I do come from a life of ease…I see that now. Though, had I never come here, I would swear my life had its share of hardship and peril. But I had never seen death up close before. I had seen the dead…people who had died of a sickness, or in an accident… but to see killing up close, at its most brutal…with edged weapons used to stab and hack and slash… to see the blood and bone… and the guts…and their eyes as they die…"

Raymond had to shake the images from his head before turning to face Hanshee. When he next spoke, shame and regret shaped his words.

"I am sorry that, even for an instant, I thought you were a murderer," Raymond said. "Back in Aggipoor you did what was necessary and you saved us; you saved me."

Hanshee remained silent. He felt Raymond was just now coming to terms with a truth he had avoided since their escape from the first city. It was a truth most warriors took for granted, but for someone like Raymond it was clearly a huge hurdle that must be overcome before he could truly move forward in this world. Hanshee knew that constant exposure to battle drove some men mad. How much greater would be the impact on one who had never seen, nor truly imagined, the grim, messy reality of a life-or-death struggle?

Hanshee felt compelled to offer a silent prayer for Ray's sanity before he spoke

"Then it is the death of Botha that troubles you?"

Raymond dropped his head to gather his thoughts, considering the question carefully before replying.

"He was a sadist, a butcher, an evil man. That was plain for all to see," he said.

"But he did not attack us. I did not have to fight him," Hanshee finished the thought for him.

Raymond looked sheepishly up at his protector. "Yes," he said, "that's part of it, I think."

"Botha's slaying was a calculation," Hanshee said. "We were in a camp full of armed warriors. Though welcomed by the priest, it was clear Galin only tolerated us. We would have been provided for the entertainment of his men if not for Jusaan."

Hanshee locked eyes with Ray.

"Do you remember that morning?"

"How could I forget it?" asked Raymond. "I had never seen anything so brutal, so…sickening, in my life. Even your killing of the guard of Aggipoor was merciful by comparison."

"You are right, Way-mon. It was brutal, and sickening. In Botha there was corruption, an evil that should not be allowed to exist. I saw a chance to remove an evil and, as Maiyochi, I must always stand against evil.

"But even more," he continued, "there were messages being sent that day. The brutality of the morning, though presented as entertainment for the men, was meant as an embarrassment to the priest and a challenge to me. Had we shown weakness Galin would have had us killed in our sleep, again to embarrass the priest, and all would have claimed ignorance."

"Killing you in your sleep is probably as difficult as killing you when you are awake," Raymond said. Hanshee dipped his head in gracious acceptance of the complement before continuing.

"But it was also a challenge to me, by Galin, put forth before all of his men. In a camp of armed warriors, weakness will invite attack. My defeat of Botha… *how* I defeated Botha… was a message to all. To Jusaan, it gave strength, so he could hold his head high and not be cowed by Galin and the warriors that surrounded him. To Galin and his men, the message was clear: the very best among them would perish if he were to try me, on orders or no. And, Way-mon, it allowed me to punish evil as it should be punished! I was needlessly brutal in the slaying of the beast, so that all would think twice before again having sport with human life."

Only the crackling of the logs broke the silence as Raymond digested the logic and the truth behind Hanshee's words. Hanshee scanned his face for some sign of understanding, while Raymond continued to scan the flames as he considered all that had been said. Presently, Raymond turned back to Hanshee.

"The Citadel guard in the training yard yesterday? He was a challenge in the same way as was Botha, right?"

"In a way, yes," said Hanshee.

"But?" Ray pressed.

"The situation was more dangerous," said Hanshee. "There had already been an attempt on our life, by poison. I expected another. Four warriors stepped forth in the training yard, all ready to test me. Weakness would encourage attack but a strong and swift end to one of their number…"

"It made the others fall back," finished Ray.

"The opponent was stopped, or at least stalled, feeling the need to rethink an attack at that time," said Hanshee. "Stopped or stalled; either gives us the space to escape, which we did."

Hanshee could see that, although Raymond nodded his head in acknowledgement, he still struggled with the need to take a human life. He sensed this would be a continuing struggle for Ray. Still, he thought progress was being made, and Raymond was beginning to erase the picture of him as a bloodthirsty and thoughtless killer. Hanshee took the opportunity of Ray's slowly changing mindset to press him on one more point.

"Way-mon," he said, "I fear before our journey is over, you will be called upon to defend yourself. When you do, it is most important that you triumph. You must be able to make the journey to the Blue Mountains with or without me."

These words fell heavily on Raymond's mind.

"Hanshee, I'm not a warrior."

Leaning forward, Hanshee reached out a reassuring hand and grasped Ray's forearm. Mustering all the confidence he could, he spoke.

"Not yet, but you have the spirit of a warrior! I will continue to train you, Way-mon. When the day comes, you will do what you must."

Chapter 22

The next month was marked by more winter storms. High winds and copious snowfall combined to make everyday life in the mountain kingdom of Pith difficult for all.

For the farmers and the growers, the winter harvest was rushed in an effort to save as much of the crop as they could before it was ruined by the cold. Those herders who were tardy bringing their cattle and sheep down from the high elevations were finding more and more lost to cold and starvation. Even in the valley of Stronghold itself, the early snows and the deep accumulations meant the livestock had to be fed from the stores of hay and grain much earlier than was normal in the winter.

The harshness of the early winter cut short the time for slaughter which, along with the animals lost to cold, starvation, and predation, meant shortages of meat for the taverns and the butcher shops, as well as shortages of leather, horn, and bone for the craftsmen. The cities bore the brunt of this, but almost everyone in the nation was in some way affected by the various shortages and hardships caused by the weather. Indeed, only the woodsmen, those who made a living in the winter months by gathering firewood for sale to the populace, seemed to thrive in the worsening weather.

The military, now in the middle of training for their anticipated campaign to return to the motherland, found their efforts ground to a halt. Now the various barracks were not just full but overcrowded due to the heavy recruiting that had taken place to fill the ranks for the coming expedition. The pressure caused by large numbers of armed and aggressive men living in confined spaces made for an atmosphere of smoldering hostility and violent conflict based on age, rank, social standing, family, mother tongue, or simple proximity. The officers were at wits' end as the number of assaults, injuries, and occasional deaths, continued to climb.

The cities and towns were of no help. There was a reason most training garrisons were located far from population centers. Those allowing any soldiers at all often limited their hospitality to officers, or regulars in small groups. This was hardly enough to release the growing pressure in the overcrowded garrisons.

No shortages were evident in the Citadel. King Ammon IV, his nobles, priests, and fortunate guests, continued to exist as if the hardships being experienced across the land were nonexistent. The Citadel Guard were aware of the worsening conditions, but their duty ended at the Citadel walls. Additional forces were brought in to address any issues that might arise if those in the city discovered just how well those in the Citadel continued to live. These newcomers were more than happy to be assigned duties in the "land of plenty".

As honored guests of the Royal House, the routine established for Hanshee and Raymond showed little change They still had much more time on their hands than Hanshee was accustomed to, but this only served to provide more consistent training for Ray.

On a typical day, they arose early for a session of pre-dawn exercise before partaking of the morning meal. After the meal, which Hanshee characterized as much too rich to eat on a daily basis, they spent the next couple of hours discussing things such as the warrior's code, philosophy, tactics, and strategy. This was initiated by Hanshee so Raymond would better understand the thought processes necessary for a fighting man's survival.

This was followed by stretching and more exercise in the form of drills, where Hanshee would instruct Raymond on the mechanics and targeting of a proper block, parry, or strike. Ray hated these sessions, as they were mostly consumed with repetition. It seemed to him he would perform a motion hundreds of times before Hanshee was satisfied with his balance, leverage, and power. Then he would have to duplicate that exact form hundreds more times before Hanshee believed it was taking hold in his subconscious mind. "Becoming one with you," is how Hanshee described it.

Ray was always happy when the midday meal arrived.

There would sometimes be additional lessons after the midday meal, mostly archery, the bow and arrow being the only weapon Hanshee would allow Ray to train with at this point. After the intense exertion of the morning training, Raymond regarded archery as relaxing. Despite the weather, he came to enjoy the time spent in their private courtyard and quickly developed a level of skill with the bow surprising even him.

Late afternoons were not the busiest of times around the Citadel, and it had become customary for Jusaan to stop by briefly to check up on his charges. Though he was still responsible for their comfort, Hanshee and Raymond were thankful he had delegated the bulk of these responsibilities to Laretha. Jusaan's visits were more along the lines of maintaining contact and control over the empire's two most valued guests. They were, after all, the keys to his future.

Another afternoon occurrence that was beginning to increase in frequency were informal sessions with King Ammon IV. These sessions were first explained as a time the monarch had chosen to become better acquainted with the royal guests. These meetings were sometimes held over a late midday meal or, if later in the day, over goblets of hot spiced wine. Jusaan would usually arrive at the guest quarters with a retinue of four armed guards; a precaution against another attempt on the life of the Harbinger. They would escort Hanshee and Raymond to a parlor just off of the royal chambers, or sometimes the royal library, or wherever the King might decide was appropriate for the day. Food and drinks would be served and King Ammon would attempt to engage in polite conversation with Hanshee.

At least that is how it began.

Jusaan would sit in, as the King was not as accomplished in speaking or understanding the old tongue. Raymond's attendance was requested so that Hanshee would feel more at ease. Usually, before Jusaan would ask Hanshee the King's question, he and the King would briefly discuss what to ask and how it should be posed. This was done in the Pithian tongue, a bastardized language which included the different languages and dialects from the tribes and cultures the Pith had assimilated over their long journey from the Blue Mountains to Stronghold. Although many of the proper names for objects and places survived, the conversational language of Pith bore almost no resemblance to the old tongue.

This was no impediment to Raymond, who had been able to understand and speak the Pithian language since their days in the Southern Mountains under Galin. He had mastered a facial expression of bored distraction when accompanying Hanshee wherever Jusaan had determined he needed to be. His real mission, one he was now quite good at, was to hear what others were saying in languages they thought would mask their thoughts and intentions from their guests.

So it was that, after the very first session with the King, Raymond informed Hanshee the conversation between Ammon and Jusaan centered on the best ways to interrogate him without appearing to interrogate him. Hanshee had speculated about this and was glad Raymond was there to confirm it. Putting their heads together, they determined Hanshee should play along as best he could. He would be truthful in his descriptions of his people and their culture, but provide only enough detail to keep the interest of their hosts piqued. In this way they could keep the game going, while unbeknownst to their Pithian hosts, they would enhance their own intelligence-gathering.

One of the topics touched upon with some frequency was different routes to and from Hanshee's home on the western slopes of the Blue Mountains. These mountains were known in the east to be of such height as to be impossible to cross. Many times, Hanshee was asked about the existence of high mountain passages connecting the eastern and western slopes. He was also asked about the theory that, at the northernmost ranges, there were places where the mountains decreased significantly in height and could safely be crossed. This assumed the cooperation of the extreme weather normal for that region of the world.

There was, of course, the passage followed by the ancient Pith on their journey out of the mountains so long ago, but that route was known to be hazardous and fraught with perils even then. In the almost 1,000 years since, the small desert region that began at the eastern edge of the corridor had, due to changes in weather patterns and upheavals in the landscape, expanded to the point it was now referred to simply as "the Great Desert". It was so immense and so daunting that it was thought to be impassible by a large force.

Many were the times Ammon had Jusaan steer the conversation to how Hanshee had navigated the various dangers keeping their two worlds separated. Equally interesting to the King, though he would deny it, was how Hanshee intended to return to his people once his exile into the nations of the east concluded.

Thanks to Raymond, Hanshee knew these questions were critical to the King's ambition of bringing to fruition the Fourth Prophesy. Hanshee wanted to avoid answering them and did so artfully for several sessions. Upon discussing possible answers with Ray, it occurred to them that, in this instance, the truth would not only be of no use to the Pith, it might actually dissuade them from attempting to reach the Blue Mountains by a similar route.

When next Hanshee was asked about his journey to the west, he offered an honest, if abbreviated, response.

Handling these queries as he and Raymond had discussed, Hanshee informed the King there was indeed a secret west-to-east passage through the Blue Mountains. Unfortunately, it was a one-way passage. When greeted by the perplexed expressions following his pronouncement, Hanshee explained that the passage started on the western slopes of the mountains, in a cave about three-quarters of the way to the crest.

When asked if he knew the way, Hanshee claimed ignorance, saying his people had carried him to this secret place blindfolded.

He said the cave extended into the mountain for some distance and seemed to become narrower as it progressed. Hanshee thought they walked into the depths of the cave for about a day, although he admitted it was difficult to tell, as there was no sun or moon visible by which to determine time. They walked by torchlight, deeper and deeper into the darkness until a dim shaft of light told them they were nearing another break in the rock.

The cave ended in a narrow opening about the height of a man. As Hanshee claimed to have soon discovered, this opening was on the eastern side of the mountain, about 200 feet up the smooth, sheer face of a cliff. Hanshee had been lowered down by rope. The only way to get back up to that particular cave was to be hauled back up by rope. Once he and his provisions had been lowered, and the rope pulled back up, it was then his task to make his way down the eastern slopes of the mountain.

And so, he explained, even if one could identify that particular cliff face, and that particular opening high up its face, which he doubted, one could only reach it with the help of someone already there to haul him up. He had never considered it a place to return to when his exile was complete.

Finishing this story, Hanshee smiled hugely, as if very pleased to be sharing it with those who had so graciously taken him in. In truth, he smiled at the frustration on the faces of his hosts, a frustration evident in their tone of voice, as they spoke between themselves about the information he had shared.

Presently, Jusaan turned to Hanshee with another question from the King, this time concerning the Great Desert and how he had managed to cross it. Was the expanse really so wide? Was it really so sparse of life? Were there any provisions or water to be had there?

Hanshee's voice took on a tone of dread as he discussed the Great Desert. It was indeed great and indeed a desert, he said, so it was appropriately named. He described it as a directionless wasteland of blowing sand, with the occasional rocky outcropping. Traveling light and swift, as a lone man can, it had taken him almost an entire moon to make the crossing. There was little vegetation to be found there. If not for his provisions, he would have starved.

Then his face lit up as he revealed he had found plenty of water! His people had given him a map drawn on a piece of hide. It marked several water holes he was told would get him through the desert alive, and they had been right! He had followed the course set on the map, a jagged, zigzag course with no rhyme or reason, but at the end of every line had been a watering hole, sometimes with enough water for three or four men!

This pronouncement again caused frowns to appear on the faces of his hosts, as they realized they could not possibly cross such a desert, even with a small scouting party, much less the two expeditionary forces training to make the journey.

After a few minutes of aimless conversation, the King had Jusaan ask Hanshee how he intended to make it back to his people. Hanshee responded that part of his ordeal was to wander the east until he had discovered another way to return. He did not know how long he would wander, but he expected the answer to come to him in a dream, or so he had been told.

After more idle chatter, and a few more drinks, the King stood, signaling the gathering was over and they could take their leave. Hanshee and Raymond were glad to be excused. Once back at their quarters they laughed about the dismay on the faces of Jusaan and Ammon after hearing Hanshee's stories of the journey away from his homeland.

"They were really at a loss as to how to press you without pressing you," Ray laughed. "When you told them about the water holes in the Great Desert... *enough for three or four men* ... their faces completely sunk! It was all I could do to pretend I didn't understand."

Hanshee gave a chuckle at the memory of King Ammon's expression going from one of pleased anticipation to one of disappointment. Then he brought Raymond back to earth by taking on a more serious tone.

"They will call for us again soon," he said. "And they will be better prepared."

Hanshee was right. They were called to sit with the King the very next day, and this time there were several maps lying haphazardly on the table where they were being served.

So anxious was King Ammon to get the questioning underway that Jusaan, in an attempt to slow His Majesty down, peppered a liberal amount of small talk with every question that the King wanted addressed. The King's frustration was obvious; he almost fumed at the fact his simple questions took so long for the priest to translate, and even longer before the Harbinger supplied anything close to an answer. At one point he snatched up a map, furiously unrolled it and, between clinched teeth, spat out a direct question to Hanshee while repeatedly stabbing his finger on a particular point on the map for emphasis.

Hanshee looked from the King to the Jusaan and back again, as if trying to understand what was expected of him. King Ammon looked from Hanshee to Jusaan and back again, his frustration causing him to forget Hanshee did not speak the Pithian tongue and struggling to understand why his questions were never truly answered.

Jusaan, looking from Ammon to Hanshee and back again like a spectator at a tennis match, tried to appease, yet rein in, his monarch. All the while apologizing to Hanshee, hoping the King's display of frustration would not drive him to silence.

After a short time, seeing that this was getting nowhere, the King dismissed his 'honored guest' with an impatient wave of his hand. Jusaan rose with the intention of escorting Hanshee and Raymond to their quarters, but he sank slowly back into his seat, remaining almost motionless under the raptor-like stare of his angry liege.

This parting scene led to another bout of mirth once the guards had deposited Hanshee and Raymond in their quarters for the evening.

****

The following day was bright, cold, crisp, and clear; a truly magnificent winter day. Hanshee and Raymond were expecting that the scene from the day before would give the King pause in his pursuit of intelligence but, to their surprise, there was a knock on the outer door of their chambers about an hour after the midday meal.

Raymond, now well-schooled in his duty as an acolyte of the warrior-priest, hurried to open the door. There he found four guards who were prepared to escort them into the presence of the King. Hurriedly donning their robes, they fell in with them, the two guards in front leading the way, their shields shining, their short swords in polished scabbards, while the remaining two, with swords, bows, and quivers filled with arrows, brought up the rear. As they proceeded down the corridor, Raymond spoke to Hanshee in a tongue only they understood.

"I wonder where we will sit with His Majesty today," he asked casually. "Probably in the map room, so he won't run out of charts to stab at."

This brought a quick smile to Hanshee's lips, before he again took up the mantle of the stoic warrior-priest.

Through massive doors they passed, and up a circular stone stairwell, before passing through double doors and turning left down a long, wide hallway. Here the walls were recessed at intervals to allow for displays of various trophies and artifacts thought to be both decorative and important by the staff of the Royal House.

It was as they proceeded down this hallway that a stray thought lingered in Raymond's mind, and he wondered why he had never before seen archers inside either of the main Citadel buildings.

Then something else caught his attention. He no longer heard the sound of footsteps behind them. Still keeping pace with the two forward guards, Raymond glanced back to see why.

He first noticed the other two guards were no longer behind them, which he had already surmised when he could no longer hear their footsteps. Casting his eyes back the way they had come, he caught sight of them. Instead of turning left down the long hall, the two guards had come to a halt after passing through the double doors. They now stood with their backs to the wall directly behind them.

Why'd they stop there, Raymond wondered, as he again turned to face the guards leading the way. Something made him take another look back, and this time what he saw sent a chill through his entire body.

The two guards were notching arrows!

Turning to face front once again, Raymond was unsure of what he had witnessed. Was this a threat to him and Hanshee? Was this a dangerous situation, or was he on the verge of overreacting? His mind seemed to be working in slow motion as he studied the guards walking before them, proceeding them down the hall as if all was well. It was not until the guard directly in front of him quickly stepped to his left, toward a recess in the wall, that everything fell into place, and Ray's thoughts instantly went from sluggish and confused to assured.

Acting on instinct, Raymond screamed Hanshee's name as he lunged to his right, throwing his shoulder into his friend with as much force as he could muster, knocking Hanshee toward the recess in the wall to his right; the recess into which the other guard was ducking. As soon as he shouldered Hanshee out of the way, Ray felt a hard blow to the right side of his upper back.

Something hit him like a sledge hammer, spinning him around and sending him crashing into the stone wall beyond the recess to his right! As his left shoulder slid slowly down the wall, the shaft of the arrow protruding from his back and dragging on the stones finally broke, allowing him to fall freely into an almost sitting position, his shoulder and the remains of the arrow stabilizing him as he looked to his left at the scene unfolding before him.

He first caught sight of Hanshee, pulling a bloody knife from the lower jaw of the guard before him.

After being pushed into the recess in the wall where the guard had taken cover, Hanshee had thrown his weight against the guard, pulled the guards own blade from the sheath at his belt, and drove it upward into the soft pallet of his lower jaw, through the upper jaw, and into his brain. The guard now stared into space, wide eyed, his right hand locked on the hilt of his short sword and still moving spastically as if trying to draw it and join the combat.

Without any regard for the guard's unlikely success, Hanshee turned and faced the other guard who had ducked into the recess on the other side of the hallway.

After his initial move toward the recess on the left, the first guard spun around and found the acolyte knocked down and bleeding-out against the far wall. An instant later he spotted Hanshee, the Panther, moving with the speed of his namesake and skewering his companion, but with his unprotected back towards him. Seeing his opportunity, the guard drew his short sword and quickly advanced on the exposed back of their primary target.

He had covered half the distance between them when Hanshee spun on him with such speed and ferocity that he had only enough time to raise his sword above his head. Before he could bring it down in a killing blow, he found it held motionless, his right upper arm caught in the iron grip of this warrior-priest from hell.

Even while dealing with the shock and blossoming pain of being impaled by an arrow, Raymond still registered the surprise in the eyes of the guard that anyone could move so fast yet be so strong. He saw how the guard, with his left arm, tried in vain to bring his shield to bear, but Hanshee had positioned his right forearm to block such a move. Now Raymond saw the eyes of the guard, already widened in surprise, go wider still as Hanshee twisted his right arm and plunged the knife blade, fresh from the skull of his companion, into the guard's left side, through his ribcage, his lung, into his heart.

Then Raymond witnessed a feat of strength that had him, even in his injured state, gasping in astonishment!

Hanshee, left hand still holding onto the dying guard's right upper arm, and right hand holding tight to the hilt of the knife protruding from the guard's ribs, hoisted the guard off of his feet, pivoted in the direction of the surprised archers, and sprinted toward them!

Although both archers had a second arrow notched, they had not fired as they expected their brethren to move in and finish any killing left undone. Facing the spectacle of this crazed warrior-priest who, in the blink of an eye, had killed the first of their companions, and was now speeding toward them behind the quickly dying body of the other, they were both of the same mind and loosed their arrows simultaneously. One arrow struck the airborne guard in his lower right back with enough force that the tip completely penetrated his body and tore the fabric of Hanshee's robe about chest high. The second arrow struck the dying guard in the back of his skull, putting an end to any suffering he might have felt.

Hanshee never missed a step.

Not slowing down, even after feeling the impact of the two arrows, he heaved the body of the now dead guard to his left and out of his way, pulling the knife free as he went, and then bore down on the two archers who were both struggling to get another arrow notched. Having covered half the distance when he discarded his "human shield" he was betting he could cover the remaining thirty feet and reach the archers before they could notch and let fly with another pair of arrows.

Raymond took in this unfolding scene as if it were happening in slow motion. He saw that the guard to Hanshee's left was possessed of a cooler head than his companion, who fumbled ineptly while glancing between his arrow and the onrushing Hanshee.

When Hanshee was about twenty feet away, the cooler of the two archers had notched his arrow and was beginning to raise his bow to shooting position. Hanshee saw this too, and flicked his right arm up and forward like a striking whip, sending the knife that he had pulled from the side of the dead guard spinning toward the head of the archer! This threw the archer completely off of his shooting position as he contorted his body to avoid the bloody knife. The other guard, already panicked at the sight of the advancing Hanshee, let his arrow slip between his fumbling fingers as he involuntarily dodged the knife not even thrown at him!

Continuing the motion used to release the blade at the head of the guard, Hanshee dove for the hard stone floor, tucking his body into a perfect forward roll, while simultaneously reaching into his robe and pulled out his own ever-present blade.

Even as he twisted to avoid the knife thrown by his intended prey, the cool-headed archer released his arrow into the center of Hanshee's chest... or where his chest had been a split-second before. As the arrow passed above him, Hanshee completed his roll by extending himself forward, right arm leading the way, and plunging his knife into the archer's torso. The blade entered right below the sternum and proceeded at an angle up into the heart.

As the killing blow struck home, Hanshee turned his face to the right and gazed into the panicked eyes of the second archer. Having bent to retrieve his fallen arrow, the second archer's face was almost level with Hanshee's, who greeted him with teeth bared and a wide-eyed stare; a look that spoke of a rage-fueled insanity! Bellowing at the top of his lungs, the guard dropped both bow and arrow and bolted through the doorway to his left, just as the body of his comrade collapsed onto the cold stone floor.

Hanshee yanked his blade from the chest of the dying guard, looked briefly after the one that had fled, then turned and bolted back down the hallway. Passing the first two guards he had killed, he slid to a halt and knelt beside Raymond.

The real pain was now beginning, and it promised a fierceness the likes of which Raymond had never felt before. He closed his eyes and ground his teeth as Hanshee gently pulled him away from the wall in order to examine his wound. Then, as Hanshee lay him down in a pool of his own blood, his world thankfully went dark.

Chapter 23

Hanshee worked tirelessly over his friend.

It had taken too long for him to solicit help in getting Raymond back to their quarters and onto the table. He had not wanted to leave him lying bleeding and unconscious, but leave him he did, sprinting back up the hallway and through the same doors the archer had used to escape. There he paused and looked both ways for help. Seeing no one, Hanshee let loose with a high-pitched war cry that would have shook the dead.

Only seconds passed before footsteps were heard rushing down corridors below before ascending the circular stairwell two steps at a time. When the three Citadel Guards reached the corridor above, they pulled up in their tracks upon finding 'the Panther' standing alone in this part of the Royal House.

Holding up both hands to assure the guards he was unarmed and unhurt, he looked to the first and said in a loud voice, "Jusaan." The guard responded with a look of confusion, prompting Hanshee to speak again, this time louder and more insistently: "Jusaan!" Hanshee's eyes darted from one face to another when the guards again failed to react. Finally, he approached the lead guard and, grabbing him by his shoulders, stared into his eyes while shaking him and shouting, "Jusaan!"

He pushed the soldier toward the stairwell so hard that he stumbled, almost falling on his face before righting himself and looking back at the angry visage of Hanshee. Amazed at the stubbornness of the fellow, Hanshee pointed to the stairwell and bellowed, "Jusaaaaaaaaaan!"

"Damn it, man, he wants you to go and get the priest Jusaan!" one of his companions shouted. Understanding finally dawned on the face of the dense guard.

"Hurry!" his companion shouted, and the guard turned and dashed down the stairs as quickly as he had come up.

Hanshee followed the man with his eyes until he was sure he had finally caught on. Turning back to the two remaining guards, he motioned for them to follow, and sprinted back through the portal of the double doors and down the hallway to where Raymond was lying.

The guards, at first startled by the unexpected bloody carnage that lay before them, soon focused on where Hanshee had knelt and saw that the acolyte of the Panther lay unconscious, an arrow having pierced his back and now become visible as its head passed through his chest and tented the front of his robe. Hanshee looked pleadingly at the two guards, the language barrier preventing him from asking for the help he needed, but one of the guards, the one who had urged his fellow to go find Jusaan, saw instantly what Hanshee wanted, and turned to the second, instructing him to fetch a pallet on which to lay the acolyte so he could be carried to aid.

Raymond's prone body was laid as gently as possible onto a hastily retrieved pallet and the two guards, taking opposite ends, hoisted it into the air and headed back toward the double doors. Just as they reached the doors, Jusaan came bursting through, a look of stark panic in his eyes. He first saw the dead archer lying against the wall to his right, and then his head pivoted to his left and saw the two guards carrying a pallet with a bloody Raymond on it.

Now his eyes truly widened and he let loose with a shuddering moan that would have ended in a dejected sob had he not spied Hanshee who approached from behind the guard holding the rear of the pallet.

"Oh, my brother!" Jusaan exclaimed as he rushed forward to try to embrace Hanshee, relieved that it was only the acolyte who apparently had been killed. Hanshee stopped him with an iron grip on both his upper arms and forced the Council Priest to focus on his face.

"He is not dead," Hanshee said, as he stared into Jusaan's again startled eyes. Since Jusaan spoke the 'old tongue', Hanshee knew he would be understood.

"We must return to our quarters, quickly!" Hanshee said, shoving the priest toward the door and motioned for the two guards to follow. Hanshee and the third guard took up the rear as Jusaan, already winded from sprinting to get there, was now being pushed by the intensity of Hanshee's demand to be taken to their apartments as quickly as possible.

Once they arrived, Hanshee had Jusaan instruct the guards to place Ray on the large table. He then pulled his own knife, still bloody from killing the first archer, and proceeded to cut off Ray's blood-stained robes.

Jusaan wanted to send for the royal physician but Hanshee refused, instructing him instead to send for Laretha. Once she arrived, Hanshee had Jusaan tell her to bring as many clean cloths as she could find, and to boil a pot of water. He then had Jusaan excuse the three guards as he pulled what he needed from his bag and went to work to save his friend's life.

****

It was now well past the hour for the evening meal. Hanshee had been working nonstop on Ray for over six hours. Jusaan had rushed to bring the royal physician, only to find that, once Laretha had returned with clean cloths and water, Hanshee had bolted the door from within. None but he would be allowed to treat the acolyte. The physician, Jusaan, and King Ammon IV who had been alerted of the assassination attempt, could only await the outcome. They hoped the impending death of the acolyte would not throw off their plans for the spring.

The arrow had struck Ray on the right side of his upper back, its head partially shattering on the scapula, before proceeding into the chest cavity and coming to a stop against a rib. The force of the arrow had sent Ray's body into a spin, only coming to rest when his back struck the stone wall. This sent the shaft deeper into his body, pushing the partial head remaining on the arrow past the rib, through his pectoral muscle, and out of his chest.

The miracle was that the partial arrow head only lacerated the outer edge of Ray's lung, and his internal organs were otherwise intact. The hard part was opening him up further to remove the fragments of the arrowhead that were still inside.

There was considerable bleeding.

Hanshee had feared that Ray was losing too much blood while still on the cold floor of the corridor, but now, with all the additional bleeding after removing the bolt from his chest, cutting a larger entrance and exit wound and having to feel around to locate the pieces of arrowhead, removing them and then suturing his wound both internally and on the surface, Hanshee was amazed when he saw Ray's chest continue to rise and fall with even shallow breaths.

Laretha was a huge help, almost instinctively knowing what Hanshee needed and quickly bringing it to him, removing bloodied rags and making sure there was plenty of hot water to sterilize blades and clean the wounds. She even placed several blades in the fire, knowing that cauterization would be needed if ever they were to stop the wounds, both back and front, from bleeding Raymond completely out.

Somewhere in the middle of all this, Hanshee had taken time to prepare more of the mixture he had given Raymond when he first found him and pulled him from the river. The concoction would not only deaden the pain and keep Raymond unconscious, it would slow his metabolism so he would not need as much oxygen. This would be vital after having lost so much blood.

Hanshee was hopeful Raymond's body would replenish its blood supply to the point where the potion would no longer be needed. Then the real healing could begin.

Getting Ray to swallow the mixture was as difficult now as it had been on that day by the river. After first packing the initial wounds, Hanshee and Laretha had to prop him up and spoon small amounts into his mouth, holding his nose to induce an automatic swallowing reflex. It was crude, but effective, as long as none of the mixture went into his windpipe.

When they determined he had swallowed enough, they again laid him prone and proceeded on to the difficult portions of the treatment.

As Hanshee examined an exhausted Laretha, the bloody mess around the table, and his own red-stained hands, he at least could be content in the knowledge that he had done all that he was able to do and Raymond, still taking shallow regular breaths atop the table, at least had a chance.

After Laretha helped him to clean up the room, and brought him food and drink to replenish him and carry him through the night, he showed her out, stopping at the door to thank her wordlessly as they shared no common language. He smiled a smile of relief, touched her face, and gave a slight nod in acknowledgement of her effort. She knew what he was saying, and smiled a tired smile of a burden shared, a battle finished, and a hope that their efforts would prove to be enough.

After she left, Hanshee made a point of checking the outer corridors and was somewhat relieved to find the guard had been doubled. Still, upon returning to his quarters, he bolted the door and moved a heavy chest of drawers in front of it to further dissuade any attempt to open it during the night. After stoking both fires, Hanshee bedded down beside the table where the heavily sedated Raymond slept a peaceful sleep, masking the fact that he was in a fight for his life.

Chapter 24

High Priest Mayhew was reclining in his private quarters in the Temple's estate at the foothills of the northern mountains known as Stronghold's Crown. He very much enjoyed the estate, one of the many perks accompanying his title. There was peace and quiet there, a needed break from the schemes and intrigues of life in the Temple, which was compounded by being so close to the royal court. Here he needn't worry about the King; here he was his own king. His every word was ironclad law. Here he lived as had high priests of the past, as the monarch he secretly wished to be.

Presently, he was ruminating on what delicacies would be served him for an evening meal. Although the food from the Temple's kitchens was the talk even of those in the Royal House, Mayhew always reserved the very best for the estate. The very best food prepared by the very best chef, prepared only for him. Of course, the help was fortunate to have access to his leavings, if there were any. Sometimes even this annoyed him. Be it power and influence, or the sumptuous fare of his dinner table, the high priest did not like to share.

A knock on the outer door lifted him from his happy thoughts, abruptly bringing him back to the world.

Who would dare knock on my door so close to the hour of the evening meal? he wondered angrily. He counted on his aide to handle trifling matters, intruding on him only if necessary. A moment later, there was a soft tap on his door, followed by a pregnant silence.

"Enter!" Mayhew lifted his voice in an unnecessary shout.

A whisper would have sufficed for the aide on the other side of the door. He had been holding his breath with anticipation of a word, but Mayhew wanted his displeasure at being disturbed known.

Quickly the door opened and the nonplussed aide walked through, looking around until he saw the Lord High Priest lounging in his great chair by the roaring fireplace. He made a beeline for Mayhew, ending by kneeling before his master, head down, left arm outstretched, left hand holding a small bamboo canister recently pulled from the leg of a pigeon. Mayhew snatched the canister from the extended hand, after which the aide stood and withdrew to a respectable distance while Mayhew read the message contained therein.

His brow furrowed as he reread what was printed on the small strip of paper. After reading it a third time, he tossed it into the fireplace where it was instantly incinerated. He remained staring into the flames in deep thought, until a slight shuffling of feet reminded him his aide was still in the room.

"Thank you," the high priest said, with uncharacteristic courtesy. "You are excused."

The aide silently bowed and took his leave, amazed by his master's civility.

The Lord High Priest continued to regard the flames as his mind worked. Once again, he recalled the simple wording of the message: Four assassins killed. The Harbinger lives.

"So, Galin has finally made his play," Mayhew said quietly to no one. "This time he cannot deny his hand, or his failure... at least not to me."

He thought briefly of again summoning the commander to a meeting, where he would make sure to gloat at both the lack of finesse and the lack of results in this latest attempt on the life of the Harbinger. The thought was quickly discarded. Galin would never meet with him under these circumstances. Not after their last meeting, where he had lied about his first unsuccessful attempt at eliminating their mutual problem. He had too much pride for that.

But Mayhew, too, was a proud man, and he did not take kindly the insinuations by Galin that, because he was of the Temple, he was too soft to take the actions that a situation such as this required. Of course, those of the Temple were no longer the 'warrior-priests of old', but the Temple still had its ways. It's very secret ways.

It was then the lord high priest made his decision. Tonight, he would use the balcony staircase and ascend to the roof of his private quarters. There he would light a signal fire, adding the special powder that would make it a blue flame, one which could only be seen from the mountain peaks directly above the estate. Then he would wait.

He hoped he would not have to wait long.

****

Just as a blue flame was dying out at an estate somewhere at the base of Stronghold's Crown, a flame of a different sort was being lit at the Royal House of the Citadel.

It was a white-hot flame, glowing in the eyes of His Majesty King Ammon IV.

Upon hearing the news of the latest attempt on the life of the Harbinger, the King had first called his trusted Chief Advisor, Lord Cecil. He then released him on the Citadel like a hound straining at his leash for the hunt. Cecil's instructions were to bring his King "every detail of the attempted assassination, so that the proper heads could be taken."

Lord Cecil, an intimidating figure standing a very stout six and a half feet tall, was possessed of one of the sharpest minds in the empire. It did not take him long to ascertain the details of the act, as well as they could be fathomed with so many of the principles being dead. His only delay was in speaking with the Harbinger himself about the attempt on his life. He had been accompanied by Jusaan, who acted as translator.

The Harbinger, having tended to his acolyte himself, and having barricaded them both in their quarters, had not been eager to deal with him. Still, Cecil persisted and, with the help of the priest, had gleaned what information he could from the stoic warrior-priest.

It was not until early the next morning that he was able to report to Ammon IV with all he had learned about the events of the day just past.

"Four men, informed by someone familiar with current events and routines inside the Citadel, were provided with uniforms and weapons stolen from supplies allotted to the guards assigned to the Royal House," Cecil said. "They were then able to enter the compound unmolested, due in part to the recent influx of new guards. Somehow knowing of the series of meetings between His Highness and the royal guests, even to what time they usually took place, these men were able to approach the guest quarters in formation, with no one voicing any concern to their presence and none the wiser concerning their intentions.

"These men were able to impersonate the actual guards to the point where the Royal Guests allowed themselves to be escorted to one of the mid-level halls, usually a quiet part of the House during that time of day. There the intention of the imposters was to dispatch the Harbinger and his acolyte. Two of the imposters carried bows, which apparently were the first option for their assault. By this fact, it can be surmised that they were somewhat aware of the capabilities of the Harbinger, who the soldiers have named 'The Panther', and planned to safely kill him from a distance. It can likewise be surmised that the two imposters carrying weapons for close combat were there to ensure the deaths should the archers miss or simply wound their quarry."

Cecil paused to make sure that His Highness Ammon IV was following all that he had thus far relayed. Satisfied, he continued:

"Your Highness, to refer to the Harbinger as a 'true warrior-priest of old' is no exaggeration. These four fellows, obviously having had some type of military training, and armed with knives, swords, bucklers, bows and arrows, fared poorly against him. Three of them, the two swordsmen and one archer, were killed on the spot. The body of the second archer was found not too long ago, having been stabbed from behind before his throat was slashed. Although the Harbinger's acolyte has suffered a life-threatening wound, having taken an arrow in his back, the Harbinger had not one scratch upon his person. Through the translation of Council Priest Jusaan, he informed me of the combat, absent the details of exactly how he managed to kill the three."

Ammon had been standing before the fireplace as Cecil made his report, chin down, arms laced across his chest, with his right hand periodically making the journey up to his face to stroke his beard. It was a pose he often struck when absorbing and digesting information. Upon realizing that Cecil had stopped talking, he raised his head, turned, and faced his Chief Advisor.

"What do you know of the assassins?" he asked. "Who are they? Where are they from? Do you think they served with our military?"

"We know little about them, my liege," replied Cecil. "One of them, the archer killed at the scene, has been tentatively identified by a current Citadel Guard who served with the Second Expeditionary Force. According to him, this man was a scout and an excellent archer, well trained and disciplined; a good soldier who recently completed his twenty-year stint. On the others, we have no history as yet."

Anticipating his King's next question, Cecil continued.

"Of the person who helped them - for they certainly needed help with uniforms, locations, and the palace routine - we have nothing. I would surmise that there was a prearranged place of meeting, probably for payment for services rendered, after the deed was done. The archer that escaped most probably made it to this location and was quickly dispatched. I would wager this was to be the fate of all, as it was the only way to tie up that particular loose end. His body was found by a kitchen worker who was taking refuse out to a compost pile, but it does not appear that he was killed there."

"And how do you know this? asked the King.

"There was very little of his blood there, Your Highness," Cecil said. "Undoubtedly he was killed elsewhere and transported there during the night."

"And what," asked the King, "has my Chief Advisor surmised concerning who would most likely want to sabotage our plans? Who among our many citizens would have the gall to stand against the prophesy of The One Spirit?"

"On that matter, my liege, I could put forth an intelligent argument connecting this act to a number of your subjects, and for a myriad of reasons. In fact, were I not who I am, I could make a reasonable argument that I should be suspected. Thus is the broad fog of suspicion hiding from us the identity of the true culprit."

Ammon could only stare at Cecil after this pronouncement.

"It just so happens," Cecil continued, "that most, if not all, of those most worthy of our suspicion, were not present anywhere near the Citadel compound at the time of the attempt on the Harbinger's life."

"Is that important?" asked the King.

"My liege," said Cecil, "assassination at this level is a very delicate thing. Delegation is hardly an option. Few would trust its machinations to your average underlings because of the added burden of having to leave one more body to ensure one's own safety. That last body would be the most likely to lead back to he who had put the plan in place."

Ammon thought about this for a moment before nodding his head in agreement.

"Where does this leave us?" the King sighed. "I now have enemies inside the Temple or inside the Royal House, or maybe both! My plans, so far along already, are in jeopardy from forces unknown to me, while I, the King, am powerless in the grip of this conspiracy!

"Your plans remain in place, my liege," Cecil assured him, replacing the hat of investigator with that of counselor. "You have but to reinforce your protection for our guests... well... likely just one guest, as the acolyte is not expected to survive.

"Meet with Colevant. Is he not the commander of the City Garrison, from which the finest are selected to serve as Citadel Guard? Impress upon him the seriousness of the current situation and allow me to continue my inquiries into the assassination attempt. I will eventually ferret out the one, or ones, behind this mischief."

****

Thus, it was that Colevant was the first to experience the white-hot fire in the eyes of His Highness King Ammon IV.

Upon meeting with him, King Ammon made it abundantly clear that, as commander of the City Garrison, Colevant would be held personally responsible in the event of another episode such as the one just past. When Colevant dared to speak in his own defense, stating that he should not be held responsible if someone outside his command attempted to take the life of the Harbinger, King Ammon made himself perfectly clear.

"You are correct in that point, commander," the King graciously conceded, "but should someone outside your command *succeed*, who shall I hold responsible?"

Colevant could only stare in stony silence.

"Were I you, commander," the King continued, "I would double the guard in the Royal House, and I would hand-pick every man assigned there, because every guard there will bear the responsibility of your head, along with their own, should an assassination attempt, successful or not, arise from their ranks. Do you understand?"

"I understand, my liege," said Colevant.

"And should an attempt on the life of the Harbinger... from any quarter... be successful," the King said, leaning menacingly into the face of his subject, "my anger would be surpassed only by the amount of blood needed to quench it! I would make sure that your entire family would head the line!"

Chapter 25

The sun had just set on another clear and cold mid-winter day. Mayhew knew this to be the time of signaling and took his place beside a large window in his quarters looking out upon the nearest peaks of the northern mountain range. This is where his blue flame would be acknowledged, if its message had been received.

As he waited, he tried to come to terms with the steps he was preparing to take to influence the direction of the empire.

He had dealt with the Masscus family before, though not frequently. Their patriarch had journeyed down the mountain to pay homage and pledge fealty when Mayhew had first been ordained as high priest of the Temple of The One Spirit. It was a ritual that had taken place after every ordination, upon the new high priest's first visit to the temple estate at the base of Strongholds Crown. There had been other meetings over the years; small but important tasks he had needed carried out, and instances where he had called them down from the mountain to reward them for their fealty and services.

Several years had passed since the last time their presence had been requested. Since that time, the old patriarch had died, or so Mayhew had been informed. The high priest felt a shudder run down his spine as he recalled how he had come by the knowledge. A message had been left inside his personal quarters, under the very noses of his guard and his staff. Not one of them, indeed no one in the whole of the estate, claimed to have seen or heard anything. Yet the message was there, laid on a pillow at the foot of his bed while he slept.

While he slept!

Mayhew had not known quite how to take that message. Oh, the news it conveyed was straightforward enough, but the method of its delivery was... disturbing. Was it a demonstration of their proficiency for his benefit? Was it a threat on his life or on the wellbeing of the Temple; a statement that even within his personal sanctum, surrounded by his guards, he was never out of their reach?

Mayhew cursed his paranoia. An overactive mind, possessed of vision and imagination, could sometimes be a double-edged sword. Too often he attributed his own penchant for schemes and plots to those about him, even when they had repeatedly shown themselves to be of the simplest, most innocuous sort, content with where the currents of life took them, or with what those currents allowed to drift their way. He had chosen then to see the message for its surface meaning, and not attach any ulterior motives to its method of delivery. Still, the memory of its delivery caused him to wonder, and at times to shudder.

Well, soon he would allay some of his doubts and wonderings. If all proceeded as intended, he would meet with the new patriarch this very night. Having allowed his mind to drift while deep in thought, he refocused on the quickly darkening mountains outside his window, and saw what he had been searching for: three torches glowing in the distance, the center torch higher than the other two. He would receive three visitors this night. One of them would be the new patriarch of the Masscus clan.

****

Seenio Masscus looked down upon the estate of the high priest of The One Spirit and smiled a smile of satisfaction long deferred. Soon he would meet His Eminence, Lord High Priest Mayhew, the man who held the position his family was sworn to serve. He had laid eyes on the high priest several times, once from the foot of his bed while he slept. That had been a demonstration for one who had not called upon their services in a while; to let him know that the skills sworn to be used in support of the Temple remained undimmed and were available to him at a moment's notice.

Seenio sometimes thought that the pride in his skills he had demonstrated that night might have been a mistake. He had received no summons since then, and he dared not show his face to the high priest of The One without an invitation.

He had been arrogant enough to access the high priest's bedchamber uninvited, to leave a note in order to demonstrate his prowess. It was the insolence of youth and of power newly acquired.

Since that day he had often pondered on the wisdom of subtlety, while hoping for an opportunity to serve the high priest and perchance find redemption for his earlier rash actions.

Maybe it had been because he had ascended to head the family at such a young age that he had felt the need to prove himself. He had always done everything at an age earlier than most in his clan. As a youth he had displayed the courage, the guile, the savagery, and the physical attributes of one beyond his years. He had been separated from the herds earlier than most and thrust into training. He was named "the Beast" when not yet past his twelfth winter, a name he had taken great pride in and had worked every day to affirm.

His father, too, was proud of his youngest son, and after his thirteenth winter Seenio was allowed to lie with the females who were of age, and produce offspring of his own. Two of them stood beside him now: his oldest son and daughter.

A female, even though his daughter, participating in a meeting such as this had not occurred in generations. But she had trained with her brothers and had proven herself at least their equal, and often their superior, in courage, guile, and skill. When she learned of this pilgrimage, she had petitioned her father, begging him to allow her to accompany him. In a moment of weakness completely out of character, Seenio had acquiesced.

Casting a casual glance behind him, Seenio saw that the torches were getting low. He had lit the three torches with his own hands as the sun was setting behind the western slopes, placing them in the rock wall. The center torch was placed higher up the wall than the other two, alerting the high priest that his summons had been received and would be obeyed this very evening by the patriarch of the clan. Satisfied the torches had served their purpose, Seenio spoke to his firstborn son, Mem.

"Douse the flames," he said. "It is time."

Mem hesitated, pretending that his Chief was not addressing the first-born male to perform a menial task when a woman was present. This lasted but for a moment, then he rose from his squatting position near the edge of the ledge designated as the place of signaling, and did as he was commanded, his hesitation having sent the message he dared not deliver directly.

Seenio took no obvious notice of this small protest. He had seen it's like many times before from his son. He had decided long ago not to pitch the boy from a height, as was his right as a sire. He had let the occasional beating suffice as punishment for a child's insolence. After all, it was no small thing to feel threatened by a woman, though she be your older sibling, for your customary place as heir to the family seat.

He snorted as Mem moved in the direction of the torches, believing himself to have become much too soft.

He blamed the boy's mother, who he maintained had manipulated his youth into feelings of fondness for her and the children she had borne him. Maybe those who had whispered that a boy of his age was too young to lie with a woman were right. Surely his sire would never have indulged such a streak of insolence in him as he had with his own firstborn son.

And to consider the wishes of a daughter to ascend to the position of "Reaper"?

Seenio shook his head as he considered all the complications that affection had imposed on his life. He glanced back at Nola, his daughter, sitting cross-legged near a large rock. He knew she had chosen that spot because of its shadow, which shielded her from the light of the torches and allowed her to keep her night vision.

Seenio's lips twisted into a slight smile.

"Let us be off," he said, starting down the rocky path to the manor below.

****

Mayhew found himself pacing back and forth before the fireplace in his bedchamber. Looking back at his life, his entry into the priesthood, his ascension to the high seat, he could not recall ever having felt as apprehensive as he did at this moment. He knew he should remain calm, but he was about to come face to face with that which was not merely a bad dream or an imaginary monster hiding under the bed. To most they were rumors, rumors of legends based on events that occurred a long, long time ago, and only the High Priest ever knew that the nightmare was reality. The secrecy that having such a weapon at one's disposal required was an awesome weight to bare.

That was the crux of it, he thought. They are a weapon, and they are completely at his disposal. Their pledge had been given centuries ago, and according to the writings of past high priests, they have unfailingly lived and died by that pledge ever since. They are sworn to serve he who holds the mantle of high priest, meaning they are sworn to Lord Mayhew, to use as he would, in achieving whatever end he desired.

So, why am I so nervous? Mayhew wondered.

Because, he answered himself, *it is not every day that the monster crawls from under the bed to look you in the eye.*

This thought brought a smile to his face, quickly erased by the next thought; *How much control can one truly have over a monster?*

He had sent his personal assistants away for the evening in preparation for this meeting. He should have released the guards also, but that might have caused undue suspicion among his staff. If he were honest with himself, he would admit the thought of releasing his guard for the evening had terrified him. His every instinct told him to double the guard.

Again, Mayhew forced a smile, trying to reassure himself that all of his apprehension was uncalled for and, based on all he had read from his predecessors, he was the one in control here. This thought, followed by a few deep breaths, allowed him to clear his mind and banish those silly fears from his head. He could feel his racing heartbeat start to slow and his...

Knock!

Mayhew's breath caught in his chest when he heard the single knock that was the signal that his guests had arrived. Taking time again to regain the slim level of control he had briefly attained, he moved over to the door of his private balcony, paused for a second, and opened it.

They entered on an icy wind, flowing smoothly and silently into the chamber as if one with the winter breeze. The cold of the night air galvanized Mayhew's senses and, after firmly closing the door, he found the courage to turn and regard his visitors.

They had moved to stand before the fire, but Mayhew felt they did not seek its warmth so much as its light, so as to reveal themselves to their sovereign.

Reaching deep inside for the aloof dignity that his title demanded, the lord high priest approached those who had entered, calling upon all of his hard-won authority to project to them, and to reassure himself, that *they* were the ones who were under scrutiny here.

"M'lord," the one in the middle said in a rich baritone.

The words were unexpected, as was the motion that swiftly followed. The speaker stepped forward and, taking a knee, grasped Mayhew's right hand and planted a kiss on the backhand side. The move took Mayhew by surprise and he called upon all of his self-control so as not to snatch his hand away.

Having paid proper respect, the man resumed his position between the two still standing, all three staring silently at the high priest. Shadows from the flickering fire hid their piercing eyes, allowing Mayhew the luxury of looking them up and down while not feeling that he, too, was being weighed.

They are tall, he thought without considering that, to him, almost everyone was. They were all of the same stature, about six feet, give-or-take, their soft boots adding little to their height. They were clothed in heavy woolen robes decorated with thick fur around the hoods that were pulled up over their heads causing Mayhew to struggle to see their faces. Apparently, the center figure picked up on this and, loosening his robe, allowed it to drop to the thickly carpeted floor. Those on either side of him did the same, allowing Mayhew to take in these three who stood before him.

They were two men and a woman. All were fair of skin, though deeply tanned, and with long, reddish-brown hair falling past their shoulders. He could not be sure, as both men wore full beards, but Mayhew thought the facial features of the three were very similar. They were dressed alike, in wool tunics covering shirts of heavy cloth, with sleeves falling three-quarters down their arms. The tunics were belted, but no weapons were visible upon them. Looking down, Mayhew noted that the soft leather boots overlapped leggings of fur that began just above their ankles and were held in place by two thick leather straps tied off just below the knees.

Those were the similarities. Mayhew had to look more closely to find the differences.

All were considered young by his standards, the man in the middle appearing to have seen years totaling somewhere in the mid-to-late thirties. His companions were younger, though carrying an air of maturity that made it hard to gauge their ages. Mayhew guessed they were in their early twenties, their bodies long and lean and hard, with no unneeded weight or fat. He in the center also had the long, lean look, but with added muscle that filled out his form to just short of stout. Taking another look, Mayhew felt these three probably were related. As they stood before him, they reminded him of a lion and two newly grown cubs.

"M'lord?"

Again, the baritone voice spoke.

"How should I address you?" Mayhew asked the man standing in the center, the only one to have spoken since their entrance.

The man stepped forward, this time not taking a knee. His bearing was proud as he looked into Mayhew's eyes. "I am called Seenio, patriarch of Clan Masscus... the Clan of the Reaper," he said, using the name bestowed by myth and legend upon his family. "With me is my firstborn, Nola, and my first son, Mem."

Mayhew noted the use of the term "Clan of the Reaper," an identifier mentioned in the writings of his predecessors. Mayhew also noted that Seenio spoke the Pithian tongue as if it was his first language.

There was a brief moment of silence before Mayhew responded.

"I am Lord Mayhew, High Priest of the Temple of The One Spirit and Keeper of the Secrets."

Upon hearing these words, Seenio motioned to his companions. The three of them took a knee, the younger two moving forward in order to kiss the back of Mayhew's right hand. Then Seenio again spoke.

"You are our sovereign," Seenio said. "We know no king; we bow only to the Lord High Priest of the Temple of The One Spirit."

Mayhew recognized these words too, as coming from the writings of his fellow high priests. Along with the single knock and other signs, they establish the identity of those standing before him and confirmed their loyalty to the lord high priest alone.

"It is good of you to come," Mayhew said, feeling a bit more in control. "Was your journey pleasant?"

Even as he spoke the words, Mayhew recognized how foolish they must sound, given their reason for being here and the nature of their relationship with him. Still, he was surprised when Seenio smiled at the question.

"We noticed m'lord left his guards posted in order to test our skills," Seenio said, interpreting the pleasantry as a challenge. "And yet we reached your quarters unseen and without taking a life."

The patriarch stated this with pride, assuming they had passed a final test laid out by their sovereign. *Now, like puppies,* Mayhew thought, *they wish a pat on the head.*

"You have done well," he said, "as I knew that you would. The service of your clan to the High Seat, though necessarily a secret from all others, is well known and appreciated by he who sits there. Allow him to serve you this one time."

With that, another coded saying to reassure his visitors that he was, indeed, the High Priest and Keeper of the Secrets, he directed the trio to a small, round table. They sat while Mayhew served them hot spiced wine, the very best available.

With the rituals now complete and Mayhew's confidence renewed, he launched into his reason for the signal and what would be required of these Reapers.

His Reapers.

****

They sat crouched around the small fire that, along with their heavy cloaks, provided all the warmth they needed. They had sat with Lord Mayhew for quite some time, and though his quarters were warm and comfortable and his hot spiced wine delicious, Seenio had nevertheless been anxious to be nestled within the confines of his mountains. The world below could be a complicated place. Here he was sovereign, and that was all.

The three of them had been watching the dancing flames while Seenio contemplated all he had heard this night. Of course, Nola worried that they had ruined their night vision, but they were presently within the friendly confines of their mountains and felt supremely safe here.

At length Seenio rocked back onto his heels and cleared his throat, much as his father had done, signaling he was ready to speak.

"Mem will take the lead in this killing," he said, and saw his son's eyes take on a light of their own, not a reflection from the fire. He knew Mem had felt insulted when his sister was introduced to the lord high priest as the firstborn. Seenio did not make his decisions based on the feelings of others, but he felt that giving lead in this killing to his eldest son was a good decision, as well as one that would help soothe his son's injured dignity. Turning toward Mem, he continued.

"You will take your younger brothers, the twins, and scout everything about the eastern wall of the Citadel, the Royal House, and the terrain surrounding it. You will choose an approach and retreat. The kill will be made at close quarters, with a blade. An arrow is not as certain. You will take no trophies for yourselves, only his right hand to be presented to m'lord as proof of fealty.

"Make your plan," Seenio finished, "and bring it to me. When you have received my blessing, you may move forward."

Mem felt he should have been insulted anew by the way his father laid out the basics of the task, as if this would be his first kill, but he was happy nonetheless. He did not know why this warrior-priest was to be killed, but to be given the lead in an assault inside the Royal House was an honor indeed. Still, he could not help but raise a question.

"I could perform this killing more easily and with less chance of discovery were I to go alone."

Seenio had known something like this was coming and thus did not release his temper. He knew his children well.

"With less chance of discovery, perhaps," Seenio said patiently, "but did you not hear the words of m'lord? This is no ordinary priest, but a warrior-priest of old. He has already slain five of the best warriors sent against him, his only known weapon a knife taken from his attackers. You will take your brothers, and Nola will accompany you to observe only."

Knowing how Mem felt about this last pronouncement and feeling left out until this moment, Nola smiled in her brother's direction... just because. Then, emboldened by her small triumph, she spoke up.

"How dangerous could this old warrior-priest be?" she asked. "The high priest looks as if he knows little about the ways of killing. He is short, and plump, and..."

THWAACK!

Seenio's short but powerful backhand blow sent his daughter sprawling into the darkness, with only her boots and leggings visible in the small circle of light cast by the fire. When she had regained her composure and returned to the fire, her head bowed and her bloodied lips unmoving, he spoke.

"Never question the word of the lord high priest again," he said.

Epilogue

Running… running… running… fast as I can… why so slow? …it's coming… it's gonna catch me… what is it?… it's bad… it's coming and it's bad… it's gonna catch me… I have to run faster! …why am I moving so slow… my legs… I'm trying as hard as I can… why am I moving so slow? …why are my legs moving so slow… and… why can't I open my eyes? …it's coming and I can't see… can't open my eyes to see it… where?… I can't run and I can't see it… I can't see what it is… I can't see where it is and… but I gotta run faster!… why are my legs… my arms… moving so slow?… there's Hanshee!… he's over there! …I'm coming! …I'm trying! …why can't I run faster! …wait up! …wait for me! …Please! …please… please… why can't I open my eyes? …damn… he's not there anymore… where did he go… away… why did he go away… damn… my eyes… and…

…It's so cold in here! Put more wood on the fire, Laretha… more wood… MORE WOOD!… IT'S SO DAMN COLD! … ooooohhh, that's so much better… Just hold me, Laretha… aaaww… ooohhh… what? …no, don't leave me… I get so cold…why are you smiling at me? … don't leave me… I get sooo cooold… put more wood on the fire… come back to bed… come back to me… please… it's still so cold… It's burning my feet! The fire, it's burning my feet! … but they're so cold… my feet are so cold… got to get them out of the fire… they're burning… why can't I move my feet out of the fire? ...before they burn up... but they're so cold... I'm trying... as hard as I can, I'm trying... why can't I... open my eyes?...

...so dizzy... been spinning around... everything's going by so fast... stop! ...stop spinning! ... there... that's better... there's... there's Jusaan... where's Hanshee... Jusaan... just smiling and smiling and... I've gotta find Hanshee... we've gotta go... Jusaan has tricks... he's a tricky one... we've gotta go before... we start spinning around and around and... I'm getting so dizzy... where does Hanshee keep going to... where does this thing... stop spinning... there's Hanshee! ... no, that's not Hanshee... that's the King... he's just smiling and smiling... just like Jusaan... and Laretha! ...they're all smiling and smiling and... where's Hanshee... is he smiling too? ...why can't I find Hanshee... getting so dizzy... the whole world is spinning and... and I can't... can't stop it... I can't open my eyes...

...I heard that! ...I heard that! ...what was that... what was... Hanshee? ...what was that... over there... waaay over there... what was... where are you Hanshee... we've got to go before... wait up... I'm running as fast as I... why won't my legs move faster... I'm.... I'm... running... wait up... Hanshee... don't leave... me... DAMMIT I'M TRYING! ...my legs... my... they just won't... MOVE FASTER DAMMIT! ... move fast... move faster, dammit... move... why won't my legs move faster... they're coming... they're coming to get... Hanshee! ...where are you Hanshee! ...my eyes... I can't get my eyes open! ...I can't... open my eyes...

...thank God... Hanshee... I've been trying to find you... where are you... where are we going... where are... there they are! ...all of them... and there's so much blood! ...so much... where did they come from... all of them... all of them are there...

Botha... the three thieves in the tiny city... the tiny city... and there's that big guard... that great big guard with his arm cut off... and his guts cut out... and so much blood... blood everywhere... where are you Hanshee... there you are... you're covered in the blood... it's everywhere, all over everything... it's... so much... Botha is bleeding from everywhere... so much of it... where are you going, Hanshee? ...wait for me... Wait For Me! ...I'm coming... I'm moving as fast as I... my legs are so slow... why can't I... open my eyes? ...

Where the hell am I? wondered Raymond when his eyes finally opened.

THE END OF BOOK II

About the Author

Phillip L. Johnson is a retired analyst living in Columbia, South Carolina. A graduate of the University of South Carolina, he and his wife Louise have raised two sons and are surrounded by family and friends. After spending a career in the Insurance industry, he now has the time to do what he really wanted to be doing all those years behind a desk, writing stories of excitement and adventure.

Note from the Author

Word-of-mouth is crucial for any author to succeed. If you enjoyed *The Maiyochi Chronicles: Stronghold*, please leave a review online—anywhere you are able. Even if it's just a sentence or two. It would make all the difference and would be very much appreciated.

Thanks!
Phillip L. Johnson

We hope you enjoyed reading this title from:

www.blackrosewriting.com

Subscribe to our mailing list – *The Rosevine* – and receive **FREE** books, daily deals, and stay current with news about upcoming releases and our hottest authors.
Scan the QR code below to sign up.

Already a subscriber? Please accept a sincere thank you for being a fan of Black Rose Writing authors.

View other Black Rose Writing titles at
www.blackrosewriting.com/books and use promo code
PRINT to receive a **20% discount** when purchasing.

Ingram Content Group UK Ltd.
Milton Keynes UK
UKHW041819080323
418238UK00001B/2